Six Feet Four

Jackson Gregory

SAGEBRUSH
Large Print Westerns

First published in Great Britain by Melrose
First published in the United States by Dodd, Mead

First Isis Edition
published 2017
by arrangement with
Golden West Literary Agency

A catalogue record for this book is available
from the British Library.

ISBN 978–1–78541–387–2 (pb)

Published by
F. A. Thorpe (Publishing)
Anstey, Leicestershire

Set by Words & Graphics Ltd.
Anstey, Leicestershire
Printed and bound in Great Britain by
T. J. International Ltd., Padstow, Cornwall

This book is printed on acid-free paper

To
E. M. Gregory
"Here's Your Book"

CONTENTS

CHAPTER
ONE

The Storm

All day long, from an hour before the pale dawn until now after the thick dark, the storm had raged through the mountains. Before midday it had grown dark in the cañons. In the driving blast of the wind many a tall pine had snapped, broken at last after long valiant years of victorious buffeting with the seasons, while countless tossing branches had been riven away from the parent boles and hurled far out in all directions. Through the narrow cañons the wet wind went shrieking fearsomely, driving the slant rain like countless thin spears of glistening steel.

At the wan daybreak the sound filling the air was one of many-voiced but subdued tumult, like the faraway growling of fierce, hungry, imprisoned beasts. As the sodden hours dragged by the noises everywhere increased steadily, so that before noon the whole of the wilderness seemed to be shouting; narrow creek beds were filled with gushing, muddy water; the trees on the mountainsides shook and snapped and creaked and hissed to the hissing of the racing wind; at intervals the thunder echoing ominously added its boom to the general uproar. Not for a score of years and upward had such a storm visited the mountains in the vicinity of the old road house in Big Pine Flat.

Night, as though it had leaped upon the back of the storm and had ridden hitherward on the wings of the wind all impatience to defy the laws of daylight, was in truth mistress of the mountains a full hour or more before the invisible sun's allotted time of setting. In the storm-smitten, lonely building at the foot of the rocky slope, shivering as though with the cold, rocking crazily as though in startled fear at each gust, the roaring log fire in the open fireplace made an uncertain twilight and innumerable ghostlike shadows. The wind whistling down the chimney, making that eerie sound known locally as the voice of William Henry, came and went fitfully. Poke Drury, the cheerful, one-legged keeper of the road house, swung back and forth up and down on his one crutch, whistling blithely with his guest of the chimney and lighting the last of his coal oil lamps and candles.

"She's a Lu-lu bird, all right," acknowledged Poke Drury. He swung across his long "general room" to the fireplace, balanced on his crutch while he shifted and kicked at a fallen burning log with his one boot, and then hooked his elbows on his mantel. His very black, smiling eyes took cheerful stock of his guests whom the storm had brought him. They were many, more than had ever at one time honoured the Big Pine road house. And still others were coming.

"If Hap Smith ain't forgot how to sling a four horse team through the dark, huh?" continued the landlord as he placed still another candle at the south window.

In architectural design Poke Drury's road house was as simple an affair as Poke Drury himself. There was but one story: the whole front of the house facing the country road was devoted to the "general room." Here was a bar, occupying the far end. Then there were two or three rude pine tables, oil-cloth covered. The chairs were plentiful and all of the rawhide bottom species, austere looking, but comfortable enough. And, at the other end of the barn like chamber was the long dining table. Beyond it a door leading to the kitchen at the back of the house. Next to the kitchen the family bed room where Poke Drury and his dreary looking spouse slept. Adjoining this was the one spare bed room, with a couple of broken legged cots and a washstand without any bowl or pitcher. If one wished to lave his hands and face or comb his hair let him step out on the back porch under the shoulder of the mountain and utilize the road house toilet facilities there: they were a tin basin, a water pipe leading from a spring and a broken comb stuck after the fashion of the country in the long hairs of the ox's tail nailed to the porch post.

"You gents is sure right welcome," the one-legged proprietor went on, having paused a moment to listen to the wind howling through the narrow pass and battling at his door and windows. "I got plenty to eat an' more'n plenty to drink, same as usual. But when it comes to sleepin', well, you got to make floors an' chairs an' tables do. You see this here little shower has filled me all up. The Lew Yates place up the river got itself pretty well washed out; Lew's young wife an' ol' mother-in-law," and Poke's voice was properly modified, "got scared clean to pieces. Not bein' used to our ways out here," he added brightly. "Any way they've got the spare bed room. An' my room an' Ma's . . . well, Ma's got a real bad cold an' she's camped there for the night. But, shucks, boys, what's the odds, when there's fire in the fire place an' grub in the grub box an' as fine a line of licker as you can find any place *I* know of. An' a deck or two of cards an' the bones to rattle for them that's anxious to make or break quick . . . Hap Smith *ought* to been here before now. You wouldn't suppose . . ."

He broke off and looked at those of the faces which had been turned his way. His thought was plain to read, at least for those who understood recent local conditions. Hap Smith had been driving the stage over the mountains for only something less than three weeks; which is to say since the violent taking off of his predecessor, Bill Varney.

Before any one spoke the dozen men in the room had had ample time to consider this suggestion. One or two of them glanced up at the clock swinging its pendulum over the chimney piece. Then they went on with what they were doing, glancing through old newspapers, dealing at cards, smoking or just sitting and staring at nothing in particular.

"The last week has put lots of water in all the cricks," offered old man Adams from his place by the fire. "Then with this cloud-bust an' downpour today, it ain't real nice travellin'. That would be about all that's holdin' Hap up. An' I'm tellin' you why: Did you ever

4

hear a man tell of a stick-up party on a night like this? No, sir! These here stick-up gents got more sense than that; they'd be settin' nice an' snug an' dry like us fellers, right now."

As usual, old man Adams had stated a theory with emphasis and utterly without any previous reflection, being a positive soul, but never a brilliant. And, again quite as usual, a theory stated was naturally to be combated with more or less violence. Out of the innocent enough statement there grew a long, devious argument. An argument which was at its height and evincing no signs of ever getting anywhere at all, when from the night without came the rattle of wheels, the jingle of harness chains and Hap Smith's voice shouting out the tidings of his tardy arrival.

The front door was flung open, lamps and candles and log fire all danced in the sudden draft and some of the flickering flames went out, and the first one of Hap Smith's belated passengers, a young girl, was fairly blown into the room. She, like the rest, was drenched and as she hastened across the floor to the welcome fire trailed rain water from her cape and dress. But her eyes were sparkling, her cheeks rosy with the rude wooing of the outside night. After her, stamping noisily, glad of the light and warmth and a prospect of food and drink, came Hap Smith's other passengers, four booted men from the mines and the cattle country.

To the last man of them in the road house they gave her their immediate and exclusive attention. Briefly suspended were all such operations as smoking, drinking, newspaper reading or card playing. They looked at her gravely, speculatively and with frankly unhidden interest. One man who had laid a wet coat aside donned it again swiftly and surreptitiously. Another in awkward fashion, as she passed close to him, half rose and then sank back into his chair. Still others merely narrowed the gaze that was bent upon her steadily.

She went straight to the fireplace, threw off her wraps and extended her hands to the blaze. So for a moment she stood, her shoulders stirring to the shiver which ran down her whole body. Then she turned her head a little and for the first time took in all of the rude appointments of the room.

"Oh!" she gasped. "I . . ."

"It's all right, Miss," said Poke Drury, swinging toward her, his hand lifted as though to stop one in full flight. "You see . . . just that end there is the bar room," he explained nodding at her reassuringly. "The middle of the room here is the . . . the parlour; an' down at that end, where the long table is, that's the dinin' room. I ain't ever got aroun' to the partitions yet, but I'm goin' to some day. An' . . . Ahem!"

He had said it all and, all things considered, had done rather well with an impossible job. The clearing of the throat and a glare to go with it were not for the startled girl but for that part of the room where the bar and card tables were being used.

"Oh," said the girl again. And then, turning her back upon the bar and so allowing the firelight to add to the sparkle of her eyes and the flush on her cheeks, "Of course. One mustn't expect everything. And please

6

don't ask the gentlemen to . . . to stop whatever they are doing on my account. I'm quite warm now." She smiled brightly at her host and shivered again. "May I go right to my room?"

In the days when Poke Drury's road house stood lone and aloof from the world in Big Pine Flat, very little of the world from which such as Poke Drury had retreated had ever peered into these mountain-bound fastnesses; certainly less than few women of the type of this girl had ever some here in the memory of the men who now, some boldly and some shyly, regarded her drying herself and seeking warmth in front of the blazing fire. True, at the time there were in the house three others of her sex. But they were . . . different.

"May I go right to my room?" she repeated as the landlord stood gaping at her rather foolishly. She imagined that he had not heard, being a little deaf . . . or that, possibly, the poor chap was a trifle slow witted. And again she smiled on him kindly and again he noted the shiver bespeaking both chill and fatigue.

But to Poke Drury there had come an inspiration. Not much of one, perhaps, yet he quickly availed himself of it. Hanging in a dusty corner near the long dining table, was an old and long disused guest's book, the official road house register. Drury's wandering eye lighted upon it.

"If you'll sign up, Miss," he suggested, "I'll go have Ma get your room ready."

And away he scurried on his crutch, casting a last look over his shoulder at his ruder male guests.

The girl went hastily as directed and sat down at the table, her back to the room. The book she lifted down from its hanging place; there was a stub of pencil tied to the string. She took it stiffly into her fingers and wrote, "Winifred Waverly." Her pencil in the space reserved for the signer's home town, she hesitated. Only briefly, however. With a little shrug, she completed the legend, inscribing swiftly, "Hill's Corners." Then she sat still, feeling that many eyes were upon her and waited the return of the road house keeper. When finally he came back into the room, his slow hesitating gait and puckered face gave her a suspicion of the truth.

"I'm downright sorry, Miss," he began lamely. "Ma's got somethin' . . . bad cold or pneumonia . . . an' she won't budge. There's only one more bed room an' Lew Yates's wife has got one cot an Lew's mother-in-law has got the other. An' *they* won't budge. An' . . ."

He ended there abruptly.

"I see," said the girl wearily. "There isn't any place for me."

"Unless," offered Drury without enthusiasm and equally without expectation of his offer being of any great value, "you'd care to crawl in with Ma . . ."

"No, thank you!" said Miss Waverly hastily. "I can sit up somewhere; after all it won't be long until morning and we start on again. Or, if I might have a blanket to throw down in a corner . . ."

Again Poke Drury left her abruptly. She sat still at the table, without turning, again conscious of many eyes steadily on her. Presently from an adjoining room came Drury's voice, subdued to a low mutter. Then a woman's voice, snapping and querrulous. And a moment later the return of Drury, his haste savouring somewhat of flight from the connubial chamber, but certain spoils of victory with him; from his arm trailed a crazy-quilt which it was perfectly clear he had snatched from his wife's bed.

He led the way to the kitchen, stuck a candle in a bottle on the table, spread the quilt on the floor in the corner, made a veritable ceremony of fastening the back door and left her. The girl shivered and went slowly to her uninviting couch.

Poke Drury, in his big general room again, stood staring with troubled face at the other men. With common consent and to the last man of them they had already tiptoed to the register and were seeking to inform themselves as to the name and habitat of the prettiest girl who had ever found herself within the four walls of Poke Drury's road house.

"Nice name," offered old man Adams whose curiosity had kept stride with his years and who, lacking all youthful hesitation, had been first to get to the book. "Kind of stylish soundin'. But, Hill's Corners?" He shook his head. "I ain't been to the Corners for a right smart spell, but I didn't know such as *her* lived there."

"They don't," growled the heavy set man who had snatched the register from old man Adams' fingers. "An' I been there recent. Only last week. The Corners ain't so allfired big as a female like her is goin' to be livin' there an' it not be knowed all over."

Poke Drury descended upon them, jerked the book away and with a screwed up face and many gestures toward the kitchen recalled to them that a flimsy partition, though it may shut out the vision, is hardly to be counted on to stop the passage of an unguarded voice.

"Step down this way, gents," he said tactfully. "Where the bar is. Bein' it's a right winterish sort of night I don't reckon a little drop o' kindness would go bad, huh? Name your poison, gents. It's on me."

In her corner just beyond the flimsy partition, Winifred Waverly, of Hill's Corners or elsewhere, drew the many coloured patch work quilt about her and shivered again.

CHAPTER
TWO

The Devil's Own Night

Hap Smith, the last to come in, opened the front door which the wind snatched from his hands and slammed violently against the wall. In the sudden draft the old newspapers on one of the oil-cloth covered tables went flying across the room, while the rain drove in and blackened the floor. Hap Smith got the door shut and for a moment stood with his back against it, his two mail bags, a lean and a fat, tied together and flung over his shoulder, while he smote his hands together and laughed.

"A night for the devil to go skylarkin' in!" he cried jovially. "A night for murder an' arson an' robbin' graveyards! Listen to her, boys! Hear her roar! Poke Drury, I'm tellin' you, I'm glad your shack's right where it is instead of seventeen miles fu'ther on. An' ...Where's the girl?" He had swept the room with his roving eye; now, dropping his voice a little he came on down the room and to the bar. "Gone to bed?"

As one thoroughly at home here he went for a moment behind the bar, dropped the bags into a corner for safety and threw off his heavy outer coat, frankly exposing the big revolver which dragged openly at his right hip. Bill Varney had always carried a rifle and had been unable to avail himself of it in time; Hap Smith in assuming the responsibilities of the United States Mail had forthwith invested heavily of his cash on hand for a Colt forty-five and wore it frankly in the open. His, by the way, was the only gun in sight, although there were perhaps a half dozen in the room.

"She ain't exactly gone to bed," giggled the garrulous old man Adams, "bein' as there ain't no bed for her to go to. Ma Drury is inhabitin' one right now, while the other two is pre-empted by Lew Yates' wife an' his mother-in-law."

"Pshaw," muttered Hap Smith. "That ain't right. She's an awful nice girl an' she's clean tuckered out an' cold an' wet. She'd ought to have a bed to creep into." His eyes reproachfully trailed off to Poke Drury. The one-legged man made a grimace and shrugged.

"I can't drag Lew's folks out, can I?" he demanded. "An' I'd like to see the jasper as would try pryin' Ma loose from the covers right now. It can't be did, Hap."

Hap sighed, seeming to agree, and sighing reached out a big hairy hand for the bottle.

"She's an awful nice girl, jus' the same," he repeated with head-nodding emphasis. And then, feeling no doubt that he had done his chivalrous duty, he tossed off his liquor, stretched his thick arms high over his head, squared his shoulders comfortably in his blue flannel shirt and grinned in wide good humour. "This here campoody of yours ain't a terrible bad place to be right now, Poke, old scout. Not a bad place a-tall."

12

"You said twice, she was nice," put in old man Adams, his bleary, red rimmed ferret eyes gimleting at the stage driver. "But you ain't said who she was? Now . . ."

Hap Smith stared at him and chuckled.

"Ain't that jus' like Adams for you?" he wanted to know. "Who is she, he says! An' here I been ridin' alongside her all day an' never once does it pop into my head to ask whether she minds the name of Daisy or Sweet Marie!"

"Name's Winifred Waverly," chirped up the old man. "But a name don't mean much; not in this end of the world least ways. But us boys finds it kind of inter-estin' how she hangs out to Dead Man's Alley. That bein' kind of strange an' . . ."

"Poh!" snorted Hap Smith disdainfully. "Her hang out in that little town of Hill's Corners? Seein' as she ain't ever been there, havin' tol' me so on the stage less'n two hours ago, what's the sense of sayin' a fool thing like that? She ain't the kind as dwells in the likes of that nest of polecats an' sidewinders. Poh!"

"Poh, is it?" jeered old man Adams tremulously. "Clap your peep sight on that, Hap Smith. *Poh* at me, will you?" and close up to the driver's eyes he thrust the road house register with its newly pencilled inscription so close that Hap Smith dodged and was some time deciphering the brief legend.

"Beats me," he grunted, when he had done. He tossed the book to a table as a matter of no moment and shrugged. "Anyways she's a nice girl, I don't care where she abides, so to speak. An' me an' these other boys," with a sweeping glance at the four of his recent male passengers, "is hungrier than wolves. How about it, Poke? Late hours, but considerin' the kind of night the devil's dealin' we're lucky to be here a-tall. I could eat the hind leg off a ten year ol' steer."

"Jus' because a girl's got a red mouth an' purty eyes . . ." began old man Adams knowingly. But Smith snorted "Poh!" at him again and clapped him good naturedly on the thin old shoulders after such a fashion as to double the old man up and send him coughing and catching at his breath back to his chair by the fire.

Poke Drury, staring strangely at Smith, showed unmistakable signs of his embarrassment. Slowly under several pairs of interested eyes his face went a flaming red.

"I don't know what's got into me tonight," he muttered, slapping a very high and shining forehead with a very soft, flabby hand. "I clean forgot you boys hadn't had supper. An' now . . . the grub's all in the kitchen an' . . . *she's* in there, all curled up in a quilt an' mos' likely asleep."

Several mouths dropped. As for Hap Smith he again smote his big hands together and laughed.

"Drinks on Poke Drury," he announced cheerfully. "For havin' got so excited over a pretty girl he forgot we hadn't had supper! Bein' that's what's got into him."

Drury hastily set forth bottles and glasses. More than that, being tactful, he started Hap Smith talking. He asked of the roads, called attention to the fact that the stage was several hours late, hinted at danger from the same gentleman who had taken off Bill Varney only recently, and so succeeded in attaining the desired result. Hap Smith, a glass twisting slowly in his hand, declaimed long and loudly.

But in the midst of his dissertation the kitchen door opened and the girl, her quilt about her shoulders like a shawl, came in.

"I heard," she said quietly. "You are all hungry and the food is in there." She came on to the fireplace and sat down. "I am hungry, too. And cold." She looked upon the broad genial face of Hap Smith as upon the visage of an old friend. "I am not going to be stupid," she announced with a little air of taking the situation in hand. "I would be, if I stayed in there and caught cold. Tell them," and it was still Hap Smith whom she addressed, "to go on with whatever they are doing."

Again she came in for a close general scrutiny, one of serious, frank and matter of fact appraisal. Conscious of it, as she could not help being, she for a little lifted her head and turned her eyes gravely to meet the eyes directed upon her. Hers were clear, untroubled, a deep grey and eminently pleasant to look into; especially now that she put into them a little friendly smile. But in another moment and with a half sigh of weariness, she settled into a chair at the fireside and let her gaze wander back to the blazing fire.

Again among themselves they conceded, what by glances and covert nods, that she was most decidedly worth a man's second look and another after that. "Pretty, like a picture," offered Joe Hamby in a guarded whisper to one of the recent arrivals, who was standing with him at the bar. "Or," amended Joe with a flash of inspiration, "like a flower; one of them nice blue flowers on a long stem down by the crick."

"Nice to talk to, too," returned Joe's companion, something of the pride of ownership in his tone and look. For, during the day on the stage had he not once summoned the courage for a stammering remark to her, and had she not replied pleasantly? "Never travelled with a nicer lady." Whereupon Joe Hamby regarded him enviously. And old man Adams, with a sly look out of his senile old eyes, jerked his thin old body across the floor, dragging a chair after him, and sat down to entertain the lady. Who, it would seem from the twitching of her lips, had been in reality wooed out of herself and highly amused, when the interruption to the quiet hour came. Abruptly and without warning.

Poke Drury, willingly aided by the hungrier of his guests, had brought in the cold dishes; a big roast of beef, boiled potatoes, quantities of bread and butter and the last of Ma Drury's dried-apple pies. The long dining table had begun to take on a truly festive air. The coffee was boiling in the coals of the fireplace. Then the front door, the knob turned and released from without, was blown wide open by the gusty wind and a tall man stood in the black rectangle of the doorway. His appearance and attitude were significant, making useless all conjecture. A faded red bandana handkerchief was knotted about his face with rude slits for the eyes. A broad black hat with flapping, dripping brim was down over his forehead. In his two hands, the

16

barrel thrust forward into the room, was a sawed-off shotgun.

He did not speak, it being plain that words were utterly superfluous and that he knew it. Nor was there any outcry in the room. At first the girl had not seen, her back being to the door. Nor had old man Adams, his red rimmed eyes being on the girl. They turned together. The old man's jaw dropped; the girl's eyes widened, rather to a lively interest, it would seem, than to alarm. One had but to sit tight at times like this and obey orders . . .

The intruder's eyes were everywhere. His chief concern, however, from the start appeared to be Hap Smith. The stage driver's hand had gone to the butt of his revolver and now rested there. The muzzle of the short barrelled shotgun made a short quick arc and came to bear on Hap Smith. Slowly his fingers dropped from his belt.

Bert Stone, a quick eyed little man from Barstow's Springs, whipped out a revolver from its hidden place on his person and fired. But he had been over hasty and the man in the doorway had seen the gesture. The roar of the shotgun there in the house sounded like that of a cannon; the smoke lifted and spread and swirled in the draft. Bert Stone went down with a scream of pain as a load of buckshot flung him about and half tore off his outer arm. Only the fact that Stone, in firing, had wisely thrown his body a little to the side, saved the head upon his body.

The wind swept through the open door with fresh fury. Here a lamp went out, there the unsteady flame of

17

a candle was extinguished. The smoke from the shotgun was mingled with much wood smoke whipped out of the fireplace. The man in the doorway, neither hesitating nor hurrying, eminently cool and confident, came into the room. The girl studied him curiously, marking each trifling detail of his costume: the shaggy black chaps like those of a cowboy off for a gay holiday; the soft grey shirt and silk handkerchief to match knotted loosely about a brown throat. He was very tall and wore boots with tall heels; his black hat had a crown which added to the impression of great height. To the fascinated eyes of the girl he appeared little less than a giant.

He stopped and for a moment remained tensely, watchfully still. She felt his eyes on her; she could not see them in the shadow of his hat, but had an unpleasant sensation of a pair of sinister eyes narrowing in their keen regard of her. She shivered as though cold.

Moving again he made his away along the wall and to the bar. He stepped behind it, still with neither hesitation nor haste, and found the two mail bags with his feet. And with his feet he pushed them out to the open, along the wall, toward the door. Hap Smith snarled; his face no longer one of broad good humour. The shotgun barrel bore upon him steadily, warningly. Hap's rising hand dropped again.

Then suddenly all was uproar and confusion, those who had been chained to their chairs or places on the floor springing into action. The man had backed to the door, swept up the mail bags and now suddenly leaped backward into the outside night. Hap Smith and four or five other men had drawn their guns and were firing after him. There were outcries, above them surging the curses of the stage driver. Bert Stone was moaning on the floor. The girl wanted to go to him but for a little merely regarded him with wide eyes; there was a spreading pool on the bare floor at his side, looking in the uncertain light like spilled ink. A thud of bare feet, and Ma Drury came running into the room, her night dress flying after her.

"Pa!" she cried wildly. "You ain't killed, are you, Pa?"

"Bert is, most likely," he answered, swinging across the room to the fallen man. Then it was that the girl by the fire sprang to her feet and ran to Bert Stone's side.

"Who was it? What happened?" Ma Drury asked shrilly.

The men looked from one to another of their set-faced crowd. Getting only silence for her answer Ma Drury with characteristic irritation demanded again to be told full particulars and in the same breath ordered the door shut. A tardy squeal and another like an echo came from the room which harboured Lew Yates's wife and mother-in-law. Perhaps they had just come out from under the covers for air and squealed and dived back again . . . not being used to the customs obtaining in the vicinity of Drury's road house as Poke himself had remarked.

Hap Smith was the first one of the men who had dashed outside to return. He carried a mail bag in each hand, muddy and wet, having stumbled over them in the wild chase. He dropped them to the floor and stared angrily at them.

The bulky mail bag, save for the damp and mud, was untouched. The lean bag however had been slit open. Hap Smith kicked it in a sudden access of rage.

"There was ten thousan' dollars in there, in green backs," he said heavily. "They trusted it to me an' Bert Stone to get across with it. An' now . . ."

His face was puckered with rage and shame. He went slowly to where Bert Stone lay. His friend was white and unconscious . . . perhaps already his tale was told. Hap Smith looked from him to the girl who, her face as white as Bert's, was trying to staunch the flow of blood.

"I said it," he muttered lugubriously; "the devil's own night."

CHAPTER
THREE

Buck Thornton, Man's Man

Those who had rushed into the outer darkness in the wake of the highwayman returned presently. Mere impulse and swift natural reaction from their former enforced inactivity rather than any hope of success had sent them hot-foot on the pursuit. The noisy, windy night, the absolute dark, obviated all possibility of coming up with him. Grumbling and theorising, they returned to the room and closed the door behind them.

Now that the tense moment of the actual robbery had passed there was a general buzzing talk, voices lifted in surmise, a lively excitement replacing the cosy quiet of a few moments ago. Voices from the spare bed room urged Ma Drury to bring an account of the adventure, and Poke's wife, having first escorted the wounded man to her own bed and donned a wrapper and shoes and stockings, gave to Lew Yates's women folk as circumstantial a description of the whole affair as though she herself had witnessed it.

After a while a man here and there began to eat, taking a slab of bread and meat in one hand and a cup of black coffee in the other, walking back and forth and talking thickly. The girl at the fireplace sat stiff and still, staring at the flames; she had lost her appetite, had quite forgotten it in fact. At first from under the hand shading her eyes she watched the men going for one drink after another, the strong drink of the frontier; but after a little, as though this had been a novel sight in the beginning but soon lost interest for her, she let her look droop to the fire. Fresh dry fuel had been piled on the back log and at last a grateful sense of warmth and sleepiness pervaded her being. She no longer felt hunger; she was too tired, her eyelids had grown too heavy for her to harbour the thought of food. She settled forward in her chair and nodded. The talk of the men, though as they ate and drank their voices were lifted, grew fainter and fainter in her ears, further and further away. Finally they were blended in an indistinguishable murmur that meant nothing . . . In a doze she caught herself wondering if the wounded man in the next room would live. It was terribly still in there.

She was in that mental and physical condition when, the body tired and the brain betwixt dozing and waking, thought becomes a feverish process, the mind snatching vivid pictures from the day's experience and weaving them into as illogical a pattern as that of the crazy quilt over her shoulders. All day long she had ridden in the swaying, lurching, jerking stage until now in her chair, as she slipped a little forward, she experienced the sensations of the day. Many a time that day as the racing horses obeying the experienced hand of the driver swept around a sharp turn in the road she had looked down a sheer cliff that had made her flesh quiver so that it had been hard not to draw back and

22

cry out. She had seen the horses leaping forward scamper like mad runaways down a long slope, dashing through the spray of a rising creek to take the uphill climb on the run. And tonight she had seen a masked man shoot down one of her day's companions and loot the United States mail . . . And in a register somewhere she had written down the name of Hill's Corners. The place men called Dead Man's Alley. She had never heard the name until today. Tomorrow she would ask the exact significance of it . . .

At last she was sound asleep. She had found comfort by twisting sideways in her chair and resting her shoulder against the warm rock-masonry of the outer edge of the fireplace. She awoke with a start. What had recalled her to consciousness she did not know. Perhaps a new voice in her ears, perhaps Poke Drury's tones become suddenly shrill. Or it may be that just a sudden sinking and falling away into utter silence of all voice, the growing still of hands upon dice cups, all eloquent of a new breathless atmosphere in the room had succeeded in impressing upon her sleep-drugged brain the fact of still another vital, electrically charged moment. She turned in her chair. Then she settled back, wondering.

The door was open; the wind was sweeping in; again old newspapers went flying wildly as though in panicky fear. The men in the room were staring even as she stared, in bewilderment. She heard old man Adams's tongue clicking in his toothless old mouth. She saw Hap Smith, his expression one of pure amazement, standing, half crouching as though to spring, his hands like claws at his sides. And all of this because of the man who stood in the open doorway, looking in.

The man who had shot Bert Stone, who had looted a mail bag, had returned! That was her instant thought. And clearly enough it was the thought shared by all of Poke Drury's guests. To be sure he carried no visible gun and his face was unhidden. But there was the hugeness of him, bulking big in the doorway, the spare, sinewy height made the taller by his tall boot heels, the wide black hat with the drooping brim from which rain drops trickled in a quick flashing chain, the shaggy black chaps of a cowboy in holiday attire, the soft grey shirt, the grey neck handkerchief about a brown throat, even the end of a faded bandana trailing from a hip pocket.

He stood stone-still a moment, looking in at them with that queer expression in his eyes. Then he stepped forward swiftly and closed the door. He had glanced sharply at the girl by the fire; she had shaded her eyes with her hand, the shadow of which lay across her face. He turned again from her to the men, his regard chiefly for Hap Smith.

"Well?" he said lightly, being the first to break the silence. "What's wrong?"

There are moments in which it seems as if time itself stood still. During the spellbound fragment of time a girl, looking out from under a cupped hand, noted a man and marvelled at him. By his sheer physical bigness, first, he fascinated her. He was like the night and the storm itself, big, powerful, not the kind born to know and suffer restraint; but rather the type of man to dwell in such lands as stretched mile after unfenced mile "out yonder" beyond the mountains. As he moved he gave forth a vital impression of immense animal power; standing still he was dynamic. A sculptor might have carved him in stone and named the result "Masculinity."

The brief moment in which souls balanced and muscles were chained passed swiftly. Strangely enough it was old man Adams who precipitated action. The old man was nervous; more than that, bred here, he was fearless. Also fortune had given him a place of vantage. His body was half screened by that of Hap Smith and by a corner of the bar. His eager old hand snatched out Hap Smith's dragging revolver, levelled it and steadied it across the bar, the muzzle seeking the young giant who had come a step forward.

"Hands up!" clacked the old man in tremulous triumph. "I got you, dad burn you!" And at the same instant Hap Smith cried out wonderingly:

"Buck Thornton! You!"

The big man stood very still, only his head turning quickly so that his eyes were upon the feverish eyes of old man Adams.

"Yes," he returned coolly. "I'm Thornton." And, "Got me, have you?" he added just as coolly.

Winifred Waverly stiffened in her chair; already tonight had she heard gunshots and smelled powder and seen spurting red blood. A little surge of sick horror brought its tinge of vertigo and left her clear thoughted and afraid.

"Hands up, I say," repeated the old man sharply. "I got you."

"You go to hell," returned Thornton, and his coolness had grown into curt insolence. "I never saw the man yet that I'm going to do that for." He came on two more quick, long strides, thrust his face forward and cried in a voice that rang out commandingly above the crash of the wind, *"Drop that gun! Drop it!"*

Old man Adams had no intention of obeying; he had played poker himself for some fifty odd years and knew what bluff meant. But for just one brief instant he was taken aback, fairly shocked into a fluttering indecision by the thunderous voice. Then, before he could recover himself the big man had flung a heavy wet coat into Adams's face, a gun had been fired wildly, the bullet ripping into the ceiling, and Buck Thornton had sprung forward and whipped the smoking weapon from an uncertain grasp. Winifred Waverly, without breathing and without stirring, saw Buck Thornton's strong white teeth in a wide, good humoured smile.

"I know you were just joking but . . ."

He whirled and fired, never lifting the gun from his side. And a man across the room from him cried out and dropped his own gun and grasped his shoulder with a hand which slowly went red.

Now again she saw Buck Thornton's teeth. But no longer in a smile. He had seemed to condone the act of old Adams as a bit of senility; the look in his eyes was one of blazing rage as this other man drew back and back from him, muttering.

26

"I'd have killed you then," said Thornton coldly, his rage the cold wrath that begets murder in men's souls. "But I shot just a shade too quick. Try it again, or any other man here draw, and by God, I'll show you a dead man in ten seconds."

He drew back and put the bar just behind him. Then with a sudden gesture, he flung down the revolver which had come from Hap Smith's holster and more recently from old man Adams's fingers, and his hand flashed to his arm pit and back into plain sight, his own weapon in it.

"I don't savvy your game, sports," he said with the same cool insolence. "But if you want me to play just go ahead and deal me a hand."

To the last man of them they looked at him and hesitated. It was written in large bold script upon the faces of them that the girl's thought was their thought. And yet, though there were upward a dozen of them and though Poke Drury's firelight flickered on several gun barrels and though here were men who were not cowards and who did not lack initiative, to the last man of them they hesitated. As his glance sped here and there it seemed to stab at them like a knife blade. He challenged them and stood quietly waiting for the first move. And the girl by the fire knew almost from the first that no hostile move was forthcoming. And she knew further that had a man there lifted his hand Buck Thornton's promise would have been kept and he'd show them a dead man in ten seconds.

"Suppose," said Thornton suddenly, "you explain. Poke Drury, this being your shack . . . What's the play?"

Drury moistened his lips. But it was Hap Smith who spoke up.

"I've knowed you some time, Buck," he said bluntly. "An' I never knowed you to go wrong. But . . . Well, not an hour ago a man your build an' size an' with a bandana across his face stuck this place up."

"Well?" said Thornton coolly.

"At first," went on the stage driver heavily and a bit defiantly, "we thought it was him come back when you come in." His eye met Thornton's in a long unwavering look. "We ain't certain yet," he ended briefly.

Thornton pondered the matter, his thumb softly caressing the hammer of his revolver.

"So that's it, is it?" he said finally.

"That's it," returned Hap Smith.

"And what have you decided to do in the matter?"

Smith shrugged. "We acted like a pack of kids," he said. "Lettin' you get the drop on us like this. Oh, you're twice as quick on the draw as the best two of us an' we know it. An' . . . an' we ain't dead sure as we ain't made a mistake."

His candidly honest face was troubled. He was not sure that Thornton was the same man who so short a time ago had shot Bert Stone. It did not seem reasonable to Hap Smith that a man, having successfully made his play, would return just to court trouble.

"If you're on the square, Buck," he said in a moment, "throw down your gun an' let's see the linin' of your pockets!"

"Yes?" retorted Thornton. "What else, Mr. Smith?"

28

"Let us take a squint at that bandana trailin' out'n your back pocket," said Smith crisply. "If it ain't got deep holes cut in it!"

Now that was stupid, thought Winifred. Nothing could be more stupid, in fact. If this man had committed the crime and had thus voluntarily returned to the road house, he would be prepared. He would have emptied his pockets, he certainly would have had enough brains to dispose of so telltale a bit of evidence as a handkerchief with slits let into it.

"Maybe," said Thornton quietly, and she did not detect the contemptuous insolence under the slow words until he had nearly completed his meaning, "you'd like to have me tell you where I'm riding from and why? And maybe you'd like to have me take off my shoes so you can look in them for your lost treasures?" Now was his contempt unhidden. He strode quickly across the room, coming to the fireplace where the girl sat. He took the handkerchief from his pocket, keeping it rolled up in his hand; stooping forward he dropped it into the fire, well behind the back log.

Then for the first time he saw her face plainly. As he had come close to her she had slipped from her chair and stood now, her face lifted, looking at him. His gaze was arrested as his eyes met hers. He stood very still, plainly showing the surprise which he made no slightest effort to disguise. She flushed, bit her lip, went a fiery red. He put up his hand and removed his hat.

"I didn't expect," he said, still looking at her with that intent, openly admiring acknowledgment of her beauty, "to see a girl like you. Here."

The thing which struck her was that still there were men in the room who were armed and distrustful of him and that he had forgotten them. What she could not gauge was the full of the effect she had had upon him. He had marked a female form at the fireside, shawled by a shapeless patch-work quilt; out of it, magically it seemed to his startled fancies, there had stepped a superb creature with eyes on fire with her youth, a superlatively lovely creature, essentially feminine. From the flash of her eyes to the curl of her hair, she was all girl. And to Buck Thornton, man's man of the wide open country beyond the mountains, who had set his eyes upon no woman for a half year, who had looked on no woman of her obvious class and type for two years, who had seen the woman of one half her physical loveliness and tugging charm never, the effect was instant and tremendous. A little shiver went through him; his eyes caught fire.

CHAPTER
FOUR

The Ford

"These little cotton-tail rabbits," he said to her slowly, without turning his eyes from hers to those of whom he spoke, "haven't any more sense than you'd think to look at them. Once let them get a notion in their heads . . . Look here!" he broke off sharply. "*You* don't think the same way they do, do you?"

"No!" she said hurriedly.

Hurriedly, because for the moment her poise had fled from her and she knew that he must note the high colour in her cheeks. And the colour had come not in response to his words but in quick answer to his look. A young giant of a man, he stood staring at her like some artless boy who at a bend in the road had stopped, breathless, to widen his eyes to the smile of a fairy fresh from fairy land.

And her "No," was the true reply to his question and burst spontaneously from her lips. Her first swift suspicion when she had seen the bulk of him framed against the bleak night had been quite natural. But now that she had marked the man's carriage and had seen his face and looked for one instant deep into his clear eyes, she set her conjecture aside as an absurdity. It was not so much that her reason had risen to demand why a successful highwayman should return into danger and the likelihood of swift punishment. It was rather and simply because she felt that this bronzed young stranger, seeming to her woman's instinct a sort of breezy incarnation of the outdoors, partook of none of the characteristics of the footpad, sneak thief or nocturnal gentleman of the road. An essential attribute of the boldest and most picturesque of that gentry was the quality of deceit and subterfuge and hypocrisy. Consecutive logical thought being, after all, a tedious process, she had had no time to progress from step to step of deduction and inference; he had asked his question with a startling abruptness and as abruptly she had given him her answer. The rest might believe what they chose to believe. She, for her part, held Buck Thornton, whoever he might be, guiltless of the earlier affair of the evening. And, moreover, she could quite understand the impulse that sent an innocent man to toss a handkerchief into the fire and let them ponder on the act's significance. The act may have been foolhardy and certainly had the youthful flavour of bravado; none the less in her eyes the man achieved through it a sort of magnificence.

He stood looking at her very gravely and gravely she returned the look. And it was borne in upon the girl's inner consciousness that now and for the first time in her life she had come face to face with a man absolutely without guile or the need thereof. He was in character as he was in physique, or she read him wrongly. He thought his thought straight out and made no pretence of hiding it for the simple and sufficient reason that there was in all the universe no slightest need of hiding it. As she looked straight back into his eyes little flashes of impressions which had fastened upon her mind during the day came back to her, things which he suggested, which were like him. She was very tired and further she was overwrought from the nervous excitement of the evening; hence her mental processes were the quicker and more prone to fly off at wild tangents . . . She had seen a tall, rugged cedar on a rocky ridge blown through by the tempest, standing out in clear relief against the sky; this man recalled the scene, the very atmosphere. She had seen a wild swollen torrent hurtling on its way down the mountainside; the man had threatened to become like that, headlong with unbounded passion, fierce and destructive when a moment ago they opposed him . . . Again she bit her lip; she was thinking of this huge male creature in hyperboles. Yes; she was overwrought; it was not well to think thusly of any mere male creature.

And yet she but liked him the better and her fancies were smitten anew by what he did now. Having filled his eyes with her as a man a thirst may fill himself with water from a brook, he turned abruptly away and left her. He did not tarry to say "Thank you," that she had been almost eager in asserting her belief in his innocence. He did not go back to a futile and perhaps quarrelsome discussion with Hap Smith and old man Adams and the rest. He simply dropped everything where it was, shoved his big revolver out of sight under his left arm-pit and went to the long dining table.

There, his back to the room, he helped himself generously to cold meat, bread and luke-warm coffee and ate hungrily.

She sank back into her chair and let her eyes wander to his breadth of shoulder, straightness of back and even to the curl of his hair that cast its dancing shadows upon the wall in front of him. She had never had a man turn his back on her this way, and yet now the accomplished deed struck her in nowise as boorish or rude. He had paid her the tribute of a deep admiration, as clear and strong and unsullied as a racing mountain stream in spring time. The few words which he deemed necessary had passed between them. Then he had withdrawn himself from her attention. Not rude, the act savoured somehow of the downright free bigness of unconvention.

"It's silly, jumping to conclusions, any way," she informed herself. "Why suspect him just because he wears the costume of the country, has the usual red handkerchief in his possession and is tall? There are half a dozen big red handkerchiefs in this room right now . . . and this would seem to be the land of tall men."

Only once again did he speak to her that night and then just to say in plain matter-of-fact style: "You'd better lie down there and get some sleep. Good night." And this remark had come only after fifteen minutes of busy preparation on his part and curiosity on hers. He had gone out of the room into the night with no offered explanation and with many eyes following him; men began to show rising signs of excitement and to regret audibly that they had not "gathered him in." But in a few minutes he was back, his arms filled with loose hay from the barn. He spread it out in a corner, down by the long table. The table itself he drew out of the way. On the hay he smoothed out her quilt. Then, after a brief word with Poke Drury, he made another expedition into the night, returning with a strip of weather beaten, patched canvas; this he hung by the corners from the nails he hammered into a beam of the low ceiling, letting the thing drop partition-wise across the room. It had been then that he said quietly: "You'd better lie down there and get some sleep. Good night."

"Good night," she answered him. And as it was with his eyes that again he told her frankly what he thought of her, so was it with her eyes that she thanked him.

The night passed some-how. She lay down and slept, awoke, moved her body for more comfort, slept again. And through her sleep and dreams and wakeful moments she heard the quiet voices of the men who had no beds to go to; that monotonous sound and an occasional clink of glass and bottle neck or the rustling of shuffled cards. Once she got up and looked through a hole in the canvas; she had taken off her shoes and made no noise to draw attention to her spying. It must have been chance, therefore, which prompted Thornton to lift his head quickly and look toward her. The light was all on his side of the room; she knew that he had not heard her and could not see her; the tear in her flimsy wall was scarcely more than a pin-hole. He was playing cards; furthermore he was winning, there being a high stack of blue and red and white chips in front of him and a sprinkling of gold. But she saw no sign of the gambling fever in his eyes. Rather, there was in them a look which made her draw back guiltily; which sent her creeping back to her rude bed with suffused cheeks. He was still thinking of her, solely of her, despite the spoils of chance at his hand . . .

All night the storm beat at the lone house in the mountain pass, rattling at doors and windows, whistling down the chimney, shaking the building with its fierce gusts. The rain ceased only briefly when the cold congealed it into a flurry of beating hail stones; thereafter came the rain again, scarcely less noisy. And in the morning when she awoke with a start and smelled boiling coffee the wind was still raging, the rain was falling heavily and steadily.

In the dark and with the lamps burning on palely into the dim day she breakfasted. Together with several of the men she ate in the kitchen where a fire roared in an old stove, and where a table was placed conveniently. Ma Drury was about, sniffling with her cold, but cooking and serving her guests sourly, slamming down the enamelled ware in front of them and challenging them with a look to find fault anywhere. She reported that in some mysterious way, for which God be thanked, there were no dead men in her house this morning. Bert Stone was alive and showed signs of continuing to live, a thing to marvel at. And the man whom Buck Thornton had winged, beyond displaying a sore arm and disposition, was for the present a mere negligible and disagreeable quantity.

Hap Smith came in from the barn while she was eating. He was going to start right away. There was no use, however, in her attempting to make the rest of the trip with him. His other passengers would lie over here for a day or two. She looked at him curiously: why should she not go on? It certainly was not pleasant to think of remaining in these cramped quarters indefinitely.

Hap Smith, hastily eating hot cakes and ham, answered briefly and to the point. Mountain streams were all up, filling their narrow beds, spilling over. A rain like this downpour brought them up in a few hours; it would stop raining presently and they'd go down as fast as they had risen. Just two miles from the road house was the biggest stream of all to negotiate, being the upper waters of Alder Creek. It was up to Hap to make it because he represented a certain Uncle Samuel who was not to be stopped by hell or high water; literally that. He'd tie his mail bags in; leave all extras at Poke Drury's, drive his horses into the turbulent river high above the ford and . . . make it somehow. It was up to her to stay here.

He gobbled down his breakfast, rolled a fat brown cigarette, buttoned up his coat and went out to his stage. Before he could snap back his brake she was at his side.

"My business is as important to me as Uncle Samuel's is to him," she told him in a steady, matter-of-fact voice. "What is more, I have paid my fare and mean to go through with you."

He saw that she did mean it. He expostulated, but briefly. He was behind time, he knew that already they had sought to argue with her in the house, he recognized the futility of further argument. He had a wife of his own, had Hap Smith. He grunted his displeasure with the arrangement, informed her curtly that it was up to her and that, if they went under, his mail bags would require all of his attention, shrugged his two shoulders at once and high up, released his brake and went clattering down the rocky road. The girl cast a quick look behind her as they drew away from the road house; she had not seen Buck Thornton this morning and wondered if he had been loitering about the barn or had turned back into the mountains or had ridden ahead.

Alder Creek was a mad rush and swirl of muddy water; the swish and hiss of it smote their ears five minutes before they saw the brown, writhing thing itself. The girl tensed on her seat; her breathing was momentarily suspended; her cheek went a little pale. Then, conscious of a quick measuring look from the stage driver, she said as quietly as she could:

"It doesn't look inviting, does it?"

Hap Smith grunted and gave his attention forthwith and solely to the dexterous handling of his tugging reins. He knew the crossing; had made it with one sort of a team and another many times in his life. But he had never seen it so swollen and threatening and he had never heard its hissing sound upgathered into such a booming roar as now greeted them. He stopped his team and looked from under drawn brows at the water.

"You'd better get out," he said shortly.

"But I won't!" she retorted hurriedly. "And, since we are going to make the crossing . . . go ahead, quick!"

He winked both eyes at the rain driving into his face and sat still, measuring his chances. While he did so she looked up and down; not a hundred paces from them, upstream on the near bank, the figure of a man loomed unnaturally large in the wet air. He was mounted upon a tall, rangy horse that might have been foaled just for the purpose of carrying a man of his ilk, a pale yellow-sorrel whose two forefeet, had it not been for the mud, would have shone whitely. She wondered what he was doing there. His attitude was that of one who was patiently waiting.

"Hold on good an' tight," said Smith suddenly. "I'm goin' to tackle it."

She gripped the back of the seat firmly, braced her feet, set her teeth together, a little in quick fear, a great deal in determination. Smith swung his team upstream fifty paces, then in a short arc out and away from the creek; then, getting their heads again to the stream he called to them, one by one, each of the four in turn, saying crisply: "You, Babe! Charlie! that's the boy! Baldy! You Tom, you Tom! Into it; into it; *get up!*"

With shaking heads that flung the raindrops from tossing manes, with gingerly lifted forefeet, with a snort here and a crablike sidling dance there, they came down to the water's edge at a brisk trot. The off-lead, Charlie, fought shy and snorted again; the long whip in Hap Smith's hand shot out, uncurled, flicked Charlie's side, and with a last defiant shake of the head the big bay drove his obedient neck into his collar and splashed mightily in the muddy current. Babe plunged forward at his side; the two other horses followed as they were in the habit of following.

The girl, fascinated, saw the water curl and eddy and whiten about their knees; she saw it surge onward and rise about the hubs of the slow turning wheels. Higher it came and higher until the rushing sound of it filled her ears, the dark yellow flash of it filled her eyes and she sat breathless and rigid . . . A quick glance showed her the man, Thornton, still above them on the bank of the stream. She noted that he had drawn a little closer to the water's edge.

They were half way across, fairly in midstream, and Hap Smith, utterly oblivious of his one passenger, cursing mightily, when the mishap came. The mad stream, rolling its rocks and boulders and jagged tree trunks, had gouged holes in the bank here and there and had digged similar holes in the uneven bed itself. Into such a hole the two horses on the lower side floundered, with no warning and with disastrous suddenness. Then went down, until only their heads were above the current. They lost all solid ground under their threshing hoofs and, as they rose a little, began to swim, flailing about desperately. Hap Smith yelled at them, yanked at his reins, seeking to turn them straight down stream for a spell until the hole be passed. But already another horse was in and engulfed, the wagon careened, was whipped about in the furious struggle, a wheel struck a submerged boulder and Hap Smith leaped one way while Winifred Waverly sprang

40

the other as the awkward stage tipped and went on its side.

She knew on the instant that one had no chance to swim here, no matter how strong the swimmer. For the current was stronger than the mere strength of a human being. She knew that if Hap Smith clung tight to his reins he might be pulled ashore in due time, if all went well for him. She knew that Winifred Waverly had never been in such desperate straits. And finally she understood, and the knowledge was infinitely sweet to her in her moment of need, why the man yonder had been sitting his horse so idly in the rain, and just why he had been waiting.

She did not see him as his horse, striking out valiantly, swimming and finding precarious foothold by turns, bore down upon her; she saw only the yellow, dirty current when she saw anything at all. She could not know when, the first time, he leaned far out and snatched at her . . . and missed. For at the moment a sucking maelstrom had caught her and whipped her out of his reach and flung her onward, for a little piling the churning water above her head. She did not see when finally he succeeded in that which he had attempted. But she felt his two arms about her and in her heart there was a sudden glow and, though the water battled with the two of them, strangely enough a feeling of safety.

Perhaps it was only because he had planned on the possibility of just this and was ready for it that she came out of Alder Creek alive. He had slipped the loop of his rope about the horn of his saddle, making it secure with an additional half hitch; when he was sure of her he flung himself from the saddle, still keeping the rope in his hand as he took her into his arms. Then, swimming as best he could, seeking to keep her head and his above the water, he left the rest to a certain rangy, yellow-sorrel saddle horse. And as Hap Smith and his struggling team made shore just below the ford, Buck Thornton and Winifred Waverly were drawn to safety by Buck Thornton's horse.

Just as there had been no spoken thanks last night for a kindness rendered, so now on this larger occasion there was no gush of grateful words. He released her slowly and their eyes met. As he turned to help Hap Smith with the frightened horses entangled in their harness, the only words were his:

"A couple of miles farther on you'll pass a ranch house. You can get warm and dry your clothes there. This is the last bad crossing."

And so, lifting his hat, he left her.

CHAPTER
FIVE

The Man from Poison Hole Ranch

Dry town never looked less dry. As Buck Thornton drew rein in front of the one brick building of which the ugly little village could boast, the mud was above his yellow-sorrel's fetlocks. But the rain was over, the sun was out glorious and warm above the level lands and in the air was a miraculous feeling as of spring. It is the way of Dry Town in the matter of seasons to rival in abruptness its denizens' ways in other matters. The last great storm had come and gone and seeds would be bursting on every hand and eagerly now.

Because he loved a good horse, and this rangy sorrel above others, and because further he had been forced to ride the willing animal unusually hard all day yesterday, Thornton today had travelled slowly. So, long ago, he had watched the stage out of sight and now, when finally he drew up in front of the bank, he saw Hap Smith's lumbering vehicle standing down by the stable. From it he let his eyes travel along the double row of ill kept, unpainted houses. Fifty yards away a stranger would have marked only his great height, the lean, clean, powerful physique. But from near by one might have forgotten this matter of physical bigness for

43

another, noting just the man's eyes alone. Very keen, piercing, quick eyes just now, watchful and suspicious of every corner and alley, they more than hinted at a stern vigilance that was more than half positive expectancy.

Only for a moment he sat so. Then he swung down from the saddle and with spurs clanking noisily upon the board sidewalk went into the bank building.

"I want to see Mr. Templeton," he said abruptly to the clerkly looking individual behind the new lattice work. The words were very quietly spoken, the voice rather soft and gentle for so big a man. And yet the cashier turned quickly, looking at him curiously.

"Who shall I say it is?" he demanded.

"This man's town is getting citified mighty fast," the tall man grunted. "I should have brought my cards! Well, just tell him it's Thornton."

"Thornton?"

"You got it. Buck Thornton, from the Poison Hole ranch."

He spoke lightly, his voice hinting at a vast store of good nature, his eyes, however, losing meanwhile no glint of their stern light as they looked at the man to whom he was talking and beyond him watched the door through which he had entered. The cashier regarded him with new interest.

"You are early, Mr. Thornton," he said, rather more warmly than he had spoken before. "But Mr. Templeton will be glad to see you. He is in his private office. Walk right in."

Thornton stooped, his back to the wall, and swiftly unbuckled his spurs. Carrying them in his left hand he passed along the lattice work partition which shut off the cashier with his books and till, and threw open the door at the end of the short hallway. Here was a sort of waiting room, to judge from the two or three chairs, the square topped table strewn with financial journals and illustrated magazines indiscriminately mixed. He closed the door behind him, standing again for a moment as he had stood out in the street, his eyes keen and watchful as they took swift inventory of the room and its furnishings.

Before him was a second door upon the frosted glass top of which were the stencilled words: J. W. TEMPLETON, President, Private. He took a step toward the door and then stopped suddenly as though the very vehemence of the voice bursting out upon the other side of it had halted him.

"I tell you, Miss Waverly," . . . it was Templeton's voice, snappy and irritable, . . . "this thing is madness! Pure and simple, unadulterated madness! It's as devoid of sense as a last year's nest of birds; it's as full of danger as a . . . a . . ."

"Never mind exhausting your similes, Mr. Templeton," came the answer, the girl's voice young and fresh and yet withal firm and a little cool. "I didn't come to ask your advice, you know. And you haven't given me what I did come for. If you . . ."

Thornton pushed the door open, sweeping off his hat as he came in, and said bluntly,

"I don't know what you folks are talking about, but I judge it's important. And there's no sense in looseendish talk when you don't know who's listening."

The square built, square faced man tapping with big square finger ends at the table in front of him whirled about suddenly, his gesture and eyes alike showing his keen annoyance at the interruption. Then when he saw who it was he got to his feet, saying crisply:

"I'm glad it's you. This young woman has got it into her head . . ."

"You will remember, Mr. Templeton, that this is in strict confidence?"

Templeton's teeth shut with a click. Thornton turned from him and, with his spurs in one hand, his hat caught in the other, stood looking down upon the owner of the voice that was at once so fresh and young, so coolly determined and vaguely defiant. And as he looked at her there was much speculation in his grave eyes. Odd that he should stumble upon her the first thing. Odd and — natural . . .

The girl's back was to him. For a moment she did not shift her position the least fraction of an inch, but sat very still, leaning forward in her chair, facing the banker. Then after a little when it was evident that Templeton was going to say nothing more she turned slowly to the new comer, her lashes sweeping upward swiftly as her eyes met his full and steady. And the man from the Poison Hole ranch, his own eyes looking down into hers very gravely, noted many things in the quick, keen way characteristic of him.

He saw that her mouth, red lips about very white teeth, was smiling softly, confidently; and yet that the brownflecked grey of her eyes was as unsmiling, as gravely speculative as his own eyes were. He saw that her skin was a golden brown from life in the open outdoors, that she had upon the heels of her boots a pair of tiny, sharp rowelled spurs, that a riding quirt hung from her right wrist by its rawhide thong, that her cheeks were a little flushed as though from excitement but that she knew the trick of forbidding her eyes to tell what her excitement was. He saw that her throat, where her neck scarf fell loosely away from it, was very round and white. He saw that while her grey riding habit covered her body it hid none of her body's grace and strength and slender youthfulness.

While his eyes left hers to note these things her eyes had been as busy, running from the man's close cropped dark hair to his mud-spattered boots. And there came into her look just a hint of admiration which the man did not see as she in her swift examination noted the breadth of shoulder, the straight tallness of him, the clean, supple, sinewy form which his loose attire of soft shirt, unbottoned vest grey with dust, and shaggy chaps, black and much worn, in no way concealed.

"I have come," he was saying now to Templeton, speaking abruptly although his voice was as gentle and low-toned and pleasant as when he had spoken with the cashier, "three days ahead of time. It won't take me a minute to get through. And if you and the young lady will excuse me I'll say my little speech and drift, giving you a free swing for your business. Besides, I'm in a fair sized hurry."

"Certainly," said Templeton immediately, while the girl, smiling now with eyes and lips together, unconcernedly, made no answer. "Miss Waverly is planning to . . . Well, I want to talk with her a little more. Well, Thornton," and only now he put out his hand to be gripped quickly and warmly by the other's, "what is it? I'm glad to see you. Everything's all right?"

"Yes. I just dropped in to fix up that second payment."

"Shall I go out while you talk?" The girl had gotten to her feet swiftly. "If you are going to say anything important . . ."

"No, you'd better stay," Thornton said, and added jestingly: "I've got nothing confidential on my mind, and since I'm just going to hand Mr. Templeton some money, an almighty big pile of money for me to be carrying around, maybe we'd better have a witness to the transaction."

The banker looked at him in surprise.

"You don't mean that you've got it with you now? That you've just ridden in from the range and have brought it with you . . . in cash!"

For answer the cattle man slipped a bronzed hand into his shirt and brought out a small packet done up in a piece of buckskin and tied with a string. He tossed it to the shining table top, where it fell heavily.

"There she is," he said lightly. "Gold and a few pieces of paper. The whole thing. Count it."

Templeton sank back into his chair and stared at him. He put out his hand, lifted the packet, dropped it back upon the table, stared again, and then burst out irritably:

"Of all the reckless young fools in the county you two are without equals. Buck Thornton, I thought *you* had some sense!"

"You never can tell," came the quiet rejoinder from unsmiling lips. "I saw a man once I thought had sense and I found out afterwards he ran sheep. Now, if you'll see my bet I'll travel."

Templeton's desk shears were already busy. He jerked the packet open flat on the table. There were many twenty dollar pieces, some fives and tens and a little bundle of bank notes. He counted swiftly.

"It's all right. Five thousand dollars," he said crisply. "In full for second payment due, as you say, in three days. I'll note it on the two agreements. And I'll give you a receipt."

The tall man's deep chest rose and fell to a sigh as of relief at having done his errand; he placed his spurs in his hat and his hat upon a chair and began to roll a cigarette. The banker wrote quickly with sputtering pen in a book of receipt blanks, tore out the leaf and passed it across the table.

"There you are, Buck Thornton of the Poison Hole," he said with an increase of irritability in his curt tones. "And now you listen to me; you're a fool! Or else you're so far out of the world over on your ranch that you don't know what's going on. Which is it?"

"I hear a good deal of what's happening," returned Thornton drily.

"Then I suppose you realize that a man who rides day and night, through that country, carrying five thousand dollars with him, and when everybody in the country knows that according to contract he is about due to make a five thousand dollar payment, is acting like a fool with a suicidal mania?"

For a moment Thornton did not answer. He seemed so engrossed in his cigarette building that one might almost suppose that he had not heard. And then, lifting his head suddenly, his eyes keen and hard upon Templeton's, he said casually,

"I dropped in three days ahead of time, didn't I?"

"And the wonder is," snapped Templeton, "that you haven't dropped clean out of the world! If you do a fool thing like this, Buck Thornton, when your last payment is due, you can do it. But I won't go near your funeral!"

Thornton laughed easily, tucked the receipt into his vest pocket, and reached for his hat and spurs.

"I'm obliged, Mr. Templeton," he acknowledged lightly. "But we've got to admit that I got across all right this time. And, as you've heard, I suppose, right under Mr. Bad Man's nose, since I was carrying that little wad last night when Hap Smith got cleaned at Poke Drury's. Well, I'll be going. Just give that rattlesnake Pollard the five thousand and an invitation from me to keep off my ranch, remembering that it doesn't happen to belong to him any more."

He nodded and went to the door. There he turned and looked back at the girl. She had risen swiftly, even coming a step toward him.

"I haven't thanked you . . . I . . ."

Templeton looked on curiously, an odd twitching at the corners of his large mouth. Thornton threw up a sudden hand.

"No," he said hastily. "You haven't spoiled things by thanking me. And . . . We'll see each other again," he concluded in his quietly matter-of-fact way. And, his nod for both of them, he went out.

CHAPTER
SIX

Winifred Judges a Man

There was a puzzled frown in her eyes, a faint flush tinging her cheeks as, withdrawing her regard from Thornton's departure, she looked to Templeton and asked quickly:

"Why did he call Henry Pollard a rattlesnake?"

A faint smile for a moment threatened to drive the sternness away from Templeton's lips. But it was gone in a quick tightening of the mouth, and he answered briefly.

"He didn't know that you knew Pollard."

"I don't know him," she reminded him coolly. "You will remember that I haven't seen him since I was six years old. I hardly know what he looks like. But you haven't answered me; why did your imprudent giant call him a rattlesnake?"

"They have had business dealings together," he told her vaguely. "Maybe they have disagreed about something. Men out there are a little given to hard words, I think."

She sat silent, leaning forward, tapping at her boot with her quirt. Then quickly, just as the banker was opening his lips to speak of the other matter, she demanded:

"Why did you call him a fool for bringing the money here? It had to be brought, hadn't it?"

"Yes! That's just it. It had to be brought and there is not a man in all of the cattle country here who does not know all about the terms of the contract Thornton and Pollard made. Ten thousand down, five thousand in three days from now, the other five thousand in six months. Why, right now I wouldn't attempt to carry five thousand dollars *in cash* over that wilderness trail if there were ten times the amount to come to me at the end of it! It's as mad as this thing you want to do."

"He did it."

"Yes," shortly. "He did it." He gathered up the loose money, pushed a button set in the table, and upon the prompt appearance of the cashier said crisply, "Five thousand to apply on the Pollard–Thornton agreement. Put it in the big safe immediately."

"He looks as though he could take care of himself," the girl said thoughtfully when the money had gone.

Templeton whirled about upon her, his eyes blazing.

"Take care of himself!" he scoffed. "What chance has a man to take care of himself when another man puts a rifle ball through his back? What chance had Bill Varney of the Twin Dry Diggings stage only three weeks ago? Varney is dead and the money he was carrying is gone, that's the chance *he* had! What chance has any man had for the last six months if he carried five hundred dollars on him and any one knew about it? They chased off a dozen steers from Kemble's place not three days ago, you yourself know what happened at Drury's road

53

house last night, and now Buck Thornton rides through the same country with five thousand dollars on him!"

"He did it," she repeated again very softly, her eyes musing.

"And one of these days he's going to find out how simple a matter it is for a gang like the gang operating in broad daylight in this country now to separate a fool and his money! The Lord knows how a simple trick like coming in three days ahead of time fooled them It won't do it again."

"He is the type of man to succeed," she went on, still musingly.

Templeton shrugged.

"We have our own business on our hands," he said abruptly, looking at his watch. "The stage leaves in half an hour. Are you going to be reasonable?"

Then she stood up and smiled at him very brightly.

"The stage is going its way, Mr. Templeton. I am going mine."

Templeton flung down his pen with an access of irritation which brought a flicker of amusement into the bright grey eyes. But the banker's grim mouth did not relax; there was anger in the gesture with which he slammed a blotter down on the big yellow envelope on which his wet pen had fallen. After his carefully precise fashion he was reaching for a fresh, clean envelope when the girl took the slightly soiled one from him.

"Thank you," she said, rising and smiling down at him. "But this will do just as well. And now, if you'll wish me good luck . . ."

She went out followed by a look of much grave speculation.

Meanwhile Buck Thornton, leading his horse after him, crossed the dusty street to the Last Chance saloon. At the watering trough he watered his horse, and then, slackening the cinch a little, he went inside. In the front part of the long, dreary room was the bar presided over by a gentleman in overalls, shirt sleeves and very black hair plastered close to his low forehead. At the rear was the lunch counter where two Chinamen were serving soup and stew and coffee to half a dozen men. Thornton, with one of his quick, sharp glances which missed nothing in the room, went to the bar.

"Hello, Blackie," he said quietly.

The bartender, who in a leisure moment had been bending in deep absorption over an illustrated pink sheet spread on the bar, looked up quickly. For a short second a little gleam as of surprise shone in his shoe-button eyes. Then he put out his hand, shoving the pink sheet aside.

"Hello, Buck," he cried genially. "Where'd you blow in from?"

"Poison Hole," briefly. He spun a silver dollar on the bar and ignored the hand.

Blackie reached for bottle and glass, and putting them before the cowboy bestowed upon him a shrewd, searching look.

"What's the news out your way, Buck?"

"Nothing." He tossed off his whiskey, took up his change and went on to the lunch counter. Several men looked up at him; one or two nodded. It was evident that the new owner of the Poison Hole was something of a stranger here. He called an order to the Chinaman at the stove, told him that he'd be back in ten minutes and was in a hurry and went out to his horse. The bartender watched him go but said nothing.

Within less than ten minutes Thornton had left his sorrel at the stable, seeing personally the animal had its grain, and had come back to the saloon. Blackie, idle with his gazette unnoticed in front of him, saw him come in this time.

"In town for a little high life, Buck?" he queried listlessly.

"No. Business." He passed on down toward the lunch counter, and then swinging about suddenly came back. "Bank business," he added quietly. "I just paid my second instalment of five thousand dollars cash!"

For a moment he stood staring very steadily into the bartender's eyes, a great deal of significance in his look. Blackie returned his stare steadily.

"You're lucky, Buck," he offered colourlessly.

"Meaning to get the Poison Hole? Yes. It's the best cow range I ever saw."

"Meanin' to pack five thousan' aroun' in your tail pocket an' get away with it with this stick-up gang workin' the country."

Thornton shrugged his shoulders.

"There isn't any gang," he said, speaking as a man who knew. "It's one man with a confederate here and there maybe to keep him hep. Every job that has been pulled off yet was a one man job."

56

Blackie polished his bar and shook his head.

"Jed MacIntosh got cleaned out night before last," he retorted. "He'd made a clean-up right in here playin' stud. They got his wad before he'd gone to the end of the street. That was more than a one man job."

"Did Jed see more than one?" demanded Thornton sharply.

"No. Jed didn't see nothin', I guess. But we all seen the trail their horses made goin' through Jed's hay-field. There was three horses any way."

With no answer to this Thornton turned away, washed at the faucet near the back door, and settled his tall form upon one of the high stools at the counter. He ate hungrily, with no remark to the men upon right and left of him. But he heard their scraps of talk, noting that the one topic of conversation here in Dry Town was the work of the "stick-up party" manifesting itself in such episodes as the robbery and murder of Bill Varney, stage driver, the theft of Kemble's cattle, the "cleanin'" of Jed MacIntosh and, finally, the affair of last night at Poke Drury's. He listened with what seemed frank and only mild interest.

"It's a funny thing to me," one little dried-up old man with fierce moustaches and very gentle eyes was saying, "what we got a sheriff for. This sort of gun play's been runnin' high for nigh on six months now, an' Cole Dalton ain't boarded anybody in his little ol' jail any worse'n hoboes an' drunks for so long it makes a feller wonder what a jail an' a sheriff is for."

"Give him time, Pop," laughed a young rancher at his side. "You know all that's the matter with Cole Dalton

57

is he's got his election on the Republican ticket, an' you ain't never saw a man yet as wasn't a Demmy-crat as you'd admit was any 'count. Give him time. Cole knows what he's doin', an' when he does git his rope on Mr. Badman he ain't goin' to *need* no jail. Cole'll give him a firs' class funeral an' save the county a board bill."

Pop grunted, sniffed, and got to his feet to go to the door and watch the stage pull out. At the rumble and creak of the great lumbering vehicle and the quick thud of the hoofs of the four running horses several men left the lunch counter and followed him. Buck Thornton, finishing his own meal swiftly, went with the others.

Hap Smith took on fresh mail bags in front of the postoffice, slammed back his brake, and with his long whip cracking like pistol shots over his leaders' heads, drove on until he had passed the Last Chance. And then he came to a halt again, his coach rocking and rolling on its great springs, in front of the bank.

"Hi, there," he yelled mightily. "Git a move on, will you? I'm half a day late now."

Mr. Templeton himself appeared on the instant at the door, a small strong box in his hands. He tossed it up into the ready hands of the bull-necked, round-shouldered guard who sat at Hap Smith's side with a rifle between his knees, the two passengers craned their necks with much interest, the guard bestowed the box under the seat, the driver loosened his reins, threw off his brake, and the stage rocked and rumbled down the street, spattering mud on either hand, racing away upon the last leg of its two hundred and fifty mile trip to the last town upon the far border of the great state.

"And Templeton called *me* a fool!" mused the tall cattle man, a look of vast contempt in his stern eyes.

He stood a little behind the other men, looking over their heads. For only a fleeting second had his glance rested upon the stage at the bank. Then he looked swiftly at the man in front of him. It was Blackie, the bartender. When Blackie turned abruptly Thornton looked squarely into the black eyes, seeing there an unusually beady brightness, something of the hint of a quick frown upon the thin slick line of the eyebrows.

"Driver and guard will both be needing their shooting irons before they see the border, Blackie," Thornton said quietly.

And then with a short, insolent laugh he returned for the hat he had left hanging upon a nail. Blackie, making no answer, followed, going behind his bar. A little dusky red had crept up into his shallow face, his eyes burned hard into Thornton's as the man from the Poison Hole came by him.

"When you goin' back to the range, Buck?" he asked sharply.

"I'm going to start as soon as I can roll a smoke and saddle a horse," Thornton answered him, a little smile in his eyes. And then, as an after thought, "I follow the stage road for about ten miles before I turn off on the trail. Wish I could stick with them clean through."

"What for?" demanded Blackie in the same sharp tone.

59

"Oh, just to see the fun," Thornton told him lightly. "So long, Blackie."

"You seem to be mighty sure something's goin' to be pulled off this trip."

Thornton hung upon his heel, turning slowly.

"I am, Blackie," he said carelessly. And then, "Say, did you notice the two passengers in the stage?"

"No." He put a great deal of emphasis into the denial. "Who was it?"

"I thought you might have noticed. One of them was that crooked eyed jasper I saw you staking to free drinks the last time I was in town."

He stared straight into the smaller man's eyes, saw the colour deepen in his cheeks, shrugged his big shoulders and went to the door. Several of the men who had come back into the room looked after him curiously, then as though for explanation, into Blackie's narrowed eyes. The bartender's hand dropped swiftly out of sight under his bar. Thornton's back was turned square upon him. And yet, as though he had seen the gesture and it had been full of significance to him, he whirled with a movement even quicker than Blackie's had been, and standing loosely, his hands at his side, looked coolly into the bright black eyes. For a moment no man moved. Then Blackie, with a little sigh which sounded loudly in the quiet room, brought his hand back into sight, letting his fingers tap upon the bar. Thornton smiled, turned again and stepped quickly out of the door.

"As long as they don't get any closer to the Poison Hole it's none of my funeral," he muttered to himself.

"But if they do, I know one little man who could do a powerful lot of squealing with the proper inducement!"

Not turning once he passed swiftly down the street toward the stable, his meditative eyes upon the rocking stage sweeping on to the south-east, already drawing close to the first of the wooded foothills. He waited ten minutes, watching his horse eating, and then saddled and rode out toward the hills.

CHAPTER
SEVEN

An Invitation to Supper

It was hardly noon. Here the county road, cutting straight through the rolling fields, was broad, wet and black, glistening under the sun. Out yonder in front of him the stage, driven rapidly by Hap Smith that he might make up a little of the lost time, topped a gentle rise, stood out briefly against the sky line, shot down into the bed of Dry Creek and was lost to him. A little puzzled frown crept into Thornton's eyes.

"A man would almost say old Pop was right," he told himself. "This state is getting too settled up for this kind of game to be pulled off so all-fired regularly. Cole Dalton must be blind in his off eye . . . Oh, hell! it is none of my business. Any way . . . not yet."

He pulled his horse out into the trail paralleling the muddy road, jerked his hat down lower over his forehead, slumped forward a little in the saddle, and gave himself over to the sleepy thirty mile ride to Harte's Camp. He rode slowly now, allowing Hap Smith's speeding horses to draw swiftly away ahead of him. He saw the stage once more climbing a distant ridge; then it was lost to him in the steepening hills. A little more than an hour later he turned off to the left, leaving the county road and entering the mouth of the cañon through which his trail led. He would not see the road again although after a while he would parallel it with some dozen miles of rolling land between him and it.

Behind him lay the wide stretch of plain in which Dry Town was set; about him were the small shut-in valleys where the "little fellows" had their holdings and small herds of long horns and saddle ponies. Before him were the mountains with Kemble's place upon their far slope and his own home range lying still farther to the east. There were many streams to ford in the country through which he was now riding, all muddy-watered, laced with white, frothing edgings, but none to rise higher than his horse's belly.

Here there was a tiny valley, hardly more than a cup in the hills, but valuable for its rich feed and for the big spring set in the middle of it. He dismounted, slipped the Spanish bit from his horse's mouth, and waited for the animal to drink. It was a still, sleepy afternoon. The storm had left no trace in the deep blue of the sky; the hills were rapidly drying under the hot sun. Man and horse seemed sleepy, slow moving figures to fit into a glowing landscape, harmoniously. The horse drank slowly, shook its head in half tolerant protest at the flies singing before its eyes, and played with the water with twitching lips as though, with no will to take up the trail again, it sought to deceive its master into thinking that it was still drinking. The man yawned and his drowsy eyes came away from the wood-topped hills before him to the moist earth under foot. For the moment they did not seem the eyes of the Buck Thornton who had ridden to the bank in Dry Town a little before noon, but were gentle and dreamily meditative with all of the earlier sharp alertness gone. And then suddenly there came into them a quick change, a keen brightness, as he jerked his head forward and stared down at the ground at his feet.

"Now what is *she* doing out this way?" he asked himself aloud. "And where is she going?"

Though the soil was cut and beaten with the sharp hoofs of the many cattle that had drunk here earlier in the day, it was not so rough that it hid the thing which the quick eyes of the cattle man found and understood. There, close to the water's edge and almost under his own horse's body, were the tracks a shod horse had left not very long ago. The spring water was still trickling into one of them. There, too, a little to the side was the imprint of the foot of the rider who had gotten down to drink from the same stream, the mark of a tiny, high heeled boot.

"It might be some other girl," he told himself by way of answer to his own question. "And it might be a Mex with a proud, blue-blooded foot. But," and he leaned further forward studying the foot print, "it's a mighty good bet I could tell what she looks like from the shape of her head to the colour of her eyes! Now, what do you suppose she's tackling? Something that Mr. Templeton says is plumb foolish and full of danger?"

He slipped the bit back into his horse's mouth and swung up into the saddle.

64

"She didn't come out the way I came," he reflected as for a moment he sat still, looking down at the medley of tracks. "I'd have seen her horse's tracks. She must have made a big curve somewhere. I wonder what for?"

Then slowly the gravity left his eyes and a slow smile came into them. He surprised his horse with a touch of the spurs.

"Get into it, you long-legged wooden horse, you!" he chuckled. "We've got something to ride for now! We're going to see Miss Grey Eyes again. There's something besides stick-up men worth a man's thinking about, little horse!"

He reined back into the trail, rode through the little valley, climbed the ridge beyond and so pushed on deeper and ever deeper into the long sweep of flat country upon the other side. Often his eyes ran far ahead, seeking swiftly for the slender figure he constantly expected to see riding eastward before him; often they dropped to the trail underfoot to see that her horse's tracks had not turned to right or left should she leave this main horseman's highway for some one of the countless cross trails.

The afternoon wore on, the miles dropped away behind him; and he came to the end of the flat country and again was in low rolling hills. Her horse's tracks were there always before him, and yet he had had no sight of any rider that day since leaving the county road. Again much gravity came back into his eyes.

"Where's she going?" he asked himself again. "It looks like she was headed for Harte's Camp too. And then on to Hill's Corners? All alone? It's funny."

Twenty miles he had come from Dry Town. He was again riding slowly, remembering that his horse had carried the great weight of him many long miles yesterday and today. Now the hills grew steep and shot up high and rugged against the sky. The trail was harder, steeper, narrower where it wound along the edges of the many ravines. Again and again the ground was so flinty that it held no sign to show whether shod horse had passed over it or not. But he told himself that there was scant likelihood of her having turned out here; there was but the one trail now. And then, suddenly when he came down into another little valley through which a small drying stream wandered, he came upon the tracks he had been so long following. And he noted, with a little lift to the eyebrows, that here were the fresh hoof marks of two horses leading on toward the Camp.

"Somebody else has cut in from the side," he pondered. "Lordy, but this cattle country is sure getting shot all to pieces with folks. Who'd you suppose this new pilgrim is?"

Once or twice he drew rein, studying the signs of the trail. The tracks he had picked up at the stream with the print of the tiny boot were the small marks of a pony. This second horse for which he was seeking to account was certainly a larger animal, leaving bigger tracks, deeper sunk. There was little difficulty in distinguishing one from the other. And there was as little trouble in reading that the larger horse had followed the pony, for again and again the big, deep track lay over the other, now and then blotting it out.

A man, with a long solitary ride ahead of him, has much time for conjecture, idle and otherwise. Here lay the hint of a story; who was the second rider, what was his business? Whence had he come and whither was he riding? And did his following the girl mean anything?

Thornton came at last, in the late afternoon, to the last stream he would ford before reaching Harte's Camp. Another half mile, the passing over a slight rise, and he would be in sight of the end of his day's ride. He crossed the stream, and then, looking for the tracks he had been following, he saw that again the pony was pushing on ahead of him, that the horseman had turned aside. He jerked his horse back seeking for the lost tracks. And presently he found them, turning to the south and leading off into the mountains.

With thoughtful eyes he returned to his trail. He rode over the little ridge and so came into sight of the three log cabins under the oaks of Harte's place. Beyond was the barn. He would go there, find her horse at the manger. Then he would go up to the cabin in which the Hartes' lived and there find her.

Twenty minutes later, his face and hands washed at the well, his short cropped hair brushed back with the palm of his hand, he went to the main cabin. The door was shut but the smoke from the rough stone chimney spoke eloquently of supper being cooked within. But he was not thinking a great deal of the supper. He had found the pony in the barn, had even seen a quirt which he remembered, knew that he had not been mistaken in the matter of ownership of the trim boots that had left their marks at the spring, and realized that he was rather gladder of the circumstance than the mere facts of the case would seem to warrant. And then, with brows lifted and mouth puckered into a silent whistle, he read the words on a bit of paper tacked to the cabin door:

"We've gone over to Dave Wendells. The old woman is took sick. Back in the morning most likely make yourself to home. W. HARTE."

He paused a moment, frowning, his hat in his hand. It seemed to be in his thought to go back to his horse. While he hesitated the door was flung open and a pair of troubled grey eyes looked out at him searchingly; a pair of red lips tremulously trying to be firm smiled at him, and a very low voice faltered, albeit with a brave attempt to be steady:

"Won't you come in . . . Mr. Thornton? And . . . and make yourself at home, too? I've done it. I suppose it's all right . . ."

And then when still he hesitated, and his embarrassment began to grow and hers seemed to melt away, she added brightly and quite coolly:

"Supper is ready . . . and waiting. And I'm simply starved. Aren't you?"

Thornton laughed.

"Come to think of it," he admitted, "I believe I am."

CHAPTER
EIGHT

In Harte's Cabin

There was a rough board table, oilcloth-covered, in front of the fireplace. There were coffee, bread and butter, crisp slices of bacon, a dish of steaming tinned corn. There were two plates with knife and fork at the side, two cups, two chairs drawn up to the table.

"You see," she said, gaily and lightly enough, "you *have* kept me waiting."

He glanced swiftly at her as she stood by the fireplace, and away. For though twilight in the wooded country had crept out upon them he could see the look in her eyes, the set of the red lipped mouth. And he knew downright fear when he saw it, though it be fear bravely masked.

"Let's eat," he answered, having many things in his mind, but no other single thing to say to her just yet.

She flashed him a quick look and sat down. Thornton dragged back the other chair, flung his hat to the bunk in the corner of the room, and disposed his long legs uncomfortably under the small table. Inwardly he was devoutly cursing Dave Wendell for allowing anybody at his place to choose this particular time to get sick and the Hartes for going to the assistance of a ten-mile distant neighbour.

He watched the girl's quick fingers busy with the blackened coffee pot, realized at one and the same time that she had no ring upon a particular finger and that it was idiotic for him to so much as look for it, never allowed his glance to wander higher than her hands and attacked his bread and butter as though its immediate consumption were the most important thing in all the world. And she, when she felt that he was not watching her, when his silence was almost a tangible thing, looked at him with quick furtiveness. The something in her expression which had spoken of terror began to give place to the look of amusement which twitched at her lips and flickered up in the soft grey of her eyes. And since still he gave no sign of breaking the silence which had fallen over them, she said at last:

"Didn't you know all the time who I was?"

Then he looked up at her inquiringly. And when he saw that she was smiling a little of his sudden restraint fled from him and his eyes smiled back gently a little and reassuringly into hers.

"All the time?" he asked. "Meaning when?"

"Back there. On the trail," she told him.

"Well," he admitted slowly, "I guess I was pretty sure. Of course I couldn't be dead certain. It might have been anybody's tracks . . . that is," he corrected with a quick broadening of the smile, "anybody with a foot the right size to fit into a boot like that."

"Like what?" she asked in turn.

"Like the one that made the tracks by the creek where you came into the main trail, where you stopped to drink."

"You saw that?"

"If I hadn't seen it how was I to guess that it was you ahead of me?" he demanded. And when she frowned a little and did not answer for a moment he gave his attention to the black coffee which she had poured for him. "You sure know how to make coffee *right*," he complimented her with a vast show of sincerity. "This is the best I ever tasted."

"I'm glad you like it," she retorted as the frown fled before a hint of laughter. "I found it already made in the pot and just warmed it over!"

"Oh," said Thornton. And then with much gravity of tone but with twinkling eyes, "Come to think of it it isn't the *taste* of it that a man notices; it's the being just hot enough. I never had any coffee better warmed-up than this."

"Thank you." She stirred the sugar in her own cup of muddy looking beverage and without glancing up at him this time, went on, "You mean that you didn't know who I was when you saw me?"

"At the bank in Dry Town?"

"Of course not. Back there on the trail."

"I didn't see you," he told her.

Now she flashed another quick upward glance at him as though seeking for a reason lying back of his words.

"I saw *you*," she said steadily. "Twice. First from the top of a hill half a dozen miles back when you got down to look at your horse's foot. Did he pick up a stone?"

71

His eyes opened in surprise.

"I didn't get off to look at my horse's foot. And he didn't pick up anything."

"The second time," she continued, "was just when you had come to the last stream. I thought that you were going to turn off into the cañon. I saw that your horse was limping."

He shook his head. She must have seen that other fellow whose tracks Thornton had for so long seen following the tracks of her pony.

"What made you think you recognized me?" he asked.

"I didn't think. I knew."

"Then . . . how did you know?"

The surprise showing in her frankly lifted brows was very plain now.

"You were hardly five hundred yards away," she retorted. "And," with a quick, sweeping survey of him, "you are not a man to be readily mistaken even at that distance, you know."

"Meaning the inches of me? The up-and-down six feet four of me?" He shook his head. "I'm the only man in this neck of the woods built on the bean pole style."

"Meaning," she returned steadily, "your size and form; meaning the unusually wide hat you wear; meaning your blue shirt and grey neck-handkerchief . . . grey handkerchiefs aren't so common, are they? . . . meaning your tall sorrel horse that limped, and your bridle with the red tassel swinging from the headstall! *Now*," a little sharply, a little anxiously, he thought, "you are not going to tell me that I was mistaken, are you?"

She saw that his surprise, growing into sheer amazement as she ran on, was a wonderfully simulated thing if it were not real.

"You made a mistake," he said coolly. "I saw in the trail that there was another man following you. If I had known his get-up was so close to mine, I'd have done a little fast riding to take a peep at him. He turned off at the last creek, as you thought."

"You saw him?" she asked quickly.

"I saw his tracks. And," he added with deep thoughtfulness as he stared past her into the smouldering fire in the fireplace, "I'd sure like to know who he is."

Again, as she watched him, an expression of uneasiness crept into her eyes; then as he turned back to her she looked down quickly.

"Is it far to the Wendell place?" she asked abruptly. "Where the sick woman is?"

"Ten miles. Off to the north."

"Not on our trail?" anxiously.

"You're going on, further?"

"Yes. To . . ." she hesitated, and then concluded hurriedly, "To Hill's Corners."

He sat silent for a moment, his strong brown fingers playing with his knife and fork. And his eyes were merely stern when he spoke quietly.

"So you're going to Dead Man's Alley, are you?"

"I said that I was going to Hill's Corners!"

73

"And folks who know that quiet little city," he informed her, "have got into the habit of calling it by the name of its principal street . . . I wonder if you've ever been there?"

"No. Why?"

"I wonder if you know anything about the place?"

"What I've heard. What Mr. Templeton tried to tell me."

"Well," he said thoughtfully, "I don't know that I blame him for trying to turn you into another trail. He must have told you," and he was watching her very keenly, "that the stage runs there from Dry Town?"

"Yes. But I chose to ride on horseback. Is there anything strange in that?"

"Oh, no!" he said briefly. "Just a nice little ride!"

"I have ridden long trails before."

Again for a little while she watched him with intent, eager eyes; he was silent, frowning into his own cup of coffee.

"Dead Man's Alley," he volunteered abruptly, "is the worst little bad town I ever saw. And I've camped in two or three that a man wouldn't call just exactly healthy on the dark of the moon. I guess Mr. Templeton must have told you, but unless it's happened in the last month, there isn't a man in that town who has his wife or daughters there. If I were you," and he lifted his cup to his lips as a sign that he had said his say, "I'd rope my cow pony and hit the home trail for Dry Town!"

"Thank you," she said as quietly as he had spoken. "But really Mr. Templeton gave me enough advice to

74

last me a year, I think. I have made up my mind to go on to . . . to Dead Man's Alley, as you call it."

"Well," he grinned back at her as though the discussion had been of no moment and now was quite satisfactorily ended, "I ought to be glad, oughtn't I? Since my trail runs that way, and since the Poison Hole ranch is only twenty miles out from the Corners. Maybe you'll let me ride over and see you?"

"Of course. I'll be glad to have you. That is," and her smile came back, a very teasing smile, too, "if you'll care to call at the house where I'm going to stop? I'm going to stay with my uncle."

"The chances are that I don't know him. I don't know half a dozen folks in the town. What's his name?"

"His name," she told him demurely, "is Henry Pollard. I think you know him."

He flushed a little as she had hoped that he would He remembered. He knew that he had spoken this morning at the bank of Henry Pollard from whom he was buying his outfit, knew that he must have called him, as he always did when he spoke of him, "Rattlesnake" Pollard. And Henry Pollard was her uncle!

"I didn't know," he said slowly and a little lamely, "that he was your uncle. But," he added cheerfully, his assurance coming back to him, "you can't help that, you know. I don't blame you for it. Yes, I'll ride over from the ranch. It's good of you to let me."

They finished the meal in a rather thoughtful silence. Thornton made a cigarette and went to the door to look for the upclimbing moon; the girl carried her chair to the fireplace and sat down, her hands in her lap, her eyes staring into the coals.

The man was asking himself stubbornly why this girl, this type of girl, dainty, frank-eyed, clean-hearted as he felt instinctively that she was, was making this trip to that dirty town which straddled the state border line like an evil, venomous toad and sneered in its ugly defiant fashion at the peace officers of two states. He was trying to see what the reason could be that carried her through this little-travelled country to the house of such a man as not only Buck Thornton but every one in this end of the cattle country knew Henry Pollard to be; trying above all to seek the reason for her making the trip on horse back, alone, over a wild trail, when the stage for Hill's Corners had left Dry Town so little after her and must reach its journey's end well ahead of her.

And she, over and over, was asking herself why this man whom she was so certain she had seen twice that day upon the trail behind her, denied that he had been the man who got down to look at his horse's foot, who later had ridden a limping mount aside into the cañon. For she felt very sure that she had not been mistaken and, therefore, that he was lying to her. She frowned and glanced over her shoulder. She was a little afraid of a man who could look at her out of clear eyes as he had looked, and lie to her as she was so confident he had lied. She knew nothing of him save that this morning he had come to her assistance at a moment of great peril and that he was suspected by some of a certain robbery and assault . . .

"Are you very tired?"

76

She started. He had turned at last and came back to where she sat.

"No, I am not tired. Why do you ask?"

"There'll be a moon soon. We can let the horses rest a bit . . . I have ridden mine pretty hard the last few days . . . and then after moon-up we can ride on. There's another shack where a man and his wife live just a little off the trail and about seven miles further on. It'll be better than trying to make Wendell's place."

CHAPTER
NINE

The Double Theft

After that there were no more uncomfortable silences in the Harte cabin. Thornton found a lamp, lighted it and placed it on the table. And with the act he seemed to take upon himself the part of host, playing it with a quiet courtesy and gentleness fitting well with the unconscious grace of his lithe body and with the kindliness softening his dark eyes. He told her of his ranch, of the cowboys working for him, of the cattle they were running, of little incidents of everyday life on the range, seeking to make her forget that in reality they were strangers very unconventionally placed. And he did not once ask her a direct question about herself or concerning her business. That she was quick to notice.

For an hour they chatted pleasantly. Now, when Thornton got to his feet again, and went to the door to see what promise the night gave of being cloudless and to note the moon already pushing up above the jagged skyline where the trees stood upon the hill tops, she watched him with an interest that was not tinged with the vague suspicion of an hour ago. She saw that as he stood lounging in the doorway, his hands upon his hips, one shoulder against the rude door jamb, he had to stoop his head a little, and knew that he was a taller, bigger man than she had realized until now.

"If I were as big as you are," she laughed at him, "I'd be in constant fear of bumping my head in the dark."

He laughed with her, told her that he was getting used to it, and came back for his hat.

"If you'll be getting ready," he told her, "I'll go out and bring in the horses. If you're rested up?"

She assured him that she was, noted again how he stooped for the doorway, and watched him move swiftly away through the shadows cast by the trees about the cabin. She put on her hat, buckled on the spurs she had dropped on the table, and was ready. Then, before he could have gone half way to the barn, she heard swift steps coming back.

He had forgotten something; but what? She looked about her expecting to see his tobacco sack or some such article, a block of matches, maybe, which he had left behind. But there was nothing. She lifted the lamp in her hand so that the weak rays searched out the four corners of the cabin. Then she turned again toward the door.

Out yonder through the clear night came on the tall figure with the long free stride of the man of the outdoors. In a patch of bright moonlight his head was down as though his mood were one of thoughtfulness, and the shadow of his wide hat hid his face and eyes from her. In the black shade under the live oak before Harte's door he lifted his head quickly; here he came for an instant to a dead halt, half turning. It struck her abruptly that he was tense, that the atmosphere was suddenly charged with uneasiness, that he was listening as a man listens who more than half expects trouble.

"What is it?" she called. She could not make out more than the vague outline of his figure now as he stood still, his body seeming to merge into the great trunk of the tree. He did not answer. Again, head down and hurriedly, he came on. On through the thinning fringe of shadow and into the full bright moonlight.

A sudden formless fear which in no way could she explain was upon her. His actions were so strange; they hinted at furtiveness. He had been so outright and hearty and wholesome a moment ago and now struck her as anything but the big free and easy man who had supped with her. She drew back a little, her underlip caught between her teeth as was her habit when undue stress was laid upon her nerves, her breath coming a trifle irregularly. After all she was just a girl and he was a man, big, strong and perhaps brutal, of whom she knew virtually nothing. And they were very far from any other human beings . . .

He came straight on to the open door; as the lamp light fell upon him her formless fear of a moment ago was swept up and engulfed in an access of terror which made her sick and dizzy. All of the time until now, even when appearances hinted at an inexplicable duplicity, she had felt safe with him, trusting to what her natural instinct read of him in his eyes and carriage and voice. And now she clutched at the mantel with one hand while in the other the lamp swayed precariously.

The reason for her agitation was plain enough; had it been his sole purpose to strike terror into her heart he could hardly have selected a more efficient method. Across the face, hiding it entirely, leaving only the eyes to glint through two rude slits at her, was a wide bandana handkerchief. The big black hat was drawn low, now; the handkerchief, bound about the brow, fell to a point well below the base of his throat.

"Easy there," he said in a voice which upon her ears was only a tense, evil whisper. "Easy. You know what I want . . . Look out for that lamp! Making it dark in here, even setting the shack on fire, isn't going to help much. Easy, girlie."

"You . . . you . . ." she panted, and found no word to go on.

He came in and strode across the room, taking the lamp from her and setting it on the mantel. She had come near dropping it when his hand brushed hers. Again she drew back from him hastily, her eyes running to the door. But he forestalled her, closed the door and stood in her way, towering above her, his air charged with menace.

"You pretty thing!" he muttered, his tone frankly sincere though his voice was still hardly more than a harsh whisper. "If I just had time to play with you . . . I said you'd know what I want. And don't get funny with the little toy pistol you'd be sure to have in your dress. It won't do you any good; you know that, don't you?"

She did know. Her hand had already gone into her bosom where the "little toy pistol" lay against that which she had vainly thought it could guard, a thick envelope. The man came quite close to her, so close that she felt his breath stir her hair, so close that his slightly uplifted hand could come down upon her before she could stir an inch.

"You can tell Henry Pollard for me," he jeered from the secure anticipation of his present triumph, "that the unknown stranger names him seven kinds of fool. To think he could get across this way and sneak that little wad by me! And by the by, it's getting late and if you don't mind I'll take what's coming to me and move on."

Then she found her tongue, the fires blazed up in her eyes and a hot flush came into her pale cheeks.

"Big brute and cur and coward!" she flung at him. "Woman-fighter!"

"All of that," he laughed insolently. "And then some. And you? Grey eyed, pink beauty! By God, girl, you'd make an armful for a man! Soon to be queen of Dead Man's Alley, eh? I'll see you there; I'll come and pay my respects! Oh, but I will, coward that I am! But now . . ."

"There! Take it! Take it! Oh . . ."

She shuddered away from him, her face went white again, she grew cold with the fear upon her. Just then she cared infinitely little for the sheaf of banknotes in the yellow envelope which the banker had given to her. She jerked the parcel out from her dress and tossed it to him, her fingers fumbling with the botton of the thin garment under which her heart was beating wildly. And the little "toy pistol" she could have hurled from her, too. Against this physical bigness, against this insolent bravado and this swift sureness of eye and muscle, she knew the small weapon to be a ridiculous and utterly insufficient plaything.

He caught the envelope and thumbed it, tore off an end and glanced swiftly at the contents and then stowed it away inside his grey flannel shirt. Again his eyes came back to her.

"I'm in a hurry," he said swiftly. "But there's always time for a girl like you!"

She had foreseen how it would be. Now that she struggled to draw her tiny revolver and fire he was upon her, his long arms about her, his muscular strength making her own as nothing. And though he was breathing more quickly still he had his quiet insolent laugh for still further insult. Though she sought to strike at him he held her in utter helplessness. Slowly he lifted her face, a big hand under her chin. The lamp was close by; he blew down the chimney and save for the moon-light across the threshold it was dark in the cabin. With his other hand he lifted his crude mask from the lower part of his face. She sought again to strike, to batter his lips. But her heart sank as the relentless rigidity of his embrace baffled her attempt. He brought his face closer to hers, slowly closer until at last she knew the outrage of a violent kiss . . .

From outside came a little sound, not to be catalogued. It might have been only a dead twig snapping under the talons of a night bird alighting in the big oak tree. But suddenly the arms about her relaxed, the man whirled and sprang back, whipped open the door and silently was gone into the outer night.

Moaning, swaying, dizzy and sick, she crouched in a far corner. Then she ran to the door and looked out.

There was nothing moving to be seen anywhere. Just the white moonlight here, the black patches of shadow there, the sombre wall of the forest land a few yards away. Her nausea of dread, her uncertainty, had passed. With never a glance behind her she ran down toward the barn. She knew that she would be afraid to go into the black maw of the silent building for her horse and yet she knew that she must, that she must mount and ride . . . She had never until now known the terror of being alone, utterly alone in the night and the wilderness.

Suddenly she stopped to stare incredulously. About a corner of the barn, coming out into the bright moonlight, leading his own horse and her own, was Buck Thornton. She was so certain that he had gone! For the instant she could not move but stood powerless to lift a hand, rooted to the spot. She noted that his face was unhidden now, his black hat pushed far back on his head, while from his hip pocket trailed the end of a handkerchief which may and may not have had slits let in it for his eyes to peer through.

"You . . . here? Yet?" she found herself stammering at him.

"Yes," he answered heavily. "I have been all this time looking for the horses. The corral was broken; they had gotten out into the pasture."

"A likely tale!" she cried with a sudden heat of passionate fury at the man and his cold manner and his mad thought that she was fool enough to be beguiled from her knowledge of what he was. And then a fresh fear made her draw back and widened her eyes. She had not thought of madness but . . . if the man were mad . . .

But he was not mad and she knew it. His were the clear eyes of perfect sanity. He was simply . . . an unthinkable brute.

"Look," she said as his horse moved nervously. "Your horse *does* limp!"

His answer came quickly. And there was a queer note in his voice, harsh and ugly, which sent a shiver through her shaken nerves:

"A man did that while we were in the cabin. With a knife." The moon shone full in his face; she had never seen such a transformation, such a semblance of quiet, cold rage. If the man were just acting . . .

"I've just got the hunch," he said bluntly, "that I know who he is, too. And, for the last time, Winifred Waverly, I am interfering in your business and advising you the best way I know how to turn back right here and right now and forget that you've got an uncle named Pollard!"

CHAPTER
TEN

In the Moonlight

She stood there in a bright patch of moonlight looking up into his face, seeing every line of it in the rich flood of light from the full moon, wondering dully if she had lost her sense of the real and the unreal. It seemed to her so rankly absurd, so utterly preposterous that he should seek to pretend with her. For, now that she had seen the limping gait of his big sorrel, was she more than certain that this was the man whom she had seen following her in the afternoon. And as she noted again the sinewy bigness of him, the garb of grey shirt, open vest and black chaps, she told herself angrily that he was a fool, or that he thought her a fool, to pretend that he knew nothing of that thing which had just happened in the lonely cabin. Even the grey neck-handkerchief, now knotted loosely about the brown throat, was there to give him the lie ... With shame and anger her cheeks burned until they went as crimson as hot blood could make them.

It was all so clear to her. She had refused to believe that he had robbed. Hap Smith's mail bags. Why? She bit her lip in sudden anger: because he had fitted well in a romantic girl's eye! Fool that she was. She should have put sterner interpretation upon the fact that Thornton, coming rudely into the banker's private office, had admitted hearing part of her conversation with Mr. Templeton. Now she had no doubt that he had heard everything.

"Have you ever been over this trail? As far as the next ranch, seven miles further on?" he asked at last, his hard eyes coming away from the horse that stood with one foot lifted a little from the ground, the quick twitching of the foot itself, the writhing and twisting of the foreleg, speaking of the pain from the deep cut.

"No."

There was so much of hatred in the one short word which she flung at him, so much of passionate contempt, that he looked at her wonderingly.

"What's the matter, Miss Waverly?" he asked, his voice a shade gentler. "You seem all different somehow. Are you more tired than you thought?"

She laughed and the wonder grew in his eyes. He had never heard a woman laugh like that, had not dreamed that this girl's voice could grow so bitter.

"No," she told him coldly. She jerked her pony's reins out of Thornton's hand. "I am going to ride on. And I suppose you will ride that poor wounded horse until it drops!"

"No," he said. "That's why I asked if you knew the trails. I didn't notice he limped out there where I put the saddle on. It was dark under the trees, you know."

"Was it?" she retorted sarcastically, drawing another quick, searching look from him.

There was no call for an answer and he made none. He stepped to his horse's head, lifted the wincing forefoot very tenderly, and stooping close to it looked at it for a long time. The girl was behind the broad, stooping back. Impulsively her hand crept into the bosom of her dress, her face going steadily white as her fingers curved and tightened about the grip of the small calibre revolver she carried there. And then she jerked her hand out, empty.

She saw him straighten up, heard again the long, heavy sigh and marked how his face was convulsed with rage.

"I don't know why a man did that." He was only ten steps away and yet she turned her head a little sideways that she might catch the low words. She shivered. His voice was cold and hard and deadly. It was difficult for her to believe that in reality he had not forgotten her presence.

"No, I don't know why a man did that. But I'm going to know. Yes, I'm going to know if it takes fifty years."

"Where is my trail?" she called sharply. "I am going."

"You couldn't find it alone. I'm going with you."

Her scorn of him leaped higher in her eyes. It was her thought that he was going to ride this poor, tortured brute. For she knew that there was no other horse in the barn or about the camp. But he was quietly loosening his cinch, lifting down the heavy Mexican saddle, removing the bit from his horse's mouth.

"What are you going to do?" She bit her lips after the question, but it had leaped out involuntarily.

"I'm going to leave him here for the present. The wound will heal up after a while."

With the saddle thrown over his own shoulders, he ran a gentle hand over the soft nose of his horse which was thrust affectionately against his side, and turned away. She watched him, expecting him to go back to the barn to leave his saddle and bridle. But instead he set his face toward the hills beyond the cabin, where she supposed the trail was.

"I'll pick up another horse at the next ranch," he offered casually by way of explanation. "And we had better hit the trail. It's getting late."

Wordlessly she followed, her eyes held, fascinated by the great, tall bulk of him swinging on in front of her, carrying the heavy saddle with as little care to its weight as if he had been entirely unconscious of it, as no doubt such a man could be. She knew that already he had ridden sixty miles today and that it was seven miles farther to the ranch where he would get another horse. And yet there he strode on, swiftly, as though he had rested all day and now were going to walk the matter of a few yards.

She could not understand this man, whom, since she must, she followed. Had he not told her there in the cabin when he had played at hiding his identity from her, that he knew she was armed? And yet, encumbered with the saddle upon his shoulder, his right hand carrying the bridle, he turned his back square upon her with no glance to see if she were even now covering him with her revolver. And had she not called him a coward, thought him a coward? Was this the way a coward should act?

Again and again during those first minutes her hand crept to the bosom of her dress. Did he know it? she wondered. Was he laughing at her, knowing that she could not bring herself to the point of actually shooting? But then, she might cover him, call to him that she would shoot if he made her, and so force him to return the money he had stolen.

"He would laugh at me," she told herself each time, her anger at him and at herself rising higher and higher. "He would know that I could not kill him. Not in cold blood, this way!"

So Buck Thornton strode on, grim in the savage silence which gripped him, on through the shadows and out into the moonlight beyond the trees, and she followed in silence. There were times when she hated him so that she thought that she could shoot, shoot to kill. His very going with her angered her. Was it not more play-acting, as insolent as anything he could do, as insolent as his kissing her had been! She grew red and went white over it. It was as though he were laughing into her face, making sport of her, saying, "I am a gentleman, you see. I could stay here all night, and you would have to stay with me! But I am not taking advantage of you; I am walking seven miles over a hard trail, carrying a pack like a mule, that you may sleep tonight under the same roof with another woman."

Now she was tempted to wheel her horse, to turn back, to camp alone somewhere out there in the woods, or to ride the thirty miles back to Dry Town. And now, remembering the bank notes which had been taken from her, remembering the insult in the cabin, she held on after him, resolved that she would not lose sight of this man, that she would see him handed over to justice when she could taunt him, saying: "I didn't shoot you, you see, because I am a woman and not a tough. But I have given you into hands that are not woman's hands, because I hate you so!"

Her horse carried her on at a swift walk, but she did not have to draw rein to keep from passing Thornton. His long stride was so smooth, regular, swift and tireless that it soon began to amaze her. They had passed through the little valley in which Harte's place stood, and entered a dark cañon leading into the steeper hills. The trail was uneven, and now and then very steep. Yet Thornton pushed on steadily with no slowing in the swift gait, no sign to tell that he felt fatigue in muscles of back or legs.

"He must be made of iron," she marvelled.

In an hour they had come to the top of a ridge, and Thornton stopped, tossing his saddle to the ground. He had not once spoken since they left the Harte place. Now with quick fingers he made his cigarette. She stopped a dozen paces from him, and though one would have said that she was not looking at him, saw the flare of his match, glimpsed the hard set lines of his face, and knew that he would not speak until she had spoken. And the lines of her own face grew hard, and she turned away from him, feeling a quick spurt of anger that she had so much as looked at him when he had not turned his eyes upon her. He smoked his cigarette, swept up saddle and bridle, and moved on, striking over the ridge and down upon the other side.

It was perhaps ten minutes later when she saw, far off to the left, the glimmer of a light, lost it through the trees, found it again and knew that it told of some habitation. They came abreast of a branch trail, leading toward the lighted window; the girl's eager eyes found it readily, and then noted that Thornton was passing on as though he had seen neither light nor trail. She spoke hurriedly, saying:

"Isn't that the place? Where the light is?"

"No," he told her colourlessly and without turning. "That's the Henry place. We're going on to Smith's."

"Why don't we stop here? It's nearer. And I'm tired."

"We can stop and rest," he replied. "Then we had better go on. It's not very much further now."

"But why not here?" she cried insistently in sudden irritation that upon all matters this man dictated to her and dictated so assuredly. "One place is as good as another."

"This one isn't, Miss Waverly. There's a tough lot here, and there are no women among them. So we'll have to make it to Smith's. Do you want to rest a while?"

"No," she cried sharply. "Let's hurry and get it over with!"

He inclined his head gravely and they went on. And again her anger rose against this man who seemed over and over to wish to remind her that he was a gentleman. As though she had forgotten any little incident connected with him!

Again they made their way through lights and shadows, down into ragged cuts in the hills, over knolls and ridges, through a forest where rain-drops were still dripping from the thick leaves and where she knew that without him she never could have found her way. And not once more did they speak to each other until, unexpectedly for her, they came out of the wood and fairly upon a squat cabin with a light running out to meet them through the square of a window.

"Smith's place," he informed her briefly.

Already three dogs had run to meet them, with much barking and simulated fierceness, and a man and a woman had come to the door.

"Hello," called the man. "Who is it?"

"Hello, John. It's Thornton. Howdy, Mrs. Smith." Thornton tossed his saddle to the ground, pushed down one of the dogs that had recognized him and was leaping up on him. "Mrs. Smith, this is Miss Waverly from Dry Town. A friend of the Templetons. She'll be grateful if you could take her in for the night."

Man and wife came out, shook hands with the girl, the woman led her into the cabin, and Smith took her horse. Then the rancher saw Thornton's saddle.

"Where's your horse?" he asked quickly.

"Back at Harte's. Lame."

In a very few words he told of a deep knife cut beneath the fetlock, explained Miss Waverly's presence with him, and ended by demanding,

"Who do you suppose did that trick for me, John? It's got me buffaloed."

Smith shook his head thoughtfully.

"By me, Buck," he answered slowly. "Most likely some jasper you've had trouble with an' is too yeller to get even any other way. I haven't seen any of your friends from Hill's Corners stickin' around though. Have you?"

"No. But Miss Waverly saw somebody on the trail the other side of Harte's this afternoon. Mistook him for me until I told her. A big man about my size riding a sorrel. Know who it was?"

Again Smith shook his head.

"Can't call him to mind, Buck. It might be Huston for size, but he hasn't got a sorrel in his string, an' then he's took on too much fat lately to be mistook for you. Go on inside. You'll want to eat, I guess. I'll put up the lady's horse an' be with you in two shakes."

"Thanks, John. But I had supper back at Harte's. Can you let me have a horse in the morning? I'll send him back by one of the boys."

"Sure. Take the big roan. An' you don't have to send him back, either. I'm ridin' that way myself tomorrow, an' I'll drop by an' get him."

"Which way are you ridin'?"

"To the Bar X. I got word last week three or four of my steers was over there. I want to see about 'em. Before," he added drily, "they get any closer to Dead Man's."

Thornton's nod indicated that he understood. And then, suddenly, he said,

"If you're going that way you can see Miss Waverly through, can't you? She's going to the Corners."

Smith whistled softly.

"Now what the devil is the like of her goin' to *that* town for?" he demanded.

"I don't know the answer. But she's going there." And as partial explanation, he added, "She's Henry Pollard's niece."

For a moment Smith pondered the information in silence. Then his only reference to it was a short spoken, "Well, she don't look it! Anyway, that's her lookout, an' I'll see her within half a dozen miles of the border. You'll turn off this side the Poison Hole, huh?"

"I'll turn off right here, and right now. I've got a curiosity, John," and his voice was harder than Winifred Waverly had ever heard it, "to know a thing or two about the way my horse went lame. I'm going to sling my saddle on your roan and take a little ride back to Harte's. Maybe I can pick up that other jasper's trail in the cañon back there."

The two men went down to the stable, and while the rancher watered and fed the pony Thornton roped the big roan in the fenced-in pasture. Ten minutes after he had come to the Smith place he had saddled and ridden back along the trail toward Harte's.

The two women in the cabin looked up as Smith came in.

"Where's Mr. Thornton?" his wife asked.

"He's gone back," Smith told her. He drew out his chair, sat down and filled his pipe. Before Mrs. Smith's surprise could find words the girl had started to her feet, crying quickly:

"Gone back! Where?"

"To Harte's. A man knifed his horse back there." He stopped, lighted his pipe, and then said slowly, with much deep thoughtfulness, "If I was that man I'd ride some tonight! I'd keep right on ridin' until I'd put about seven thousand miles between me an' Buck Thornton. An' then . . . well, then, I guess I'd jest naturally dig a hole an' crawl in it so deep nothin' but my gun stuck out!"

"What did he say?" she asked breathlessly.

"That's jest it, Miss. He didn't say much!"

CHAPTER
ELEVEN

The Bedloe Boys

All thoughts of denouncing Buck Thornton before these people fled before the girl had followed the rancher's wife into the cabin. They spoke of him only in tones warm with friendship and with something more than mere friendship, an admiration that was tinged with respect. They had known him since first he had come into this country, and although that had been only a little more than a year ago, they had grown to know him as men and women in these far-out places come to know each other, swiftly, intimately.

He was a favourite topic of conversation and they talked of him naturally, readily, and Mrs. Smith, fluently. She recounted, not guessing how eagerly the girl was listening to every word, many an episode which in the aggregate had given him the reputation he bore throughout these wild miles of cattle land, the reputation of a man who was hard, hard as rock "on the outside," as she put it, hard inside, too, when they drove him to it, but naturally as soft-hearted as a baby. She wished *she* had a boy like him! Why, when she and John hit hard luck, last year, what with the cattle getting diseased first and her and John getting laid up next, flat of their backs with the grip, that man was an angel in britches and spurs if there ever was an angel in anything! He'd nursed them and cooked for them, and lifted her out of her bed while he made it up himself, just as smooth and nice as you could have done, Miss. And he rode clean into town for a doctor, and brought him out and a lot of store stuff that was nice for sick folks to eat. And he'd paid the doctor, too, and laughed and said he'd come some day and borry the money back when he got busted playing poker!

"And then, all of a sudden, when you'd have thought he was soft that way clean through," she went on, her eyes blazing now at the memory of it, "them Bedloe boys come over lookin' for trouble. An' Buck sure gave it to them!"

"Tell me about it," the girl said quickly. "Who are the Bedloe boys? What did they do?"

"The Bedloe boys," Mrs. Smith ran on, eager in the recounting, "belong over to the Corners. Or the Corners belongs to them, I don't know which you'd say. Never heard of them boys? Well, most folks has. There used to be lots like the Bedloe boys when I was a girl, Miss, but thank gracious they're getting thinned out powerful fast. First an' last an' all the time they're rowdies an' gunfighters an' bad men. There's more of their kind in Hill's Corners, but these are the worst of the outfit. They keep close in to the Corners, seeing it's right on the state line, where they can dodge from one state to another when it comes handy. Which is right often.

98

"There's three of 'em. Charley an' Ed an' the youngest one everybody calls the Kid. That's three an' I guess there's a good many more would be glad of the chance to shoot Buck up. I guess the Bedloes heard that time that John was sick. Anyway, they come over, all three of 'em, hunting trouble. Buck was out in the barn, feeding the horses, an' they didn't know he was on the ranch. The Kid, he's the youngest of the mess an' the worst an' the han'somest, with them little yeller curls, an' his daredevil blue eyes, come on ahead, riding his horse right up to the door, yelling like a drunk Injun an' cussing so it made a woman wonder how any woman could ever have a son like him. He tried to ride his horse right in the door, an' when it got scared of me an' John lyin' in bed, an' rared up, the Kid hit it over the head with the gun in his hand, an' slipped out'n the saddle, laughin' at it stagger.

"But he come on in an' Charley come in, too. Ed Bedloe was out in the far corral, gettin' ready to throw the gate open an' turn out the cows an' stampede 'em off'n the ranch. What for?" She lifted her bony shoulders. "Oh, nothin'. They'd jus' had trouble with my John about six months before, an' was taking a good chance to smash up things in general about the ranch. They swore they was going to burn the cabin an' the barn an' scatter the stock an' do anything else they could put their hands to. An' while they was in here, cussing an' abusing my John, who couldn't even get up an' grab his shotgun in the corner, an' insulting me all they could lay their dirty tongues to, there's a step at

99

the door right behind 'em, light as a cat, an' here's Buck come in from the barn.

"I wish you'd seen that man's eyes! Then you'd know what I mean when I say he gets hard, hard an' bitter sometimes. An' his voice — it was so low an' soft you might 'a' thought he was putting a baby to sleep with it! There was two of them boys, big an' ugly-mean, an' they both had guns on, in sight. There was jus' one of Buck Thornton, an' I didn't know yet he ever toted a gun. He uses his hands, mostly, I reckon, Buck does. He didn't say much. He just got them two hands of his on Charley Bedloe's neck, an' I thought he was goin' to break it sure. An' Charley got flung clean out in the yard before the Kid had finished going for his gun! You wouldn't believe a man could be that quick.

"Quick? It wasn't nothin' to his next play. I tell you the Kid's hand was on the way to his gun an' Buck didn't have a gun *on* him, you'd have said. An' then he *did* have a gun, an' John an' me didn't even see where he got it, an' he didn't seem to be in a hurry, an' he'd shot before the Kid could more'n pull his gun up!"

"He killed him?"

"He could have killed him just as easy as a man rolls a cigareet! There wasn't six feet between 'em. Only men like Buck Thornton don't kill men unless they got to, I guess. But he shot the Kid in the arm, takin' them chances as cool as an icicle; an' when the Kid dropped his gun an' then grabbed at it with his other hand, Buck shot him in the left arm the same way. An' then, using his hands, he threw *him* out. An' I don't believe Charley Bedloe more'n got on his hands an' knees outside! An' then somehow Buck has a gun in each hand, and has stepped outside, too. And I reckon the Bedloe boys saw the same thing in his eyes me an' John saw there when he come back in. Anyway, they got on their horses an' we ain't seen hide nor hair of 'em since."

Miss Waverly sat very still, leaning forward a little, her eyes big and bright upon the eyes of this other woman. The man, despite her calmer judgment, appealed to her imagination . . .

"You'd think," Mrs. Smith went on, "that that man would be tired enough for one day, wouldn't you? Ridin' all day, walking seven mile toting that big saddle on his back; an' now he goes an' starts out to ride the Lord knows how far. What do you suppose a man like him is made out'n?"

Smith answered her out of the corner of his mouth from which a slow curl of smoke was mounting:

"Sand, mostly."

No, the girl could not say to these people that which she had to say of Buck Thornton. She switched the conversation abruptly, asking them to tell her of Hill's Corners.

She knew something of the place already. Mr. Templeton had told her a great deal when insistently urging her not to do the thing she had determined to do and she had thought that he exaggerated merely in order to turn her aside from her purpose. She had even heard far-reaching rumours of the border town in Crystal City, where her own home had been for the five years since the deaths of her parents. These rumours, too, she had supposed inflated as rumours will be when they are bad and have travelled far. Now it was a little anxiously that she asked for further information, and not altogether because she sought some new topic.

"She's Henry Pollard's niece, Mary," Smith said rather hurriedly. The girl glanced at him sharply. There was something in his tone which told her that he was warning his wife, cautioning her to speak guardedly of Pollard or not at all.

When, an hour later, she went to bed, she lay long sleepless, wondering, nervously dreading the morrow. For these people who should know gave Hill's Corners the same name that Mr. Templeton had given it, the same name it bore as far as Crystal City and beyond. It was one of those far removed towns which are the last stand of the lawless, the ultimate breastwork before the final ditch into which in his hour the gunfighter has finally gone down. Desperate characters, men wanted in two states and perhaps in many more, flocked here where they found the one chance to live out their riotous lives riotously. Here they could "straddle" the line, and when wanted upon one side slip to the other. And hereabouts, for very many miles in all directions, the big cattle men, the small ranchers, the "little fellows," all slept "with their eyes open and their gun-locks oiled."

But, she tried to tell herself, Henry Pollard had sent for her, he was her own mother's brother, he would not have had her come here if it were not safe. He had written clearly enough, had told her in his letter that he could not leave the Corners, that he must have the money, that there were hold-up men in the country who would not hesitate to rob the stage if they learned that he had five thousand dollars in it, that she could bring the bills which Templeton would have ready for her and that there would be no suspicion, no danger for her. And she would believe her uncle, would believe that these people had had trouble with the Bedloes and perhaps others in the town, and that they warped the truth in the telling. For was any more faith to be put in the word of the Smiths than in that of Buck Thornton himself? And did she not know him for what he was, a man who was not above assaulting a defenceless girl, not above robbery?

Wearied out, she went to sleep, her last waking thoughts trailing off through the night after a man who could laugh like a boy, whose eyes could grow very gentle or very, very hard and inexorable.

In the morning John Smith's first words to her drove again a hot, angry flush into her face. For he told her that Thornton, before he would ride away last night, had made sure that Smith would accompany her, showing her the way and "taking care of her." She bit her lip and turned away. She was grateful that soon breakfast was eaten, the horses saddled and once more she was riding out toward the south-east. Smith rode at her elbow.

All morning they rode slowly, over rough trails in the mountains where a horse found scant foothold, where they wound down into deep, close walled cañons where the sunlight was dim at noon, where the pines stood tall and straight in thick ranks untouched by an ax. They came out into little valleys, past a half dozen ranch houses, saw many herds of cattle and horses, crossed Indian Gully, topped another steep ridge and at last looked down upon the Poison Hole ranch.

The ranch lay off to the east as they looked down upon it, a great sweep of rolling hills sprinkled with big oaks looking like shrubs from their vantage point, cut in two by the Big Little River, along the banks of which and out in the meadow lands many herds of cattle ranged free. Rising in his stirrup Smith pointed out to her the spot near the centre of the big range where Buck Thornton's "range house" was, a dozen miles away over the rolling country. And then he swung about and pointed to the south, saying shortly:

"Yonder's the country you're lookin' for. We strike due south here along the edge of the Poison Hole ranch. When we get to that next string of hills you can see the hills of three states, all at once and the same time. And you can see the town you're headed for; it sets on top a sort of hill. Down yonder," and he swung his long arm off to the south-west, "is the Bar X outfit; that's as far as I'm going. But, if you want company, one of the boys will sure be glad to ride on with you. The Corners is only about a dozen mile from there on."

CHAPTER
TWELVE

Rattlesnake Pollard

It was barely noon, the air clear, the sky cloudless, when Winifred Waverly rode into Hill's Corners. She had shaken her head at the suggestion of further escort. Here, in the open country and in the full sunlight, she was grateful for the opportunity of being alone.

At the foot of a gentle eminence she entered the narrow, winding street of the town, a crooked little town physically both in the matter of this meandering alley-like thoroughfare and in the matter of the hastily builded, unprepossessing houses; a crooked town in its innermost character, it was easy to believe. On either hand as she rode forward were low, squat, ugly shacks jammed tight together or with narrow passageways between their unlovely walls, these spaces more often than not cluttered and further disfigured by piles of rusty tins, old clothing and shoes and other discarded refuse. As she rode farther she saw now and then the more pretentious buildings, some with the false fronts which deceived nobody, the houses appearing shoddy and aged and sinister, one here and there deserted and given over to ruin, disintegration and spiders spinning unmolested in dark corners.

The nrst peculiar impression created upon her was that some evil charm was over the place, that in the sweet sunlight it lay drugged, that in those rows of slatternly shacks where the sunlight did not enter men either hid in dark secrecy or lay in some unnatural stupour. The whole settlement seemed preternaturally quiet; the fancy came to her that the town had died long ago and that she merely looked on its ghost.

She had shrunk before now at the thought of men coming to the doors to stare after her, and perhaps even to call coarsely after her; now it seemed the dreariest thing in all the world to ride down this dirty, muddy street and see no man or woman or child, not so much as a saddled horse at a hitching pole. She came abreast of the most pretentious building of Hill's Corners; its swing doors were closed, but from within she heard a low, monotonous hum of languid voices. Upon the crazy false front, a thing to draw the wondering eye of a stranger, was a gigantic and remarkably poorly painted picture of a bear holding a glass in one deformed paw, a bottle in the other, while the drunken letters of the superfluous sign spelled: "The Brown Bear Saloon." Almost directly across the street from the Brown Bear was a rival edifice which though slightly smaller was no less squat and ugly and which bore its own highly ambitious sign: a monster hand clutching a monster whiskey glass, with the illuminating words beneath, "The Here's How Saloon." That the two works of art were from the same brain and hand there was no doubting. In the inscriptions the n's and s's were all made backwards, presenting an interesting and entirely suitable air of maudlin drunkenness.

The girl hurried by. There were other saloons, so many, so close together that, used as she was to frontier towns, she wondered at it; she saw other buildings whose signs informed her they were store and postoffice, drug store, blacksmith shop and restaurant. And now the first visible token of life, a thin spiral of smoke from "Dick's Oyster House." She passed it, pushing her horse to a gallop. She had seen the two or three men upon the high stools at the counter taking their coffee and bacon. They had swung about quickly, like one man, at the cook's grin and quiet word. One of them even called out something as she passed; another laughed.

As she rode down the tortuous street, fairly racing now, the blood whipped into her face, she caught a glimpse of a man standing by his horse, preparing to swing up into the saddle. His eyes followed her with a look in them easy to read and unpleasant; something too ardently admiring to be trusted. She had seen the man's face. He was a big man, broad and straight and powerful, builded like a Vulcan. He was branded unmistakably as a rowdy; his very carriage, a sort of conscious swagger, the bold impudence of his face told that. The laughing face stood out before her eyes as she rode on, evil and reckless and handsome, with very bright blue eyes and hair curling in little yellow rings about the forehead from which the hat was pushed back. It was her first glimpse of the youngest of the Bedloe boys, the worst of them, the "Kid."

She knew that she would find her uncle's house at the end of the street. Mr. Templeton had told her that, and had described it so that she could have no trouble in knowing it. And as she rode on, making the curve of the long, crooked lane which had come to be known as Dead Man's Alley, she found time to wonder that such a town could be so silent and deserted with the sun so high in the sky. For she had not learned that here men did in their way what men do in larger cities, that they turned the day topsy turvy, that the street seethed with surging life through late afternoon and night and the dark hours of the morning, that the saloons stood brightly lighted then, that their doors were filled with men coming and going, that games ran high, voices rose high, while life, as these men knew it, ran higher still.

At last she came to Henry Pollard's house. It stood back from the street in a little yard notable for the extreme air of untidiness the rank weeds gave it and for its atmosphere of semi-desertion among its few stunted, twisted, unpruned pear trees. The fence about it had once been green, but that was long, long ago. The doors were closed, the shades close drawn over the windows, the house still and gloom-infested even in the sunlight.

Stronger and higher within her welled her misgivings; for the first time she admitted to herself that she was sorry that she had tried to do this thing which Mr. Templeton had told her was madness. She hesitated, sitting her horse at the gate, with half a mind to whirl and ride back whence she had come. And then, with an

108

inward rebuke to her own timidity, she dismounted and hurried along the weed bordered walk, and knocked at the door.

There came quick answer, a man's voice, heavy and curt, crying:

"Who is it?"

"Are you Mr. Pollard?" she called back, her voice a little eager, more than a little anxious.

"Yes." There was a note as of excitement in the voice. "Is that you, Winifred?"

"Yes, uncle. I . . . I . . ."

She faltered, hesitated, and broke off pitifully. She had heard the eagerness in Pollard's voice, guessed at what it was that he was thinking, knew that now she would have to tell him that she had failed in the errand which he had entrusted to her, that she had let a man rob her of the five thousand dollars of which he stood so urgently in need. Oh, why had she attempted to do it, why had she not listened to Mr. Templeton? And, now, what would her uncle say?

"Just a minute, Winifred. I'm a little under the weather and am in bed. Now." She heard no footsteps; yet there was the noise of a wooden bar being drawn away from the door. "Come in. You'll pardon me, being in bed, my dear. And fasten the door after you, will you, please?"

She stepped across the threshold and into the darkened house, her heart beating quickly. As she slipped the bar back into its place she saw that there was fastened to the end of it a cord which passed through a pulley over the door and then ran down the hallway, disappearing through another door at the left. So, following the cord, she went on slowly.

The outside of the house had given her a certain impression. Now, in a flash, that impression was superseded by a new one. Here was the home of a man of means, the heavy, rich furniture spoke of that, the painting there in the living room into which she glanced, the tastefully papered walls, the thick carpet muffling her footfalls. If only the curtains were thrown back, if only the sun were looking in upon it all!

And now the man. Henry Pollard, whom she had not seen since she was a very little girl and then only during his short visit at her father's house, struck her as being in some way not entirely unlike this habitation of his. A gentleman gone to seed, was that it?

His manner was courteous, courtly even, his speech soft, his eyes gentle as they rested upon her, gentle and yet eager. There was something fine about his face, about the eyes and high forehead, and yet alongside it there was something else which drove a little pain into the girl's eyes. The mouth was hard, there were deep, set lines about it and about the eyes there was a hint of cruelty which not even his smile hid entirely. And though she strove to smile back bravely as she came forward to kiss him, she knew that she was disappointed, and a little uneasy.

She knew that Henry Pollard must be about fifty; she saw that he looked to be sixty. He had pulled himself up against his pillows and had drawn on a dressing gown to cover his shoulders. He was well groomed; he had had a shave yesterday; he did not look sick. But

110

he did look old, like a man who had aged prematurely and suddenly; and he did look worried and tired, as though he had not slept well last night.

"I am alone just now," he smiled. "Mrs. Riddell is keeping house for me, but I heard her go out a little while ago. For something for breakfast, I suppose. You are looking well, Winifred. I knew you would be pretty. Now, sit down."

No word yet of her errand, no query as to its success. She was grateful to him for that. She wanted a moment, time in which to feel that she knew him a little bit, before she could tell him. But she saw in his eyes that he was curbing his eagerness, and that she would have to tell him in a moment.

"I am sorry that you are sick, Uncle Henry," she said hastily, taking the chair near his bed. "It isn't anything serious, is it?"

"No, no." His answer was as hasty as her question had been. "Just rheumatism, Winifred. I'm subject to it here of late."

Then she saw that he had sat stiffly, that his shoulder, the left shoulder, was carried awkwardly and was evidently bandaged.

"I'm sorry," she said again. And then, determined to tell him before he should ask, "Uncle, I . . ." Oh, it was so hard to say with him looking at her with those keen, bright eyes of his! "You should have got some one else to help you. I have failed . . . I have lost your money for you!"

She dropped her face into her hands, trembling, striving to keep her tears back, feeling now, as she had not felt before, as if she had been altogether to blame for all that had happened, as though it had been her carelessness that had cost her uncle his five thousand dollars. And when at last he did not speak and she looked up again, she saw that his eyes had not changed, that there was no surprise in them, that if he felt anything whatever he hid it.

"Don't cry about it, my dear," he said gently. He even smiled a little. "Tell me about it. You were robbed of it? Before you had more than got out of sight of Dry Town?"

"How do you know?" she cried.

"I don't know, my dear. But I do know that the stage came on through, with no attempt at a hold-up, and I guessed that our little ruse didn't fool anybody. When I got the empty strong box from the bank I knew pretty well what to look for."

"But," she told him, flushed with her hope, "we'll get it back! For I know who robbed me, I can swear to him!"

Pollard's hand, lying upon the bed spread, had shut tight. She noticed that and no other sign of emotion.

"And *I* know!" he said harshly. "Yes, I'll get it back! Now, tell me how it happened."

"It was a man named Buck Thornton . . ."

She saw the quick change of light in his eyes and in the instant knew that if Buck Thornton hated Henry Pollard he was hated no less in return. Further, she saw that back of the hatred there was a sort of silent laughter as though the thing she had said had pleased this man as no other thing could have pleased him, that

112

in some way which she could not understand, this information had moved him as he had not been moved by news of his heavy loss. And she wondered.

"You are ready to swear to that?" he asked sharply, his eyes searching and steady and eager upon hers. "You will swear that it was Thornton who robbed you?"

"Yes," she cried hotly as she remembered the insult of a kiss and in the memory forgot the robbery itself.

"I'll get him now," he muttered. "Both ways; going and coming! Tell me all about it, Winifred."

She began, speaking swiftly, telling him of her meeting with Thornton at the bank, of her suspicion that he had overheard her talk with the banker. Then of her second meeting with the man after she had seen him on the trail behind her, the encounter at the Harte cabin . . . A sudden banging of the kitchen door, and he had stopped her abruptly, putting his hand warningly upon her arm.

"Later. It can wait. That is Mrs. Riddell. She will show you to your room. And it will be better, my dear, if you say nothing to her. Or to any one else just yet."

She got to her feet and went to the door. Turning there, to smile back at her uncle, she saw that his pillows had slipped a little and that under them lay a heavy revolver. And she surprised upon the man's face a look which was gone so quickly that she wondered if she had seen right in the darkened room, a look so filled with malicious triumph. Instead of being profoundly disturbed by the tidings of her adventure, the man appeared positively to gloat ... Now, more than ever, did she regret that she had come to the town of Dead Man's Alley.

CHAPTER
THIRTEEN

The Ranch on Big Little River

Buck Thornton had returned to the Poison Hole ranch. But first he had ridden from the Smith place down the trail to Harte's, where he made swift, careful search for some sign to tell him who was the man who had lamed his horse maliciously and seemingly with no purpose to be gained. Further, he had sought for tracks to tell him from where this man had come, where he had gone. When he had found nothing he went, he hardly knew why, to the cabin, pushed the door open and entered. And instead of learning anything definitely now he was merely the more perplexed.

By the fireplace lay a chair, overturned. There had been some sort of hurried movement here, perhaps a struggle. The table had been pushed to one side, one leg catching in the rag rug and rumpling it. He struck a match, lighted the lamp and sought for some explanation. When had this struggle, if struggle there had been, occurred? It must have been after he and Miss Waverly had set out on the trail to Smith's, he told himself positively. Then there had been two people here in the meantime, for it takes two people to make a tussel. And they had gone. Who could it be? Was he after all to find a clue to the man who had maimed his horse?

Looking about him curiously it chanced that he found something that drove a puzzled frown into his eyes. It had caught in the frayed edge of the rug, and to have been so caught and so left meant that it had been done during the struggle he had already pictured. He took it up into his hand, trying to understand. For it was the rowel of a spur, a tiny, sharp, shining rowel that had come loose from a spur he remembered very well. And he remembered, too, that Winifred Waverly had had her spurs on when she came out to him at the barn!

"It happened while I was out after the horses!" He sat down, the shining spiked wheel lying in the palm of his hand, his brows drawn heavily. "While I was out there . . . it happened. Some jasper came in here, there was some sort of a tussle . . . and she didn't say a damned word about it!"

Yes, he was certain now that something *had* happened during the brief time between his going out for the horses and the girl's coming to him at the barn. Something that had changed her, that had killed her friendliness toward him, that had made her cold and cruelly different.

"The same man who slipped his knife across my horse's foot came in here and saw her while I was out for the horses," he said slowly. "The same man. It must have been. And she could tell me who it was and she didn't. Why? After they had struggled here, too! Why?"

He could see no reason in it all, no reason for her silence, no reason for a man's malicious cruelty to a horse. Nor were these the only things which he could not understand. Groping for the truth, he began carefully to run over the things which had seemed strange to him and which now struck him as being connected in some plan darkly hidden.

The girl was Henry Pollard's niece. He began with that fact. She was on her way to Pollard's and on an errand which the banker Templeton had called mad and dangerous. Some man had followed her, a man whom she had twice seen on the trail and whose outfit resembled Thornton's, resembled it too closely to be the result of chance! The same headstall with the red tassel, the same grey neckhandkerchief, a sorrel horse . . .

"By God!" whispered the cowboy, a sudden light in his eyes, "he lamed my horse so it would limp the same as his! So she'd be sure she had seen me on the trail behind her! And when she came out and saw my horse limping she *knew* I had lied to her!"

But why? Why? What lay back of all this?

In the end he put out the light, slipped the spur rowel into his vest pocket, and went out to his horse. Then when an hour's search brought him no nearer to the hidden truth for which he was groping, he gave up trying to pick up this other man's trail in the rocky soil about Harte's place and turned back toward the south-east and his own ranch.

"I'm going to have a talk with you, Miss Grey Eyes," he said softly. "I've got to give you back your spur, and I'm going to ask you some questions."

He rode late into the night, stopped for a few hours under the stars with saddle blanket for bed, and in the dawn pushed on again.

For the few days which followed he had, in the stress of range work, little time for thought of the riddle which had been set for him to solve, and when he had time after the day's work he was tired and ready for sleep. He was working short handed now for the very simple and not uncommon reason that he was spending no dollar which he did not have to spend. The payments he had already made to Pollard had been heavy for him, and there was yet another five thousand dollars to be forthcoming in six months. The contract was clear upon the point, and he knew that if he failed to meet his obligation Henry Pollard would be vastly pleased, being in a position to keep the fifteen thousand which had been paid to him and to get his range back to boot.

Perhaps because Henry Pollard had never lived upon the ranch during the twenty years he had owned it improvements were few and poor. There was the barn, too small now, which must come down in another year; there was the old corral which was little used since Thornton had had the newer, bigger one builded. Then, for ranch house, there was a single room cabin, its walls of heavy logs from the hills at the head of the Big Little River, its door of great thick planks rough and nail studded, its roof of shakes. A hundred yards from it, at the foot of the knoll upon which the ranch house stood, was a similar cabin, a dozen feet longer, serving as the men's bunk house.

Big Little River wound about the foot of the knoll, separating Thornton's cabin from the bunk house, three or four feet deep here and spanned by a crude footbridge. In its windings it made a sort of horseshoe about the knoll so that looking out from the door of the cattle man's cabin one saw the sluggish water to east, west and north.

Upon the third morning after his return to the range Thornton rose early, scowled sleepily at the little alarm clock whose strident clamour had startled him out of his sleep at four o'clock, kicked off his pajamas and with towel in hand started down to the river for his morning plunge. Subconsciously he noted a scrap of white paper lying upon the hewn log which served as doorstep, but he paid no heed to it. He had his dip, diving from the big rock from which most mornings of the year he dived into the deepest part of the stream; and in a little came back through the brightening daylight rosy and tingling and with the last webs of sleep washed out of his brain. Again he noted the paper; this time he stooped and caught it up. For now he saw that it was folded, carefully placed where he must see it, pinned down with a sharp pointed horseshoe nail.

"Now who's sending me letters this way?" he demanded of himself.

And he flushed a little and called himself a fool because he knew that he half expected to find that it was a note from a certain girl with unforgettable grey eyes. But before he had read the few words, as soon in fact as his eyes had fallen upon the uneven, laboriously

119

constructed letters of the lead-pencilled scrawl, he knew that this did not come from her hand. The signature puzzled him; it consisted of two letters, initials evidently, a very large j, not capitalized, followed by a very small capital C.

"Now, who's J.C.?" he muttered. "I can call to mind no J.C. who would be writing me letters!"

As he read the note a look of astonishment came into his eyes. It ran:

"Deer buck, I am shure up against hard luck. Dont know nobody but you can give me a hand remember that time down in El paso I was yore freind. Come to old shack by Poison hole tonight & dont tell nobody & bring sum grub Buck remember El paso.

"j. c.

"p. s. I was yore freind buck."

Thornton remembered. He went slowly about his dressing, turning again and again to look at the note he had placed upon his little pine table. That had been five years ago. He was riding between Juarez and El Paso, having just sold a herd of steers from the range he had owned in Texas then. He had been detained in the Mexican town until after dark, and before its lights had ceased winking behind him he had known that though his precaution of taking a check instead of gold had saved his money to him it had not saved him from coming very close to death. There were still three scars, two in the shoulder, one in the right side, to show where the bullets had bitten deep into him, from behind. He had been searched swiftly, roughly, his clothing torn by the hurried fingers of the man who had shot him.

It had been close to midnight when his consciousness came back to him. A little man, hard featured but gentle fingered, was working over him. It was Jimmie Clayton. And Clayton had found the crumpled check in the darkness, had gotten the wounded man on his own horse, had taken him to El Paso, and finally had saved his life, nursing him, working over him day and night for the two weeks in which his life was in danger.

Since then Thornton had seen little of Clayton. He had known even at the time of the shooting that the man was as hard a character as his close-set, little eyes and weasel face bespoke him; he had come to know him as an insatiate gambler, the pitiful sort of gambler who is too much of a drunkard to be more than his opponent's dupe at cards. He had found him to be a brawler and very much of a ruffian. But though he did not close his eyes to these things they did not matter to him. For gratitude and a sense of loyalty were two of the strong silver threads that went to make up the mesh of Buck Thornton's nature, and it was enough to him that little Jimmie Clayton had played the part of friend in a town where friends were scarce and at a time when but for a friend he would have died.

It was not alone the fact of Clayton's turning up here and now that surprised the cattle man; it was the fact of his turning up anywhere. For he had thought that Clayton, weak natured and so very often the other man's tool, was serving time in the Texas penitentiary. For, three years ago, rumour had brought to him word of a sheriff's clean-up, and the names of three men who had been working a crude confidence game, bold rather than shrewd, and Jimmie Clayton's name was one of the three. He had heard only after the men had been convicted and sentenced for five years apiece, and had at the time regretted that he could not have known sooner so that in some way he might have returned the favour he had never forgotten.

At last having dressed, he shoved the letter into his pocket, and went down to the bunk house for breakfast. To the cook and to the three men already at the table he had little to say, so full were his thoughts of Jimmie Clayton. He was wondering what "hard luck" the little fellow had run up against, why he was hiding out at a place like the Poison Hole shack, how he had gotten the letter to the range cabin, and, if he had brought it himself, why he had not made himself known last night.

He gave his few, succinct orders for the day, made his hurried meal, and went to the corral for his horse. And all that day he rode hard out in the broken country where the eastern end of the range ran up and back into the gorges of the mountains, shifting herd, collecting stragglers, bringing them down into the meadow lands where the feed was abundant now that he had sold the cattle he had had ranging there in order that he might raise the money to make up the five thousand dollars for Henry Pollard.

As he rode he spoke seldom to the horse running under him or to the boys with whom he worked, his thoughts flying now to another horse, lamed from a knife cut, now to a girl whose spur rowel he carried in his vest pocket, now to a man whose appealing letter he carried in another pocket. And he was glad when the day was done and the boys raced away through the dusk to their supper.

Not infrequently did he ride on after he had told the others to "knock off," working himself harder than he could ask them to work, riding late to look at the water holes or find a new pasture in some of the little mountain valleys or to bring in a fresh string of saddle horses for the morrow's riding. So now, as darkness gathered, he watched the boys scamper away to their food and smoke and bunks, and rode on slowly toward the north.

He chose this time, the thickening darkness before moonrise, for he had caught the insistent plea for secrecy running through the lines of the letter. And so, though he was not a little impatient and curious, he let his tired horse choose its own loitering gait, willing that the night draw down blacker about him.

He crossed the Big Flat, rich grassy land watered by the Big Little River, and struck off into the hills that closed in about it, following the river trail. It was very still, with no sound save the swish of the water against the willows drooping downward from its banks, no light save the dim glimmer of the early stars. For two miles he followed the stream, then left it for a short cut over the ridge, to pick it up again upon the farther side. Now he was in a tiny valley with the mountains close to the spot which gave its name to the range.

Big Little River writhed in from the east, twisted out to the south. And in the shut-in valley it made and left behind it to all but cover the entire floor of the valley a lakelet of very clear water not over a quarter of a mile from edge to edge, but very deep. Upon the far side, a little back and close under the overhanging cliffs, there was a great, jagged-mouthed, yawning hole, of a type not uncommon in this part of the western country, from which heavy, noxious gases drifted sometimes when the wind caught them up, gases which for the most part thickened and made deadly the dark interior. There were skeletons to be seen dimly by daylight down there, ten feet below the surface of the uneven ground, the vaguely phosphorescent bones of jack rabbits that had fallen into this natural trap, of coyotes, even of a young cow that had been overpowered before it could struggle upward along the steep sides. And the odour clinging to the mouth of the hole was indescribably foul and sickening.

Not a pretty place, and yet some man many years ago had builded him a habitation here that was half dugout, half log lean-to. The door of the place faced Poison Hole, and was not two hundred yards from it. The hovel had been in disuse long before Buck Thornton came to the range save as a shelter to some of the wild things of the mountains.

From the southern shore of the lake Thornton stared across the little body of water trying to make out a light to tell him that Clayton was expecting him. But there was no fire, and the stars, reflecting themselves in the natural mirror, failed to show him so much as the outline of the lean-to in the shadows of the cliffs. He turned down into the trail which ran about the shore, passed around the western end of the lake, and riding slowly, his eyes ever watchful about him as was the man's habit, he came at last to the deserted "shack."

CHAPTER
FOURTEEN

In the Name of Friendship

Twenty yards from the door he drew rein, sitting still, frowning into the darkness. Not for the first time was he realizing that the note might not be from Clayton at all; that some other man could have known of his debt of gratitude to the little fellow who had befriended him five years ago; that the name might have been used to draw him here, alone and very far from any ears to hear, any eyes to see, what might happen. He could name a half dozen men who were not above this sort of thing, men who had, some of them, sworn to "get him." There were the Bedloe boys, the three of them. There were two other men who do not come into this story. There was Henry Pollard.

"And it would be almighty like Pollard to put up a job like this," he told himself grimly. "He could afford to pay a man a good little pile to get me out of the game, and keep the money I've paid him and get back his range besides. And I reckon the Kid would be one of a dozen who would take on the job dirt cheap!"

He reined his horse a little deeper into the shadows. Then he slipped swiftly from the saddle, one end of his thirty-feet rope in his hand, the other end about the horse's neck, and with a quick flick of the quirt sent the animal trotting ahead to swing about and stop when the rope drew taut. He half expected his ruse to draw fire from somewhere in the darkness. Instead there came a low voice, sharp and querulous, through the open door.

"That you, Buck?"

"Yes. That you, Clayton?"

"Yes. Are you alone?"

"Yes."

Then Thornton came on swiftly, coiling his rope as he walked. For he had recognized the voice.

"What's the matter, Jimmie?" He was at the door now, peering in but making nothing of the blot of shadows.

"Come in," Clayton answered. "An' shut the door, Buck. I'll make a light when the door's shut."

He stepped in, dropping his rope, and moving slowly again, his back against the wall. For after all he would not be sure of everything until there was a light, until he saw that he was alone with Clayton.

A match sputtered, making vague shadows as it was held in a cupped hand. It travelled downward to the earthen floor, found the stub of a candle, and then the greater light, poor as it was, drove out the shadows. And Thornton saw that it was Jimmie Clayton, that the man was alone, and that evidently his note had put it mildly when he had said that he had struck "hard luck."

The man, small, slight and nervous looking, lay upon a bed of boughs, covered with an old saddle blanket, his eyes bright as though with fever or fear. The skin of his face where it was seen through the black stubble of beard looked yellow with sickness. The cheek bones stood out sharply, little pools of shadow emphasizing the hollowness of his sunken cheeks. Above the waist he was stripped to his undershirt; a rude bandage under the shirt was stained the reddish brown of dried blood. A quick pity drove the distrust out of the eyes of the man who saw and who remembered.

"You poor little devil!" he said softly. He reached out his hand quickly, downright hungrily, for Jimmie's.

Clayton took the hand eagerly and held it a moment in his tense hot fingers as his eyes sought and studied Thornton's. Then he sank back with a little satisfied sigh, lying flat, his hands under his head.

"I'm sure gone to seed, huh, Buck?" he demanded.

"It's tough, Jimmie. Tell me about it."

The broken line of discoloured teeth showed suddenly under the lifted lip.

"It ain't much to tell, Buck," Clayton answered slowly as the snarl left the pinched features. "But it's somethin' for a man to think about when he lays in a hole like this like a sick cat. But, Buck," and he spoke sharply, "didn't you bring no grub with you?"

"Yes, Jimmie. Wait a minute." Thornton stepped outside, not forgetting to close the door quickly after him, jerked the little package from his saddle strings where it had posed all day as his own lunch, and brought it back into the dugout. "I didn't know just what you wanted, but here's some bread and a hunk of cold meat and here's some coffee. We'll get it to boiling in a minute, and . . ."

128

"An' a drink, Buck?" eagerly. "You brung a flask, didn't you?"

"Yes, Jimmie," Thornton assured him with a quiet smile. He whipped the flask from his pocket and removing the cork held it out. "I remember that you used to say a meal without a drink wasn't any use to you."

Clayton put out a swift hand for the flask, shot it to his lips, and the gurgle of the running liquor spoke of a long draught.

"Now, the grub, Buck." He sat up, a little healthier colour in his cheeks. "Let the coffee go; it'll come in handy tomorrow."

Thornton made a cigarette and leaning back against the door watched this outcast who bore the brand of the hunted on his brow, whose eyes were feverish with a hunger that was ravenous.

"Poor little old Jimmie," he muttered under his breath.

Clayton picked over the contents of the little package with hasty fingers, pushing the bread aside, eating noisily of the meat. When at last he had finished he rolled up the remainder of the lunch in the greasy paper, thrust it under the corner of his blanket, and put out his hands for the tobacco and papers.

"I ain't even had a smoke for three days, Buck. Hones' to Gawd, I ain't."

"Now, Jimmie," Thornton suggested when both men were smoking, and Clayton again lay on his back, resting, "better tell me about it. Can't I move you over to my cabin?"

"No, Buck. You can't. An' I'll tell you." He broke off suddenly, his eyes burning with an anxious intensity upon Thornton's. Then, with a new note in his voice, a half whimper, he blurted out, "Hones' to Gawd, I'll blow my brains out before I let 'em get me again! But you wouldn't give me away, Buck, would you? You'd remember how I stuck by you down in El Paso, won't you, Buck? You wouldn't give a damn for . . . for a reward if they was to offer one, would you, Buck? 'Cause you know I'd shoot myself if they got me, an' you don't forget how I stuck to you, do you, Buck?"

"No, Jimmie," came the assurance very softly. "I don't give a damn for the reward and I don't forget. Pull yourself together, Jimmie."

"Then here it is, an' I'll give you my word, s'elp me Gawd, that every little bit of it is like I'm tellin' you. I ain't stringin' you, Buck, an' I am puttin' myself in your hands, like one friend with another. That's right, ain't it?"

"That's right, Jimmie. Go ahead."

"They had me in the pen, then; you knowed that, Buck? Run me in, by Gawd, because I happened to be havin' a drink with a man named Stenton an' a man named Cosgrove an' a dirty Mex as was all crooked an' was wanted for somethin' they pulled off back down there . . . I don't know rightly what it was, damn if I do, Buck! But they wanted *somebody*, an' they got the deadwood on them jaspers, an' me bein' seen with 'em, they put me across, too. Put me across three years ago, Buck! An' it was hell, jes' hell, that's all Hell for a man like me, Buck, as is used to sleepin outdoors an' the fresh air blowin' over the big ranges, an' horses an' things. An' . . . well, I stood it for three years, Buck. Three years, man! Think o' that! *You* don't know what it means. An' then, when I couldn't stand it no longer," and his voice dropped suddenly and the look of the hunted ran back into his eyes, "I broke jail. An' I got this."

He touched his fingers gingerly to the bandaged side, wincing even with the gesture.

"Two bullets," he muttered. "Colt forty-fives. An' I been like this nine days. Or ten, I ain't sure. *An'* nights, Buck. The nights . . . Gawd!"

Thornton, his lips tightening a little, watched the man and for a moment said nothing. And then, suddenly, his voice commanding the truth:

"Don't hold back anything, Jimmie," he said. "It'll be all over the country in a week, anyway. How'd you make your get-away? Did you have to kill anybody?"

He had his answer in the silence which for ten seconds Clayton's twitching lips hesitated to break. When spoken answer came it was broken down into a whisper.

"I . . . I wasn't goin' to hurt anybody, Buck. Hones' to Gawd, I wasn't. An' then, then I got hold his gun, an' I seen he was goin' to fight for it, an' I . . . I *had* to shoot! I didn't go to kill him, Buck! An' he shot me firs' with the other gun . . . you oughta see them holes in my side! . . . an' . . . ." He stopped abruptly, and then, a little defiance sweeping up into his eyes, rushing into his voice, he ended sulkily, "The son of a — had it comin' to him!"

For a long time Buck Thornton, sunk into a deep, thoughtful silence, said nothing. Jimmie's account of an adventure of this kind was sure to be garbled; considering it in an attempt to get to the truth at the bottom of it was an occupation comparable to that of staring down into muddy water in search of a hidden white pebble. He knew Jimmie Clayton. He knew him as perhaps Clayton did not know himself. The man had been sent to state's prison, not because of the company he kept, but because, in Jimmie's own words, "he had it comin'." He had known long ago that Jimmie Clayton would end this way, or worse. Now Clayton was giving his own version of the killing of the guard, and this version would probably be a lie. But through all of these considerations which Thornton saw so clearly there was something else; something seen as clearly, looming high and distinct above them: Jimmie had played the part of friend when but for a friend Thornton would have died. That counted with Buck Thornton. And now Clayton had sent for him, had entrusted into his hands all hope of safety. And he was not this man's judge.

While the cowboy sat silent and thoughtful Jimmie Clayton was watching him, watching him with anxiety brilliant in his eyes, his tongue moistening, constantly moistening the lips which went dry and parched and cracked. Thornton knew, without lifting his eyes from the pool of shadow quivering at the base of the candle stub.

"You ain't goin' back on me, Buck!" The wounded man had drawn himself up on his elbow. "I'll leave it to you, Buck, if I didn't stick by you when you was in trouble. Remember, Buck, when I found you, out on the trail between Juarez and El Paso. And you don't care a damn about the reward, Buck; you said so, didn't you?"

"Jimmie," said Thornton slowly, lifting his eyes from the floor to meet both the pleading and the terror in Clayton's, "I'm going to do what I can for you. But I don't quite know what is to be done. They're going to be on your trail mighty soon if they're not on it now. Can you ride?"

"I can't ride much, Buck." And yet Clayton's voice rang with its first note of hope. For if Thornton knew him, then no less did Clayton know Thornton. And Buck had said that he was going to help him. "I rode them two hundred miles getting here, me all shot to hell that away. An' I rode into your camp las' night to leave the letter. An' I guess if it had been half a mile fu'ther I wouldn't never have made it back."

"Why didn't you come in at my cabin? I'd have fixed you up there."

"I come awful near it, Buck! I wanted to. But I didn't know. There might 'a' been some of the other boys bunkin' there an' I wasn't takin' chances."

"I see. Now, let's see what we're goin' to do."

He stood whipping at his boots with his quirt, trying to see a way. This lonely place might be a safe refuge for a few days. But range business sometimes carried his men this far, and soon or late some one would stumble upon Clayton's hiding place. Clayton's voice, eager again and confident, broke into his thoughts.

"I got to find somebody as'll give me a lift, ain't I? A man can't go on playin' a lone han' like I'm adoin' an' get away with it long. Now, I got to be be laid up here four or five days, anyway, until I can ride again. You can keep your punchers away from here that long, can't you?"

"Yes. I can give them plenty to do on the other end."

"That's good. An' you can ride out again, at night, you know, Buck, an' smuggle me some more grub, can't you?"

"Yes. But . . ."

"Wait a minute! I know a man in Hill's Corners as'll give me a han'. I done him favours before now, same as I done for you, Buck. An' he knows the ropes up here. You can git word to him, can't you? An' then I'll drift, an' he'll look out for me, an' you'll be square with what I done for you, Buck. Will you do it?"

"Yes, Jimmie. I'll do it. I'll ride in and see your man at the Corners. Who is it, Jimmie?"

"An' you won't tell nobody *but* him, will you, Buck?"

"No. I won't tell any one else. Who is it?"

"It's a man as may be crooked with some," said Clayton slowly. "But he's awful square with a pal. It's a man name of Bedloe. They call him the Kid."

CHAPTER
FIFTEEN

The Kid

So the next day Buck Thornton rode away to the south and to Hill's Corners.

He had planned to have his errand over early, to have seen the Kid and to have turned back toward the ranch before noon. For he knew the town's habit of late sleeping and he wanted to be gone from it before it was awake and pouring into its long street and into its many swinging doors the stream of men whom he had no wish to see now. Perfectly well he knew how easily he could find trouble there, and it seemed to him that he had enough on his hands already without seeking to add to it.

But the press of range business kept him later than he had thought it would. And then the one horse on the range he would ride today had to be found out in the hills and roped.

"For," he told himself grimly, "if I'm going to stick my nose in that man's town I'm going to have a horse between my knees that knows how to do something more than creep! And when it comes to horses there's only one real horse I ever saw. I got you, Comet, you old son-of-a-gun!"

And his rope flew out and its wide noose landed with much precision, drawing tight about the neck of a great, lean barrelled, defiant-eyed four-year-old that in the midst of its headlong flight stopped with feet bunched together before the rope had grown taut. The animal, standing now like a horse cut from a block of grey granite, chiselled by the hands of a great sculptor who at the same time was a great lover of equine perfection, swung about upon its captor, its eyes blazing, just a little quiver of the clean-cut nostrils showing the red satin of the skin lining them. The mane was like a tumbled silken skein, the ears dainty and small and keen pointed, the chest splendidly deep and strong; the forelegs small, so slender that to a man who did not know a horse they would have seemed fragile but only because they were all bone and sinew like steel and muscle hardened and stripped clean of the last milligram of fat, as exquisite as the perfect ankle of a high bred woman.

"Part greyhound and part steam engine and part devil!" Thornton muttered with vast approval shining in his eyes. "And *all horse!* A man could ride you right through hell, Little Horse, and come out the other side and never smell your hair burn!"

He drew saddle and bridle from the animal he had been riding and turned it loose. Then coiling his rope as he went, he came up to Comet's high-lifted head. With much evident distaste but with what looked like too much pride to struggle in an encounter in which he knew that he was to be overcome, the big grey accepted the hard Spanish bit. He allowed, too, the saddle to be

136

thrown on him, only a quick little quivering of the tense flanks and a twitching of the skin upon his back showing that he felt and resented. And then with his master's weight upon him, his master's softened voice in his ear, a hard hand very gently stroking the hot shoulder, Comet shook his head, a great sigh expanded the deep lungs, and he was the perfect saddle horse with too much sense to rebel further at the knowledge that after all he is a horse and the man who bestrides him is a man. And Buck Thornton, because he knew this animal and loved him, slackened the reins a little, sensed the tensing of the powerful muscles slipping like pliant steel through satin sheaths, turned the proud head toward the south and felt the rush of air whipping back his hat brim, stinging his face as they shot out across the rolling hills.

When Comet had had his run, racing through the other herds that flung up their heads to look at him and the first half mile had sped away behind, Thornton coaxed him down into a gentle gallop, swearing at him with much soft and deep affection.

"Easy, Little Horse," he soothed. "Easy. We're going to Dead Man's. We'll go in slow and watching where we put our feet, all rested and quick on the trigger and ready to come out . . . if we *want* to! . . . like winning a race."

And Comet, snorting his dislike of any conservation of strength and energy, nevertheless obeyed. So it was a little after three o'clock when they entered the crooked, narrow street which gives a bad town a bad name.

The town had shaken off the lethargy of its morning sleep: there were many men in the street, some riding back and forth, disdaining to walk the distance of a hundred yards from a saloon they had just left to the saloon to which they were going, some sitting their horses in the shade, lounging in the saddle as a man may lounge in an arm chair, some idled on foot at the swinging doors, while many others made a buzz of deep throated voices at the bars and over the gaming tables. As Buck Thornton, riding slowly, his hat back upon his head, his eyes ranging to right and left, came into the street where Winifred Waverly had entered it last week, more than one man lifted his eyebrows on seeing him and wondered what business had brought him here. For the memory of his meeting with the Bedloes was still green, the scars which the Kid wore on his right wrist and his left arm were still fresh, and this town was the Bedloes' town in more ways than one.

He nodded to a few men, spoke to fewer, for here was he more a stranger than he was in Dry Town. Riding straight to the Brown Bear Saloon he swung down. He left his horse, trained to stand by the hour for him, at the edge of the board sidewalk, the bridle reins caught around the horn of the saddle, moved at an even pace through the men at the door and went inside.

A dozen men stood at the long bar, big men and little, dark men and light, of this nationality and that, but alike in the one essential thing that they were of the type by which the far-out places are wrested from the wilderness of God and made part of the wildness of man, hard men of tongue, of hand, of nature, hard drinkers, hard fighters. Gunmen, to the last man of them, who live with a gun always, by a gun often enough, who are dropping fast before the onrush of the civilization for which they themselves have made the way, but who will daily walk over their graves until the glimmer of steel rails runs into the last of the far places, until there be no longer wide, unfenced miles where cattle run free and rugged mountain sides into which men dip to bring out red and yellow gold.

Thornton's eyes ran down the line of them, swiftly. There was no man there whom he knew. He stepped a little to one side, the door at his left, the bare front wall at his back. He stood loosely, carelessly to judge from the little slump of the shoulders, the burning cigarette in the fingers of his left hand, the thumb of the right hand caught in his belt.

The bar was at his left, the bare floor running away in front of him, sawdust covered, the string of gaming tables stretched along the wall at his right. As by instinct his eyes lighted upon the man whom he sought. First a round topped table where three men cut and dealt at "stud"; than a faro lay-out with its quick-eyed dealer, its quick-eyed look-out upon his stool, its half dozen men playing and looking on; then the "wheel"; then a second table with six men busy at "draw." There, at this table, with his broad back to him, sat the Kid. And as usual, to complete the youthful swagger of him, he wore his two guns in plain sight.

Still the cattle man made no move, still his eyes ran back and forth, seeking, showing nothing of what they sought or of what they had found already. He marked every man in the place; saw that there were only two of them besides the Kid whom he had ever seen before, one the bartender, one a man with whom he had had no dealings; noted that neither Charley nor Ed Bedloe were in the house. He saw too that the bartender had leaned a little over his bar, saying something swiftly to the man whom he was serving; that the man turned curiously to look toward the door; while at the same time the man across the table from the Kid had given warning, and the Kid's hands had come away from his cards, dropping down into his lap.

Then Thornton came on, walking slowly, passing about the first poker table, then by the faro table, the roulette wheel, and finally to the table where the Kid sat. Bedloe had not moved again: he had not turned, his cards lay unheeded before him. The other men were silent with a jack pot waiting for their attention.

"When he turns," Thornton was telling himself, "it's going to be in the direction of his gun, and he's going to come up shooting."

There were many men there who sensed the thing he did. Not a man in the saloon whose eyes were not keen and expectant as they ran back and forth between the two, Thornton who had shot Bedloe before now, Bedloe who had sworn to "get him." A chair leg scraped and many men started as if it had been the first pistol shot; it was only the man across the table from Bedloe moving back a little, ready to leap to his feet to right or left. Somebody laughed. At the sound though Bedloe's big thick body remained steady like a rock his fingers twitched perceptibly.

140

"Bedloe," and Thornton's voice was cool and low toned, with no tremor in it, no fear, no threat, no hint of any kind of expression, "I want a talk with you."

He was not five short paces behind the brawler's back. The Kid turned a little in his chair, slowly, very slowly like a machine. His eyes came to rest full upon Thornton's. And Thornton, looking back steadily into the hard eyes, steely and blue and fearless, low lidded and watchful, knew that the man had fully expected to see straight into the barrel of a revolver. For a moment it was as though this place had come under such a spell as that in the tale of the Sleeping Beauty, with every man touched by a swift enchantment that had stilled his blood and turned his body to stone.

Thornton saw that Bedloe's hands were tense with tendons standing out sharply under the brown skin, the fingers rigid, curved inward a little, and not three inches from the grips of his guns. And Bedloe saw that Thornton carried a burning cigarette in his left hand, that his right, with thumb caught in the band of his chaps, was careless only in the seeming and that it, too, was alert and tense. And he remembered the lightning quickness of that right hand.

"What do you want?"

No bluster, no threat, no fear, no hint of expression in the voice which was as steady as Thornton's, with something in it akin to the steely steadiness of the hard eyes.

They spoke slowly, with little pauses, little silences between. The man whose chair had scraped looked uncomfortable; the muscles of his throat contracted; his

141

hand shut tight upon his cards, cracking the backs; then he pushed back his chair again, swiftly, and got to his feet. His deep breathing was audible when he stood to one side where, if there was to be shooting, he would no longer be "in line." No one noticed him.

"I want a quiet talk," was Thornton's reply. "I'm not here to start anything, Bedloe. Will you give me a chance to talk with you?"

Bedloe pondered the words, without distrust, without credence, merely searching for what lay back of them. And finally he answered with a brief question:

"Where?"

"Anywhere. In yonder," and Thornton's nod indicated the little room partitioned off from the larger for a private poker room while his eyes clung to Bedloe's. "Or outside. Anywhere."

Again the Kid pondered.

"I'm playin' poker," he said presently, very quietly. "An' I aint playin' for fun. There's one hell of a lot of money changin' han's this deal, an'," with the first flash of defiance, and much significance to words and look alike, "my luck's runnin' high today!"

"I'll wait until you play your hand," returned Thornton without hesitation. "I'll step right over here."

As he spoke he moved, walking slowly with cautious feet feeling for an obstacle over which he might stumble and so for just the one vital fraction of a second give the Kid the chance to draw first, his eyes upon the eyes which followed him. He stepped, so, about the table, to the other side, so that Bedloe, once more sitting straight in his chair, faced him over the jack pot.

142

The big blue eyed man didn't speak. It was his move and he knew it, knew that all men there were looking at him. He studied Thornton's eyes as he had never studied a man before, taking his time, cool, clear headed. He could get his gun in a flash; he could throw himself to one side as he jammed it across the table, shooting; he could do it before most men there could even guess that he was going to do it. He knew that very well. And he knew too, that although he was quick and sure on the draw, here was a man who was just that wee, deadly fraction of a second quicker.

As though he would find a flicker in the steady eyes of the other man to tell him what he wanted to know, he moved his hand, his left, a very, very little, so little that save at a time like this no man would have seen. There came no change in Thornton's eyes. The Kid lifted the hand, laying it with still fingers upon the table before him. Still nothing in Thornton's eyes to tell that he had seen or had not seen. One second more the Kid sat motionless, pondered. Then he had decided. The right hand came up and lay beside the left on the table.

A man at the bar set down his glass and the faint noise against the hard wood sounded unnaturally loud. Another man ordered a drink, and the low voice breaking the silence sounded like a shout. Men who had stood in tense, cramped positions moved, games that had stopped went on. The strain of a few moments was gone, though still no one lost sight for more than an instant of Thornton and the Kid.

Bedloe dropped his eyes to his cards, merely turning the corners as they lay flat on the table. The man who had gotten hastily out of his chair came back. The game went on as the others were going, silently and swiftly. The jack pot was opened, "boosted," and grew fat. Bedloe played a cool hand, and the impression until near the show-down was that he was not to be reckoned with. Then, a little impudently, as was his way, he shoved his pile to the centre of the table.

"See that or drop out," he said curtly.

The nervous man dropped out. Two men saw it. They both lost to the Kid's full hand.

He swept up the gold and silver and slipped it into his pocket, his hand going very close to his gun during the process but never hesitating. Then he got to his feet.

"Let's go outside," he said, turning toward Thornton.

He led the way, swinging about so that the broad of his back was to the man who followed him and the man whom he had sworn to kill. Walking so, a few paces between them, they passed by the bar, through the clutter of men about the door and out upon the narrow sidewalk. Still the Kid did not stop. He strode on, not so much as looking to see if he were followed, until he came to the middle of the narrow street. Then he came to a quick halt and turned.

"Now," said the Kid, "spit it out. If you want to finish what we begun at Smith's start in. I'm ready."

"I told you," Thornton answered him, "that I am not looking for trouble. When I am I know where I can find it." He dropped his voice yet lower so that by no possibility could any one of the men upon the sidewalk hear him, and ended, "Jimmie Clayton sent me."

"An'," asked the Kid coolly, "who the hell is Jimmie Clayton?"

"He's a poor little devil who is in need of a friend, if he's got any," Thornton returned. "And he said you were the only friend he had here."

"Maybe I am an' maybe I aint." The sharpness of suspicion was still high in Bedloe's eyes. "What about him?"

"You knew he was in the pen?"

"I ain't answerin' questions. Go ahead."

"He broke jail a few days ago. He killed his guard and got himself pretty badly shot up. I guess they're on his trail now. And he's going to swing for it if they ever get him."

"Where is he?" asked Bedloe sharply with no lessening of the suspicion and ready watchfulness.

"In the old dugout at the Poison Hole."

"How's it happen you know so much about it?"

"Jimmie was a friend to me once when I needed a friend. He got this far, he held out to ride to my cabin night before last and left a note. I took him out some grub last night. It's all I can do for him; I haven't any way to hide him out. And he's in too bad shape to ride."

"Well, where do I come in?"

Thornton shrugged his shoulders.

"That's your business, yours and Jimmie's. He said that you were a pal of his, and," he added bluntly, with a keen curious look into the Kid's steel-blue eyes, "that you never went back on a pal."

145

Behind him in the street Thornton heard the clatter of horses' hoofs coming on rapidly. He paid no attention until they were close to him, so close that from the corner of his eye he caught the flutter of a woman's skirt. Then he knew who it was before she passed on. One was Pollard looking white and sick; the other, rosy cheeked and bright eyed, was Winifred Waverly.

A quick smile drove the sternness from his eyes and he swept off his hat to her, ignoring the presence of Pollard. But into her expression as she returned his look for the moment in which she was flashing by, there came no vague hint of recognition. He turned back to Bedloe, a little flush of anger in his cheeks. The two men were very near only battle just then. For the Kid smiled.

"How do I know you're tellin' me the truth?" They had gone back to Jimmie Clayton, Bedloe speaking suspiciously again. "How do I know you aint puttin' up a game on me? It's a nice lonely place, where that dugout is."

The flush died out of the cowboy's tanned skin as swiftly as it had run into it.

"I guess you can't tell," he retorted. "Unless you go and find out. And you know if I wanted to get you I could have got you in there, and I could have got you that time at Smith's. And," with an impudence to match Bedloe's, "I could get you now!"

The Kid passed over the remark, his brows knitted thoughtfully.

146

"Well," he said in a moment, "you've shot your wad now, ain't you? I guess there ain't no call for me an' you to talk all day."

"That's all. What'll I tell Jimmie?"

"You can tell him he ain't made no mistake. You may be lyin' an' you may be tippin' me the straight. But he is a pal of mine an' a damn decent little pal, an' I'll take a chance."

"You'll get him?"

"If he's there I'll get him."

"When?"

"You'd like the time o' day to the minute, I reckon!" He laughed softly. "Jus' the first show I get, which'll be in three or four days."

"If you want a horse for him after a while, a good horse, I'll give him one. That's the best I can do. And I guess that's all, Bedloe."

Thornton stepped back toward his horse. Bedloe turned abruptly and strode through the crowd of men on the sidewalk and back to the saloon and his game, no doubt. Thornton swung up into the saddle, and riding swiftly, passed down the street and back toward the range. As he went he felt little satisfaction in an errand done, little relief to have it over. For he was thinking of the look in a girl's eyes, and again a flush ran up into his cheeks, the bright flush of anger.

CHAPTER
SIXTEEN

A Guarded Conference

With flaming eyes Winifred Waverly whirled upon her uncle.

"Why do you suffer it?" she cried hotly. "The man knows that I was not deceived by his idiotic mask, he knows that I have told you, and still you let him go free where he pleases, swagger about with brawlers like that horrible Kid Bedloe, and dribble your money over the bars for drink and over the poker tables! Why do you suffer it?"

A fleeting smile of deep satisfaction brightened Pollard's eyes. They had ridden home in silence and now, with the door barely closed behind them, she had turned upon him with her indignant question.

"I am waiting," began Pollard.

"Waiting for what?" she demanded. "Until he can have had time to squander what is rightfully yours, until there be no chance of getting it back or bringing such a man to justice!"

"You little fire-eater!" he laughed at her. "Come with me in here." He turned and led the way into the room just off the hall and at the front of the house where he had his office. When the door was closed behind him he dropped into a chair, his face a little white and drawn from the exertion of his ride, the first he had had since the girl had come. "I want to talk with you, and I don't want anybody, Mrs. Riddell in particular, to overhear. She's too fond of talking."

Winifred stood across the room from him, her quirt in her hand switching restlessly at the carpet, her eyes showing a little sympathy for his illness but more anger at Buck Thornton.

"You ask why I don't bring that man to reckoning, and I tell you that I am waiting. Then you ask, for what?" He leaned a little forward, and she saw again in his eyes the look she had surprised there on that first day she had come to Hill's Corners, a look of hate and of a sinister satisfaction. "Waiting for the time when I am sure there will be no loophole for him to crawl through! You are ready to go into a court room and swear that he robbed you; that is a great deal and it will go a long way toward convicting him. But it isn't enough. It's only your word against his; don't you see? He will swear that he did *not* rob you, won't he? We can prove that you left Dry Town with the five thousand dollars; we might even prove that you didn't bring it on to me. But we couldn't prove, beyond the last shadow of doubt, that you didn't lose it, or that somebody else didn't rob you of it."

"But," she asked, frowning in her perplexity, "what good will it do to wait?"

"Your evidence," he went on slowly, as though working the thing out for himself, "is enough to convince eleven jurors out of the twelve; now we must make sure of the twelfth. How will we do it? One way is to find the lost bank notes in Thornton's possession. The other way is to get other evidence to add to yours, cumulative evidence all of which will point one way, to one conclusion!"

"To one conclusion?" she repeated after him, prompting him, so eager was she for him to go on.

"To the fact that Buck Thornton is the man who, for six months now, has been committing the series of crimes, running the gamut from the murder of a stage driver to the theft of cattle from Kemble's place! That is the thing I am waiting for!"

She frowned. A mental picture of the cowboy rose quickly and vividly before her. She saw the clear, steadfast eyes, the free, upright carriage, the flash of a smile that was like a boy's. She had come to be firm in her belief that he was the man who had robbed her, had forced the insult of his kiss upon her, but it was hard, with that picture of him before her, to think him a murderer, too. But then, as though to sweep away her last shred of doubt, the vision widened and into it came another man: she saw Buck Thornton as she had seen him only a few minutes ago, in seeming friendly conversation with the youngest Bedloe whose eyes soiled the woman they rested upon, whose name had travelled even to her home in Crystal City and beyond as a roisterer, a brawler, a man of unsavoury deeds done boldly and shamelessly.

"I am a little sick of it all," she said wearily. "I want to go back home, uncle."

He had looked for that and had his answer ready.

"I know, Winifred. And I don't blame you. But I want you to stay a little longer, won't you? Your evidence is going to be the strongest card in our deck. Will you stay and give it?"

"How long?"

"Not long now. I expect Dalton here today."

"Who is Dalton?"

"Cole Dalton, the sheriff. He is as anxious as I am to get his hands on Thornton. The whole country has been growing hotter in its criticisms of him every day for the last six months, blaming him for not rounding up the man who has committed one depredation on top of another, and gotten away with it."

"And you are sure," she hesitated a little in spite of herself, repeating, "you are sure . . . that Buck Thornton is that man?"

"Yes. I guessed it a long time ago. I know it now that he has robbed you. You will wait a few days, won't you?"

"Yes, I'll wait. But, oh," she cried out with sudden vehemence, swinging about when half way to the door, "I hate this sort of thing! Get it over with quick, Uncle Henry!"

She left him then and went upstairs to her own room where for a little she tried to concentrate her wandering thoughts upon a book. But in the end she flung the volume aside impatiently and went to her window, staring down into the neglected tangle of the front yard and the glimpse of the street through the straggling branches of the pear trees. She tried to see only that men like Kid Bedloe and Buck Thornton were not to

151

be thought of as men, but rather as some rare species of clear-eyed, unscrupulous, conscienceless animals; that they were not human, that it would not be humane but foolish to regard them with any kind of sympathy; that the law should set its iron heel upon them as a man might set his heel upon a snake's flat, venomous head.

And she felt a hard contempt of self, she hated herself, when again and again there rose before her mind's eye the form and face of the man who surely was the worst of the lot, and yet who looked like a gentleman and who knew how to carry himself like a gentleman, who knew what courtesy to a woman was when he wanted to know, who had in a few hours made upon her an impression which she realized shamefacedly would stay with her always.

She had been in her room for an hour, driven by her loneliness had run downstairs to chat a few minutes with Mrs. Riddell in the kitchen and, unusually restless, had gone back upstairs. As she came again to her window, she saw two men leave their horses at the front gate and turn toward the house along the walk under the pear trees. Both were men whose very stature would have drawn one's thoughts away from even pleasant preoccupation, and Winifred Waverly's thoughts were sick of the channel in which they had been running.

One, the one who came on slightly in front of his companion, was very broad and heavy and thick. Thick of arm, of thigh, of neck. He was not short, standing close to six feet, and yet his bigness of girth made him seem of low, squat stature as she looked down upon him. She did not see his face under the wide, soft hat but guessed it to be heavy like the rest of him, square jawed and massive. She noted curiously that his tread was light, that his whole being spoke of energy and swift initiative, that the alertness of his carriage was an incongruity in a man so heavily built from the great, monster shoulders of him to the bulging calves.

The face of the other man she saw. His hat was far back upon his head and as he come on his dark features fascinated her. He was tall, as tall or nearly as tall as the Kid or Buck Thornton, she thought, slender, full of the grace of perfect physical manhood. There was a dash to him that, to the girl, was not without its charm. It spoke from the finely chiselled lips, curved to a still, contemptous smile, from the eyes, long lashed, well set far apart, from the swinging careless stride. A handsome devil, as handsome in his own way as the Kid in his, as defiant an insolence in his smiling eyes, as cool an assurance and a vague added charm which was not so readily classified.

The two men came to the door. She heard Pollard greet them, calling them by name, and thus learned that one was Cole Dalton, the sheriff, one Broderick. Then there came up to her the hum of voices from her uncle's office, the heavy, rasping voice which she was certain belonged to the thicker-set man, the light, careless pleasant tones of the taller man. She found herself listening, not for the words which were lost in the indistinct hum, but to the qualities of tone, idly speculating as to which man was the sheriff, which Broderick. She wondered if now they were going to arrest Buck Thornton and if Broderick were a deputy?

And again she hated herself with a quick spurt of contemptuous indignation that she allowed a feeling of sympathy for the tall cattleman to slip into her heart.

For a long time the low toned conversation in the room below her continued. At first it was her uncle who did the greater part of the talking, his utterances at once emphatic and yet guarded. She had the uneasy feeling that the tones were hushed less because of Mrs. Riddell whom she could hear clattering with her pots and pans in the kitchen, than because of herself. A little hurt, half angry that he should think of her as a possible eavesdropper, she took up her book again, turning the pages impatiently in search of the place which she had a great deal of trouble in finding since she had understood so little of what she had read that day. And even then one half of her mind was on the men below as she wondered why they should not want her to know what it was they said.

Evidently Pollard had finished what he had to say. She supposed that he had been telling them of his loss and her robbery. Then the heavy, rasping voice, Cole Dalton's she was right in guessing it to be, as guarded as Pollard's had been, broke in and for several minutes it was the only sound that came to her, save twice when a low laugh from Broderick interrupted. She frowned at that; to her it seemed that in this stern discussion which had for theme crime and retribution there was no place for a man's laughter; even then her dislike for Ben Broderick had begun.

Then Cole Dalton had finished and Broderick was talking. It was as though each man in turn were making

154

his report to the others. As before not a word came to the ears which she strove futilely to make inattentive. A certain quality in the speaker's voice drew fresh speculation from her. He spoke quietly, with no single interruption from the others and with a positiveness that was like a command, as though he whom she had thought possibly a deputy were coolly telling both Pollard and Cole Dalton what they should do, when they should do it and how. The voice was arrogant, cool and confident.

Again the sheriff's voice floated up to her, raised a little, rasping out what sounded like a protest. And Broderick's answer was another short laugh, full of contempt and followed by a few emphatic, crisp words which she did not catch.

That ended the consultation. She knew it from the silence which followed the curt finality of Broderick's retort and from the scraping of chair legs followed by the sound of the men pacing back and forth and speaking in new, unguarded tones. Now their conversation came to her for the first time.

"You'll be going out tonight, Dalton?" Pollard asked.

"No. The first thing in the morning."

"And you, Broderick?"

"I'll trot along tonight, Henry. But not," the cool voice carelessly, "until I've had something to eat. I know you're going to ask me to stay to supper!"

"What do you want to stay for, Ben?" demanded Pollard with something of irritation in the question. "Haven't you got enough on your hands . . ."

Broderick's ready laugh, slow, easy, vaguely insolent, rose clearly to Winifred's ears.

"You're sure a hospitable cuss," he retorted. "Don't be a hog on top of it, Henry. I want to see that pretty niece of yours."

The girl's cheeks went red at the light tone. She waited to hear her uncle's short rejoinder. And she heard nothing beyond the sheriff's rasping chuckle.

When Mrs. Riddell called from the foot of the stairs that supper was ready Winifred had fully made up her mind that she would not go down. She heard the three men chatting lightly and decided that she would get something to eat after they had finished and gone. But as though her uncle had caught her thought he too cams to the foot of the stairs, calling to her.

"Winifred," he was saying, "supper's ready. Sheriff Dalton is here, and Mr. Broderick, a friend of mine. I want you to tell them what you have told me."

She hesitated a moment, biting her lip. Then she answered, "All right, Uncle Henry; I'll be right down." She went to her wash-stand, arranged her hair swiftly, saw that the flush had gone out of her cheeks, that her eyes were cool and told nothing, and went down to join the three men who had already taken their places at the dinner table.

As she came through the door, her head up, her lips a little hard, Broderick was the first to see her and was upon his feet in a flash, as graceful as a cavalier, as debonair in his big boots and soft white silk shirt as though he had been a courtly gentleman dressed for the ball, his eyes frankly filled with the appreciation of her dainty beauty. Pollard, remembering, rose too, and last of all Cole Dalton, his shrewd eyes intense and keen upon her. Winifred's gaze passed by Broderick as though she had not seen him and travelled to her uncle while she waited for the introductions.

Dalton, who was first to be presented, put out a big, hard, square hand, capturing and releasing Winifred's suddenly as though it were a part of the day's work to be done and over with. He had stepped forward and now stepped back to his chair, his keen, watchful eyes never leaving her face.

Then Broderick took the hand which she did not like to refuse to her uncle's friend and guest and yet which she disliked giving him, saw the little flush which his gaze drove into her cheeks, and with a hint of laughter in his eyes bowed over it gallantly, murmuring his happiness in knowing her. And it was Broderick who stepped quickly to her chair, drawing it out for her to be seated. She found herself wondering where this man had learned to do these little things which are no part of the training of the far out cattle men.

During the first half of the meal there was no reference to the happening at Harte's Camp. Broderick, with a mood contagiously care free and sparkling, did the greater part of the talking, and though he elicited from the girl rare words beyond a brief "yes" or "no," he seemed content. And he interested her. He talked well, with little slurs of grammar that seemed rather due to the man's carelessness of nature than to ignorance, his vocabularly not without picturesque force. It seemed natural that he should do the talking,

157

that he should address himself largely to her, and that Pollard and Cole Dalton should listen and watch him.

Within ten minutes she gleaned that Broderick was a miner, that he had a claim of some sort in the mountains back of Hill's Corners, to the eastward, that a couple of years ago he had made his "pile" in the Yukon country and that he had lost it in unwise speculation, that he knew more than the names of the streets of the chief cities of both coasts, that he had strong hopes of making a strike where he was and of selling out at a good figure to a mining concern with which he was already corresponding. And yet this light miscellany of information was so brightly sprinkled into the flow of talk upon a score of other matters that it did not seem that the man was ever talking of himself.

Finally Pollard, catching a sharp look from Sheriff Dalton, got up and stepped into the kitchen where Mrs. Riddell was. The woman went out into the yard and Pollard came back. Before he had taken his chair again Dalton said abruptly, turning upon the girl:

"Pollard mentioned your seeing the stick-up man at Harte's cabin. Tell us about it."

She told him swiftly, eager to have it over with, conscious that the eyes of all three of the men watched her with a very intense interest. From her account she omitted only that which concerned her personally and alone and of which she had not even spoken to her uncle.

"You're sure it was Thornton?" demanded the sheriff when she had finished. "Dead sure?"

158

"Yes," she answered resolutely, defiant of her own self that hesitated to fix on an absent man the crime of which she believed him guilty.

Dalton sat still save for the drumming of his thick fingers upon the table cloth. Presently his big stocky body turned slowly in his chair as he looked from Broderick to Pollard, the hint of a smile merely making his eyes the harder.

"So," he said, his wide shoulders rising to his deep breath, "it looks like all we got to do is just go out and put our rope on Mr. Badman!"

"It looks like it, Cole," laughed Broderick gently. "Only when you get ready to pull off your little roping party I wish you'd let me know. He don't look like he's the kind to lie down and let you hog-tie him, does he, Miss Waverly? They say he's half Texan an' the other half panther. You want to be quick on the throw, Cole. Remember the way he got the Kid last winter!"

"The only wonder," growled Dalton, "is that the Kid hasn't taken him off our hands and got him long ago!"

"But," put in Winifred hastily, "they're friends now. Uncle Henry and I saw them talking together this afternoon."

She saw the start that her words gave the sheriff, and turning toward Broderick glimpsed a look, steely and hard and glittering with suspicion that had driven the smile from his eyes.

"If Bedloe . . ." began Dalton sharply, his great fist clenched. But he stopped short. He saw and understood the warning glance Broderick shot at him; Winifred saw, too, but did not understand.

159

"Let's go into the other room," the miner said carelessly, "and see what Henry's cigars are made out of."

They rose and went back to Pollard's office. And Ben Broderick, who had suggested cigars, was the only one of the three men who rolled his own cigarette, rolled it slowly and with deep thoughtfulness.

CHAPTER
SEVENTEEN

Suspicion

After all it seemed that for some reason the time was not yet ripe for Cole Dalton to put his rope on "Mr. Badman." For the days ran on smoothly for Buck Thornton, the weeks grew out of them and he rode, unmolested, unsuspicious of any threatened interference, about his own business.

He had gone a second time to the dugout at Poison Hole, carrying provisions enough to last Jimmie Clayton several days. Clayton seemed assured that Bedloe would look out for him now and insisted that there was danger of some of the range hands learning of Thornton's trips here. So, for a week he did not ride near the man's hiding place, and when one day he did visit the dugout again there was nothing to show that Clayton had been there and no hint of how or where he had gone. Thornton felt a deep sense of relief, believing that the episode, so far as he was concerned, was closed.

Another week and he was close to forgetting Jimmie Clayton altogether. The demands of the routine of range work kept him busy every day, early and late, and as though that were not enough to tax his endurance there came a fresh call upon him.

The stage had not been robbed that day he had seen it leaving Dry Town, and he had begun to persuade himself that the epidemic of crime from one end of the county to the other was at an end; that the highwayman had left the country while he could. But now came news of fresh outlawry, news that ran from tongue to tongue of the angered cattle men and miners who demanded more and more loudly that Cole Dalton "get busy."

Rumour flew back and forth, indignant, voluble, accusatory. It stacked crime upon crime; it mouthed the names of many men whom the county would be glad to entertain in its empty jail, the names of the three Bedloe boys, of Black Dan, of Long Phil Granger, of certain newcomers to Hill's Corners who, naturally, were to be looked upon with suspicion. It listed the depredations committed during four weeks with a result that was startling. It told of the theft of a herd of steers from Kemble's place; the shooting of Bert Stone and the looting of Hap Smith's mail bags; the robbery of Seth Powers who left the poker table at Gold Run at two o'clock one morning with seven hundred dollars in his overalls and was found at eight o'clock beaten into unconsciousness and with his pockets turned wrong-side out; the stage robbery in which Bill Varney of Twin Dry Diggings had been killed; the robbery of Jed MacIntosh in Dry Town. A hundred and fifty miles lay between the most widely removed of the places where these things had happened, but no two of them had occurred within a time too short for a man to ride from one to the other.

162

And now came the list of the bold crimes committed since the day, four weeks ago, when Buck Thornton had ridden into Dry Town with the five thousand dollars. Kemble, to the westward of the Poison Hole, told of again losing cattle, seven big steers run off in a single night, nothing left of them but their tracks and the tracks of a horse which disappeared in the rocky mountain soil; Joe Lee, of the Figure Seven Bar, to the north of the Poison Hole, reported the loss of nine cows and two horses, all picked stock; Old Man King of the Bar X grew almost speechless with trembling wrath at the loss of at least a score of cattle. And Ben Broderick, the mining man who was working his claim to the eastward of the Poison Hole, admitted quietly that a man, a big man wearing a bandana handkerchief as a mask, had slipped into his camp one night, covered him with a heavy calibre Colt, and had taken away with him a six hundred dollar can of dust.

As yet no single loss had been noted by the Poison Hole outfit. But Thornton believed that he saw the reason: now, there were few nights that found him at the range cabin or his cowboys in the bunk house. His cattle had been brought down from the mountains, herded into the open meadow lands, and the night riders kept what watch they could upon the big herds. Many a night he lay in his blankets close to the border of his range upon the south, knowing that here and there upon other borders, watching over his cattle, guarding the mouths of cañons down which a rustler might choose his way, his men lay. He began to wish that his property might be attacked, feeling secure in

163

his alertness, thinking that an over bold "badman" might come suddenly to the end of his depredations here. And yet no attack came, not so much as a wandering yearling was lost to him.

Men of the stamp and calibre of these ranchers who were hearing of a neighbour's losses only as a sort of prelude to their own, were not patient men at the best, nor did such lives as they led permit of lax hands and natures without initiative. It was in no way a surprise to Thornton, upon riding to the Bar X, to learn that the cattle men were now rising swiftly and actively to a defence of their own property. Many of them lifted frank and angry voices in condemnation of their county sheriff, many of them more generously admitted that Dalton was up against a hard proposition and was doing all that any one man could do. But they were unanimous in saying that what Cole Dalton couldn't do they would do.

This morning Thornton found Old Man King saddling his horse in the Bar X corrals and snapping out orders to his foreman and the two cowboys who sat their horses watching him with speculative eyes. His recent loss had driven him to a towering rage and his voice shook with anger in it.

"Twenty head they've took from me," he spat out angrily. "Twenty head in one night an' they think they c'n git away with it an' go on doin' jest what they damn please!" He jerked his cinch tight, climbed into his saddle and as his young horse whirled about Thornton saw that he had a rifle under his leg.

164

"Them cows," he went on wrathfully, merely ducking his head at the new comer, "will average a hundred dollars a head. Two thousan' bucks gone like a fog when the sun's up! What in hell do you fellers think I'm payin' you for?"

"It ain't goin' to happen one more time," growled Bart Elliott, the foreman whose wrath under the direct eyes of the "Old Man" was no less than King's. "I jes' wish they'd try it on again . . ."

"Ain't goin' to happen again, ain't it?" retorted King. "That's got to satisfy me, huh? Jest so long as they take a couple thousan' dollars out'n my pockets, an' then don't come back for *all* I got, it's all right, huh? Now you boys can jest nacherally take the glue out'n your ears an' listen a minute: I'm goin' to know who took them cows an' where they went, an' I'm goin' to have 'em back, every little cow brute of 'em! Git me, Elliott? An' you, Jim an' Hodge? If you fellers are lookin' for jobs where you ain't got nothin' to do you better look somewhere else. Now, listen some more."

He told them that they would find two more rifles and a shotgun at the range house. To this information he added that they could pack up some grub and hit the trail along with him. For he was going to bring his cattle back if he had to ride through three states to get them and back through hell to drive them home.

The men rode away to the range house talking among themselves, and King swung about upon Thornton.

"Hello, Buck," he said shortly.

"Hello, King. Anything I can do?"

"Not for me," said King drily. "How about yourself? Lost any cows off'n the Poison Hole?"

"Not a one. The rustlers seem to be giving me a wide berth. I've had my men out every night, though. Maybe they've got wise."

King looked at him sharply. And Thornton was vaguely aware in that swift glance of something which made but little impression on him at the time, something which he forgot even as he saw it, imagining he had misread but something to be remembered in the days that followed: it was a cool, steely look of suspicion.

"Mebbe," King grunted. "It's happenin' all *aroun'* you. I wasn't sayin' much so long's it didn't come too close the Bar X. An' now I ain't goin' to *say* much."

Thornton finished his errand with Old Man King and saw him with his men ride away into the little hills of the range. Then he was turning back toward the Poison Hole when young King, riding around the corner of the barn, called to him.

"Hello, Bud," Thornton said casually. "What's the word?"

Bud King rode up to him before he answered. Then, sitting loosely in the saddle, his eyes meditative upon one free, swinging boot, he answered.

"There's a dance over to the schoolhouse tonight, for one thing. Coming, Buck?"

Thornton shook his head.

"No. Hadn't heard of it and I guess I'll be busy enough without prancing out to dances." And then, a little curiosity in his even tones, "How does it happen you're not out hunting rustlers with the old man?"

Young King lifted his head and again Thornton saw in a man's eyes a thing which was so vague that it went almost unnoted, a look of veiled suspicion.

"The old man hunts his way and I hunt mine," Bud King said briefly. "And besides, I haven't been to a shindig for six months."

A little flush ran up into his face under Thornton's level glance, and Buck laughed softly.

"Who's the girl, Bud?" he challenged.

"Aw, go chase yourself," Bud flung back at him, but with a reddening grin. To Thornton came a swift inspiration.

"Wonder if Miss Waverly will be over from the Corners?" he asked.

"Dunno," Bud replied innocently, so innocently that Thornton laughed again.

Thornton rode back to the Poison Hole. And as he went his thoughts ran now to the mission upon which Old Man King had set forth, now upon the wisdom of shaving, putting on his best suit and new hat and going to a dance . . .

"It isn't so much I want to see her again," he told himself, "as I want to give back her spur rowel."

CHAPTER
EIGHTEEN

The Dance at Deer Creek Schoolhouse

Deer Creek schoolhouse stood in a tiny, emerald valley half a dozen miles from Hill's Corners, some fifteen miles from Thornton's cabin, its handful of barefooted pupils coming from the families scattered through the valley. It was a one roomed building with two low doors and six square windows. And yet it offered ample enough floor space and bench accommodations for the valley dances, its one room being twenty-four feet long and twelve feet wide, certainly over large for the single "school marm" and her small flock, having been constructed with an eye to just such social gatherings as the one tonight.

The teacher's desk had been taken outdoors by willing hands; the pupils' benches stood along the walls for the "women folk" during the intermissions; upon the slightly raised platform at one end of the room were the chairs for the musicians, fiddler and guitarist. And upon the floor was much shaved candle. For light there were the four coal-oil lamps with their foolish reflectors against the walls, and a full moon shining in through door and windows.

Thornton came late late that is, for a country dance It was after nine o'clock when, riding Comet, he saw

168

the schoolhouse lamps winking at him through the oaks and heard the merry music of fiddle and guitar in the frolic of a heel-and-toe polka. Already he made out here and there the saddle horses which had brought so many "stags" so many miles to the dance, and which stood tied to tree and shrub. Also there were the usual spring wagons that had brought their family loads of father, mother, son, daughter, hired man and the baby; while the inevitable cart was in evidence speaking unmistakably of mooning couples whose budding interest in each other did not permit of the drive in the family carry-all.

Thornton noted the vehicles as he passed them, and turned to look at the saddle horses, saying to himself, "So-and-so is here from Pine Ridge, So-and-so from the Corners." For hereabouts a man knew another man's horse and saddle, or wagon, as well as he knew the man himself. So when Thornton saw the buckboard near the door with its two cream-coloured mares, there was at once pleasure and speculation in his eyes, and he told himself, "Somebody is here from Pollard's."

He loosened Comet's cinch, flung the tie rope over the low limb of the big oak near Pollard's team, and leaving his horse in the shadows, went on to the open door.

Already the polka had come to its giddy end. Men and women, boys and girls, old folks with white hair and young folks in knee breeches and short skirts, laughing and talking crisscrossed the floor this way and that seeking seats. The girls and women sinking affectedly or plumping in matter-of-fact style down into their places, with languishing upward looks if they be young and in tune with the moon outside, with red faced jollity and much frankness of chatter if they were married and perhaps had a husband and children likewise disporting themselves, made long rows about the walls of the schoolhouse, looking for the world like orderly flocks of bright plumaged birds in their bravery of many hued calicos and ginghams; a gay display of bold reds and shy blues, of mellow yellows and soft pinks, with the fluttering of fans everywhere like little restless wings.

The men had left their partners, as custom demanded, and had gone to the doors, energetically mopping their brows with handkerchiefs as various in colour as the women's dresses; red and yellow silk, blue and purple, and the eternal gaudy bandana. Thornton paused at the door, losing himself among the men who had come out to stand there smoking or to wander a little away in the darkness where earlier in the evening each had hidden his personal flask under his particular bush. There would be a good deal of drinking tonight, but then that too was custom, and there was no more danger here of drunkenness than in those more pretentious balls in town where men and women partake together of heady punch.

Thornton passed words of greeting with many of these men, ranchers for the most part whom he knew well. There was Bud King, his tie a vivid scarlet, his store clothes a blue-bird-blue, the wide silk handkerchief mopping his flushed face a rich yellow; there was Hank James from the Deer Creek outfit speeding away with long strides to his own bottle under his own bush where he might conceal the tremor of the new happiness he had but come from and drink to the big-eyed girl in the pink dress with the cascades of baby-ribbon; there was Ruf Ettinger with his new overalls turned back the regulation six inches from the bottoms in a cowboy cuff that permitted of the vision of six inches of grey trouser leg below; there was Chase Harper of Tres Pinos in the smallest boots man ever wore, with the highest heels, their newness a thing of which in their pride they shrieked manfully as he walked; and there was Ben Broderick, the miner, quietly dressed in black broad-cloth, looking almost the man of the city. To him Thornton merely nodded, briefly, knowing the man but little, liking him less. But Broderick put out his hand, saying cordially:

"Hello, Buck. Going to shake a leg a little?"

"I might." They were just outside the door, and the cowboy's eyes running on past the miner sought up and down the lines of chatting women for the girl who had tempted him to his first dance in many months. He had seen Pollard's team, but he had not seen Pollard or his niece. Broderick watched him, smiling a little.

"Have a drink, Buck?" he asked, seeming not to have noticed the other's curtness of word and manner. "I've got something prime outside."

"Not thirsty right now, Broderick," Thornton returned coolly.

Then he heard a man's voice from the shadows at his back, and without turning knew that Henry Pollard was out there, just behind him. At the same instant his busy eyes found the girl he sought.

Winifred Waverly's days in Hill's Corners had had little enough of the joy of life in them for her; she had felt that she breathed an atmosphere charged with forces which she could not understand; upon her spirit had rested a weight of uncertainty and uneasiness and suspicion; the men she saw had hard, sinister faces and seemed cast for dark, merciless things; even her uncle appeared a strange sort of stranger to her and she shrank from following her natural train of surmise and suspicion when now and then she surprised a certain look upon his face or when she saw him with the type of man with whom he mixed.

Tonight it was as though after a long period of gloomy, overcast skies, a storm had passed and the sun had broken through. About her were light and music, the merry faces of children and girls with everywhere joyous, full throated, light hearted laughter. And the spirit of her ran out to meet the simple joy of the dance, glad just to be glad again.

Thornton knew that he had found her before she turned her face toward him. He recognized the trim little figure although now the riding habit was discarded for a pretty gown of white which he guessed her own quick fingers had fashioned for the dance; he recognized the white neck with the brown tendrils of hair rebelling from the ribbon-band about her head. And then, when she turned a little, he stared at her from his vantage in the outside darkness, wondering if she had grown prettier than ever in the few weeks since he had seen her, or if it were the dress and the way she wore her hair with a white flower in it, or if he had been half blind that other time.

There was a warm, tender flush upon her cheeks telling of her happiness. Her eyes shone, soft in their brightness, and her lips were red with the leaping blood of youth. She had turned to speak with Mrs. Sturgis, the stoutest, jolliest and altogether most motherly woman in the valley, and Mrs. Sturgis, watching her eyes and lips and paying no attention to her words, put out her plump hands suddenly, crying heartily:

"You pretty little mouse! If I had just one wish I'd wish I was a man, an' I'd just grab you up in my arms an' I wouldn't stop goin' until I set you down in front of a preacher. Come here an' let Mother Mary kiss you."

"There's a woman with brains for you, Buck," chuckled Broderick.

Thornton, though he agreed very heartily just then, did so in silence.

"It's Winifred Waverly," went on Broderick carelessly. "She's Henry Pollard's niece, you know. A little beauty, don't you think?"

Thornton nodded. Again he had agreed but he did not care to discuss her with Ben Broderick. The miner laughed lightly, and added for Thornton's further information,

"As keen a dancer as she is a looker. And a flirt from the drop of the hat! Had the last dance with her. Which reminds me I better hurry and down my booze and get back. I'm going to rope her for the next dance, too."

Broderick went his way for his bottle. Thornton did not speak, did not turn, did not move that a man might

173

see. But the fingers of the hand at his side twitched suddenly and for a moment were tense.

"Pollard can't help being mostly rattlesnake," he muttered angrily. "But he ought to be man enough to keep his own blood kin away from Ben Broderick's kind. Lord, Lordy, but it's sure enough hell folks can't help having uncles like Hen Pollard. Poor little girl!" And then, thoughtfully, his eyes filled with speculation as they rested upon Winifred Waverly, "Mother Mary Sturgis was absolutely right!"

Now the fiddler was tuning with long drawn bow, and the patting of the guitarist's foot told that he was ready. Thornton, tossing his hat to the teacher's desk just outside the door, entered the building and strode straight to the girl. Other men were hurrying across the floor eager to be first to ask this or that demurely waiting maiden for the dance, but Thornton was well in the lead. He nodded and smiled and spoke to many of the women whom he knew, but he did not stop until he came to Winifred Waverly and Mrs. Sturgis. There he was stopped by the older woman who had not read his intentions, and who, thinking that he was going by, took his arm in her two plump hands.

"Why, Buck Thornton, you rascal, you!" she cried heartily. "Where you been all year? I ain't seen you since I c'n remember. An' where you think you're goin', stampedin' along like a runaway horse?"

"Howdy, Mother Mary," he returned as they shook hands. "I was headed right here to see you and Miss Waverly. Howdy, Miss Waverly."

174

The eyes which the girl turned upon him were wide with surprise. She had had no thought that he would come here tonight. Surely he must know that her uncle, the man whom he had robbed, was here! And Broderick, too — another man whom he had robbed! And how many others? And yet he had come, he seemed careless and without uneasiness, he dared to speak with her quite as if that which had happened in Harte's cabin had never occurred outside of his own imaginings. He even had the assurance to put out his hand to her! As though she would touch him! . . .

"Take your pardners for a walse!" cried Chase Harper of the Tres Pinos, he of the small boots, coming in through the door, wiping his mouth and resuming his duties as "caller" of the dances. "Shake a leg, boys!"

The hurried progress of men in search of "pardners" became a race, boots clumped noisily against the floor, the cowboys swooped down upon the line of women folks, often enough there was no spoken invitation to the walse as a strong arm ran about a lithe waist, the fiddle scraped, the guitar thrummed into the tune, and with the first note they were dancing.

CHAPTER
NINETEEN

Six Feet Four!

Winifred Waverly looked steadily into Buck Thornton's eyes, suddenly determined that she would see in them the guile which must be there. Surely a man could not do the things which this man so brazenly did, and not show something of it! And she saw a glance as steady as her own, eyes as clear and filled with a very frank admiration. In spite of her, her colour rose and her eyes wavered a little. Then she noticed that Mrs. Sturgis's keen eyes were upon her, and swiftly drove the expression from her own eyes and returned Thornton's greeting indifferently. Some day her uncle would accuse this man, but she did not care to give her personal affair over to the tongue of gossip, nor did she care to have her name linked in any way with Buck Thornton's.

"May I have this dance, Miss Waverly?"

He had put out his arm as though her affirmative were a foregone conclusion. She stared at him, wondering where were the limits to this man's audacity. Then, before she could reply, Mrs. Sturgis had answered for her. For Mrs. Sturgis was a born match maker, Buck was like a son to her motherly heart, Winifred Waverly was the "sweetest little thing" she had

176

ever seen, and they had in them the making of such a couple as Mrs. Sturgis couldn't find every day of the week.

"Go 'long with you, Buck Thornton!" she cried, making a monumental failure of the frown with which she tried to draw her placid brows. "Here I thought all the time you was goin' to ask me!"

Then she jerked him by the arm, dragging him nearer, playfully pushed the girl toward him, and before she well knew what had happened Winifred found herself in Thornton's arms, whirling with him to the merry-fiddled music, putting out her little slipper by the side of his big boot to the step of the rye-walse. And Mrs. Sturgis, drawing her twinkling eyes away from them and turning upon Ben Broderick, who had arrived just too late, with as much malice in her smile as she knew how to put into it, remarked meaningly.

"A little slow, Mr. Broderick! You got to keep awake when there's a man like Buck around."

And she seemed very much pleased with the look in Broderick's eyes, a look of blended surprise and irritation.

"Thornton and her uncle are not just exactly friends," he retorted coolly.

"If they was," she flung back at him, "I'd think a heap sight more of ol' Hen Pollard!"

Mrs. Sturgis's manœuvre had so completely taken the girl by surprise that as she floated away in the cowboy's arms she was for a little undecided what to do. She did not want to dance with Thornton; it had been upon the tip of her tongue to make the old excuse and tell him that she was engaged for this walse. In that way the whole episode would have passed unnoticed. But now, if they stopped, if she had him take her to her seat and leave her, everybody would see, everybody would talk, gossip would remember that when she had first come to Hill's Corners John Smith had ridden with her as far as the Bar X, and that Smith had told there how Buck Thornton had ridden as far as his place with her; and then gossip would go on into endless speculation as to what had happened upon the trail which now made her refuse to dance with him.

That was why she hesitated, undecided, at first. Then Thornton began to speak and she wanted to know what he was going to say. Besides, she admitted to herself, begrudgingly, that she had never known a man dance as this man danced, and the magic of the walse was on her.

"I had to return something you left at Harte's Camp," were his first words. "That's the reason I rode over tonight."

"What is it?" she asked quickly.

Now suddenly there rose up into her heart a swift hope that after all he was not entirely without principle, that he had grown ashamed of having taken from a girl the money with which she had been entrusted and that he was bringing it back to her. If he were man enough to do this . . . the blood ran up higher in her cheeks at the thought . . . she could almost forgive him for that other thing he had done.

So they moved on in the dance, her hand resting lightly in his, his fingers closing about it with no hint of a pressure to tell her that again he would take what small advantage he could, his eyes looking gravely down into the eyes which flashed up at him with her question.

"Didn't you lose anything that night?" he countered. "In the cabin after I went for the horses?"

"Well?" she countered, the quick hope leaping higher within her.

"You did?"

She wondered why his eyes were so grave, so stern now, why they had ceased to say flattering things of her and merely hinted of a mind at work on a puzzle. How could she know that while she was thinking of a yellow, cloth lined envelope, he was thinking of a horse lamed with a knife, and hoping to learn from her something of the man who had wounded the animal?

"Well?" she asked again, hardly above a whisper. Did he dare even talk of it here, among all these men and women? She glanced about her anxiously to see if Pollard were in the room. "You are going to give it back to me?"

Her wonderment was hardly more than Thornton's. Why should she show this eager excitement, because of a lost spur rowel?

"I rode over to give it to you," he answered, swinging her clear of an eddy in the swirl of dancers and to the edge of the crowd. "First, though, I want you to tell me something. A man came into the cabin about three minutes before you came out to the barn, didn't he?"

She had lowered her eyes, aware that people were noticing them, her looking up so earnestly, him looking down into her face so gravely. But now, in spite of her, she looked up at him again.

"Why do you ask that?" she demanded with a flash of anger that he should continue this useless pretence. "Do you think I am a fool?"

"No. I am asking because I want to know. It's a safe gamble that the man you had a tussel with is the man who lamed my horse."

"Is it?" she asked with cool sarcasm. "And it's just as safe a gamble that he is a coward and a . . . brute!"

"I don't know about his being a coward, and I don't care about his being a brute," he told her steadily. "But I do want to know what he looks like."

Again she called herself a little fool and bit her lip in the surge of her vexation. She had been glad and over eager just now to restore her faith to this big brute of a man; at a mere word from him she had been ready to condone a crime and forgive an insult . . . She felt her face grow hot; he had kissed her rudely and she had been willing to find excuses, she had even felt an odd sort of thrill tingling through her. And now this eternal play-acting of his, this insane pretence . . .

"Mr. Thornton, this is getting us nowhere," she reminded him coldly. "If you care to be told I can assure you that I know perfectly well who the man was who . . . who came into the cabin that night. And I think that it would be for the best if you returned . . . my property!"

"I'm going to return it. Now, will you answer my question? Will you tell me who that man was?"

"Why do you pretend in this stupid way?" she demanded hotly.

"Why don't you tell me who he was?" he returned, frowning a little.

For a moment she did not answer. Then, her voice very low, she said, speakingly slowly,

"I don't tell you, Mr. Thornton, because you know as well as I do!"

She saw nothing but blank amazement in his eyes.

"If I knew I wouldn't be asking you," he informed her.

Again she looked up at him, their eyes meeting steadily, searchingly.

"You say that you don't know who it was?" she challenged. And the eyes into which she looked were as clear of guile as a mountain lake when he answered:

"No. I don't know!"

Then through lips which were moulded to a passionate scorn no less of self than of him, in a fierce whisper, she paid him in the coin of her contempt with the one word: "*Liar!*"

She saw the anger leap up into his eyes and the red run into his bronzed skin, she felt the arm about her contract tensely until for one dizzy second she thought that he would crush her. And then they were swinging on through the dance to the merry beat of the music and above the music she heard his soft laugh.

He did not look at her, nor did she again lift her eyes to his. But both of them saw Broderick where he stood near the door, his hands shoved down into his pockets, his tall, gaunt form leaning against the wall. His eyes had been following them, and there was in them an expression hard to read. It might have been anger or distrust or suspicion.

And both Thornton and Winifred as they turned in the dance caught a quick glimpse of the face of another man. It was Henry Pollard. He had evidently just come in and as evidently had not seen Thornton and his niece dancing together until this moment. And the look in his eyes springing up naked and startled was a thing easy to read. For it was the look of fear!

Winifred Waverly tried to tell herself that it was fear for her, at seeing her in Thornton's arms. But she knew that it was not. Nor was it fear for himself, not mere physical fear of Thornton. Already she knew of her uncle that the man was no coward. It was not that kind of fear; it was a fear that was apprehension, dread lest something might happen. What?

"Dread that something he did not want her to know might become known to her in her talk with Buck Thornton!"

It was as though a voice had shouted it in her ear. Where so many things were muddled in inexplicability this one matter seemed suddenly perfectly clear to her. He had not wanted her to talk with Buck Thornton! Why?

Thornton, with no farther word to her, had bowed to her, his eyes hard and stern, and taking a paper-wrapped packet from his vest pocket had given it to her, and had walked swiftly to the door near which Broderick stood. In spite of her her eyes had gone down the room after the tall figure. And then

182

something happened which could have meant nothing to any one else in the house, but which brought leaping up into the girl's heart both fear and gladness. And, at last, understanding.

Broderick, smiling, had said some light word to Thornton, laying his hand upon the cowboy's shoulder. For a moment, just the fraction of a second the two men stood side by side in the open doorway. Until they stood so, close together, a man would have said that they were of the same height. Now Winifred marked that there was a full two-inch difference and that Thornton was the taller.

Together they stepped out through the doorway. The door was low, Buck stooped his head a little, Broderick passed out without stooping!

It seemed only last night that she had made her supper in the Harte camp with Buck Thornton. She remembered so distinctly each little event. She could see him now as he had sat making his cigarette, could see him going to the door to look at the upclimbing moon. She had marked then the tall, wiry body that must stoop a little to stand in the low doorway. She had jested about his height; the six-feet-four of him, as he called it . . .

She could see again the man who had come in, masked, the man whose clothes were like the clothes of Buck Thornton even to the grey neck handkerchief. She could remember that this man had stood in the same doorway, that his eyes had gleamed at her through the slits in the handkerchief, . . . that he had held his head thrown back, that he had not stooped!

"It wasn't Buck Thornton!" she whispered to herself, her hands going white in their tense grip upon the parcel they held. "A man *did* lame his horse, a man who wanted me to think all the time that it was Buck Thornton. And that man," with swift certainty, "is Ben Broderick! Uncle Henry's friend. And Uncle knows!"

CHAPTER
TWENTY

Pollard Talks "Business"

The promise of the night flat and stale in his mouth, Thornton turned his back upon the merriment in the little schoolhouse and strode away to his horse awaiting him under the oak. He tightened the cinch with a savage jerk, coiled his tie rope and flung himself into the saddle. Did he not already have enough on his hands without running after a girl with grey eyes and a blazing temper? Had he not already enough to think about, what with guarding his range interests from a possible visit from the marauder who was driving wrath into the hearts of the cattle men and terror into the hearts of the isolated families, what with scraping every dollar here and there that he might be on time with his final payment to Henry Pollard? Must he further puzzle over the insolent whims of a captious girl?

Which was all very well, and yet as he turned Comet's head toward the Poison Hole ranch the blood was still hot on his brow, his thoughts were still busy with Winifred Waverly and the enigma she was to him, while his mind, still touched with the opiate of the loveliness of her, was filled with the picture she made in the moment of her flaming accusation.

"I have been calling her Miss Grey Eyes!" he mused angrily. "That name doesn't suit her. Little Blue Blazes would be better!"

"Mr. Thornton!"

It was Henry Pollard's voice, and for a moment Thornton had no thought of heeding it. But the voice called again, and he drew an impatient rein, waiting.

"Well," came his answer shortly. "What do *you* want?"

"I want to talk business with you or I wouldn't stop you," Pollard returned coolly. He came close to Comet's head and in the same, cool, impersonal voice continued.

"When time comes for your last payment are you going to be able to make it?"

"Until time does come," Thornton snapped at him, "it's my business what I'm going to do."

"Certainly it's your business. But since you've put fifteen thousand into it already I guess you won't slip up on the last five thousand. Now it's nearly five months until that payment falls due, isn't it?"

"Well? Talk fast, Pollard."

"I want to make you a proposition. I need money, and I don't mind saying that I need it bad! I've got a chance for something good, something big, in a mining speculation, and I'm short of cash. If I could raise the money within thirty days . . ."

Thornton laughed.

"Nothing doing, Pollard," he cut in. "When your money's due you can come talk to me. Not before."

"I said I had a proposition, didn't I?" went on Pollard evenly. "I see where I can make by it, and I'm willing for you to profit at the same time."

"Spit it out. Where do I get off?"

"You owe me five thousand yet."

"Five thousand with interest, six per cent . . ."

"Forget the interest; I don't want it. And I'll carve five hundred dollars off the five thousand too, if you'll raise it within thirty days. That is my proposition. What do you say to it?"

For a little Buck Thornton was silent, thinking swiftly. For the life of him he could not but look for some trickery in any proposition which might come from "Rattlesnake" Pollard. And when Pollard coolly offered to give away eight hundred dollars, five hundred of it principal, three hundred interest, Thornton had an uneasy sense that there was something crooked in the deal. But at the same time he knew that a year ago Pollard had been short of funds and for this reason had been driven to sell the Poison Hole. Hence it might be that now Pollard was telling the truth when he said that he needed money.

"You mean," he said presently, speaking slowly, trying to see Pollard's face in the shadows, "that if I come across with four thousand five hundred dollars in thirty days you will give me the deed to the Poison Hole?"

"That's what I mean," agreed Pollard bluntly. "It's a proposition you can take or leave alone. Only you have got to take it right now if you want it. What do you say?"

"I've got out the habit of carrying forty-five hundred around in my vest pocket . . ."

"You've got an equity of fifteen thousand in a range that is worth a whole lot more than you are paying for it, young man! The bank in Dry Town would advance you the money and never bat an eye."

Again Thornton asked himself swiftly if there were some trap here Pollard was setting for him to blunder into. But he could see none, and he could understand that matters might stand so that the smaller sum *now* would be worth more to him than the larger amount in five months.

"This is the fifteenth," replied the cowboy. "On the twenty-fifth I'll have the money ready at the Dry Town bank."

"I don't want it in the bank," Pollard told him shortly. "I want it in my fist! It's just about time for the stage to get held up again, and I'm taking no chances on this bet. You bring the money to *me* or the bet's off."

"An' *I* take the chances of gettin' held up!" grunted Thornton.

"You take all the chances there are. You stand to make eight hundred dollars, and you can take it or leave it! If you take it you can have the papers made out in town, deed and receipt and all, and I'll sign them. You can bring them to me at the Corners, or," with a little sneer creeping into his cool voice, "if you don't like the Corners, anywhere you say. And you can have half a dozen witnesses if you like."

"Why don't you ride with me into Dry Town?"

"Because I don't want to! Because, if you agree to put this thing over, I'm going to be mighty busy getting my deal in shape here and on the other side of the line."

"All right. I'll take the chance," Thornton said crisply, his voice as cool as Pollard's had been. "I'll raise the money and I'll get the papers made out. I'll bring them to you at Hill's Corners on the morning of the twenty-fifth."

He reined Comet about, turning again toward the range, and gave him his head. Pollard watched him a moment, then swinging about upon his heel, went back toward the schoolhouse. Chase Harper's voice from within rose above the fiddle and guitar, calling for the quadrille. Broderick came forward to meet Pollard.

"Well?" he asked quickly. "You made him your proposition?"

"Yes."

"What did he say?" Broderick's voice and eyes alike were eager.

"He swallowed it whole," laughed Pollard.

Broderick laughed with him, and then suddenly, the laughter going out of his voice, his hand shutting down tight upon Pollard's arm and drawing him away further from the door, deeper into the shadows, his words almost a whisper, he said:

"He danced with Winifred. You saw that?"

"Yes, damn him. That's what he came for. But I don't think that they said anything . . ."

"Shut up, man! Don't you suppose I know what you mean? I don't know what they said. It's up to you to find out. He gave her something, a little parcel done up in paper. I don't know what. That's up to you, too. And, what's more," and his voice grew harsh with the menace in it, "it's up to you that they don't see each other again! I don't think that any harm was done tonight. He went away red-mad. When I stopped him at the door for a minute he hardly knew I was there. They didn't say a word to each other the last half of their dance. She said something to him, and her eyes were on fire when she said it, like his when he went out; that put an end to their talk. They didn't even say good night."

"I've got a notion to send her away," muttered Pollard sullenly. "It was a fool idea to drag a woman into this."

"Send her away . . . now?" cried Broderick sharply. "You're the fool, Pollard. She's the best bit of evidence we've got. Keep her here, but for God's sake, man, keep her close! And let's jam this thing through to a quick finish."

"You're right, I suppose, Broderick." Pollard ran his hand across a wet forehead. "We've got to put the whole thing across in a hurry. Ten days, and we'll wind it up . . . What's Cole Dalton doing?"

"He's getting mighty hot under the collar," said Broderick grimly. "He's got to get somebody in his little old jail damn' soon, or he'll have a bunch of wild men in his hair. And he knows it. Now we can get our crop planted and things will be ripe for him to gather in in eleven days."

"Let's go inside." Pollard turned toward the front door. "I want to see Winifred. I want to see how she looks before she gets through thinking about Thornton."

And Winifred Waverly, who, after her stunned hesitation when she had seen Thornton and Broderick standing side by side in the doorway, and who had hurried out through the back door, hoping to find Thornton before he had gone, got to her feet in the black shadow where she had crouched by the schoolhouse wall, her face dead white, her eyes wide and staring, her heart pounding wildly.

CHAPTER
TWENTY-ONE

The Girl and the Game

She did not fully understand, she could not grasp everything yet, she was filled with doubts and suspicions and a growing terror. What had her uncle said to Thornton, what had the cowboy "swallowed whole"? What was the whole scheme which connected the two men, which envoluted Thornton and the sheriff, which seemed clear in one moment only to be a tangle in the next?

One thing only was perfectly clear now to the girl. And seeing it, she gathered up her skirts in her two hands and ran, ran back along the wall, keeping in the shadows, drawing close about her the dark cloak she had thrown about her white dress. She must get into the house before they came in, she must let her face show nothing, she must have time to think before she spoke with them. So she came to the back door, paused a brief moment, commanding her nerves to be steady, then slipped in, letting the cloak fall from her shoulders. She saw Bud King standing with his back to the wall watching the dancers, and going swiftly to him, putting her hand lightly upon his arm, she summoned a smile into her eyes as she cried breathlessly:

"Will you dance this with me?"

192

Young King looked at her in quick surprise, startled at the nearness of the girl for whom his eyes had been seeking, and a little flush ran up into his cheeks, a sparkle of gladness into his eyes.

"Sure," he grinned happily. "I been looking for you, Miss Waverly."

He ran his arm about her, she bent her head a little so that he could not see the whiteness of her face, and they caught the beat of the music. She lost the step, purposely that she might have a little more time before they pass down the room toward Pollard and Broderick, hesitated, taking her time to catch it, laughed at his apology for the mistake, noted that her own laugh sounded free and natural, caught the step, and swirled away into the crowd, daring now to look up laughingly into Bud's face unmindful of the havoc she was working in his soul. The two-step was lively; the room was warm, and the colour rose high in her cheeks. But still she was careful to turn her head a little as they whirled by the front door. But when, for the second time, the dance carried them to the end of the room where Pollard and Broderick were, she was so sure of herself that she sent a quick, laughing glance at her uncle. And a little of the tightness about her heart was gone as she saw the look of relief in his eyes.

King, reckless with the wine of her, demanded the next waltz, claiming that this had been only half a dance, and she gave it to him laughingly, the more pleased that she saw Broderick coming toward her and that this was the second time tonight that he had been a little too late, and that she saw a frown in his eyes as they followed her and King out upon the floor.

But she knew that if she play her part as she must play it until she could have time for the definite shaping of plans, she must dance again with Broderick. When he came for her she nodded carelessly, let him take her into his arms, and even looking up at him, forced a smile. For surely, if these men could do what they were doing and give no hint of it, she could play her part with clear eyes and a steady heart. She knew now that Ben Broderick was a highwayman, that he had forced upon her the insult of his kiss; already she suspected him of being the man who had murdered Bill Varney, who had committed crime upon crime. But she knew, too, and with as clear a knowledge, that she must give no slightest sign of what her thoughts were. And as a result Mrs. Sturgis, watching her, vowed to herself that "that Win Waverly was a little devil of a flirt!"

It seemed an endlessly long time until midnight. The lunches which had come in baskets and boxes were spread out upon the benches, coffee was made outside and brought in in steaming, blackened coffee pots to be poured into tin cups, and the supper was a noisy, successful affair. The girl so wanted to slip away, to get back into her own room at Pollard's house where she might drop all pretence and think, think, think! But she knew that she must seem to enjoy the dance, she must not let her uncle guess that the night had grown bitter in her mouth as it had in Buck Thornton's.

194

The benches were cleared and pushed back against the walls, the musicians were at it again, when Pollard came to her.

"Don't you think, Winifred, we'd better be going?" he asked quietly. "It is late, we've got a good ride ahead of us and I have a lot to do tomorrow."

But she pleaded for one more dance, and then one more, and finally with much seeming regretfulness allowed her uncle to slip on her cloak for her.

"I may be a hypocrite," she told herself a little sternly, as she sat in the buckboard at her uncle's side. "But they are playing me for a little fool! And . . . and if they knew that I guessed . . ."

She shivered and Pollard asked if she were cold.

It was a swift drive with few words spoken. Winifred, her chin sunk in her wraps, seemed to be dozing much of the way, and Henry Pollard had enough to think about to make the silence grateful. The cream-coloured mares raced out across the level land of the valley, with little thought of the light wagon and much thought of the home stable and hay. And, racing on, they sped at last through the long alley-like street of Hill's Corners, into the glaring light from the saloons, by many shadows at the corners of houses, their ears smitten by much noise of loud voices and the clack of booted feet upon the board sidewalks. When Pollard jerked in his team at his own front gate, the girl slipped quickly from the buckboard, saying quietly:

"I think I'll go right up to bed, Uncle Henry. I'm a little tired. Thank you for taking me."

And when he said, "Good night, Winifred," she called back her good night to him, and hurried under the old pear trees to the house. In the hall she found her lamp burning where Mrs. Riddell had left it for her, and taking it up she climbed the stairs to her room.

At last she was alone and could think! Her door was locked, her light was out that no one might know she was awake, and she was crouching at the open window, staring out at the night.

Out of a tangle of many doubts, suspicions and live terrors there were at first two things which caught the high lights of her understanding, standing clear of the shadows which obscured the others. Buck Thornton was absolutely innocent of the thing she had imputed to him, and unsuspecting of the evidence which was being piled up against him. And her own uncle was the friend and the actual accomplice of the real criminal.

Her thoughts harked back to the beginning of the story as she knew it, reverting to that night when she had first seen Buck Thornton at Poke Drury's road house. From that she passed in review all that she knew of him; how he had come in while she was talking with the banker about the errand which was to carry her over a lonely trail to her uncle. At first she had been quick to suspect that Thornton had overheard a part of their conversation, that he had known from the first that she was carrying the five thousand dollars. Now she realized with a little twinge of bitter self-accusation that she had been over hasty in judging the man who had been kind to her.

196

She remembered how, on the trail from Dry Town, she had seen a man following her, a man whose face, at the distance he maintained, was hidden from her by his flapping hat brim, but whom she believed to be Thornton. Upon what had she founded her belief? Upon the matter of his being of about the size and form of the cowboy, upon the fact that he rode a sorrel horse and that his clothes, even to the grey neck handkerchief, were the same! How easy, how simple a matter for another man to have a sorrel horse and to wear clothes like Thornton's!

She remembered that the cowboy's surprise had seemed sincere and lively when she had told him she had seen him; she recalled his courtesy to her in the Harte cabin, his willingness to walk seven miles carrying his heavy saddle that she might have a night's rest under a roof with another woman. Not to be forgotten was the wrath in his eye and voice when she had come upon him with his limping horse, and now, at last she knew why his horse had been lamed and by whom! For that seemingly wanton cruelty had accomplished that which it was planned to do, making her certain beyond a doubt that Thornton had lied to her, that he had been the man whom she had seen following her, hence that he it was who had robbed her and had kissed her into the bargain.

Now, in an altered mood she cast in review all that John Smith and his wife had told her of him, and she knew that her first judgment there in the storm-smitten road house, when she had deemed him clean and honest and manly, had been the right judgment; that he was a man and a gentleman; that he could be all that his eyes told of him, gentle unto tenderness or as hard as tempered steel but always . . . a man.

But there was so much which she did not grasp yet. She heard Henry Pollard return from the stable where he had left the horses and enter the house, passing down the hallway to his room. Still she sat, never stirring save for the little involuntary shiver which ran over her from head to foot, as her uncle came into the house. And still she worked at the patchwork of her puzzle, putting it together piece by piece.

"Buck Thornton didn't do it," she whispered to herself, looking up at the stars flung across the sky above the ugly little town. "Ben Broderick did do it. He robbed me of Uncle's money. And Uncle knows! I don't understand!"

But at last she thought that she did understand. Thornton was buying the Poison Hole ranch from Pollard. Already he had paid fifteen thousand dollars into the deal. Now, what would happen if it were proven that Thornton had stolen back from Pollard's emissary five thousand of that money? Thornton would go to jail and for a long time, and then . . .

But why was Pollard waiting? Why was Broderick waiting, urging the sheriff to wait? She saw it all in a flash then! They would prove . . . they thought that they were sure of proof through her! . . . that Buck Thornton had robbed her of the five thousand dollars. They would prove that Buck Thornton had killed Bill Varney; that he had robbed Hap Smith at Poke Drury's road house; they would prove that Buck Thornton was the man the whole country wanted, the man who had committed crime upon crime! She knew that he was a new man here, that he had lived on the Poison Hole ranch for only a year and that the evidence of which her own word was to have been a part, would be sufficient to prove to the countryside that Buck Thornton was the daredevil marauder they sought. And how undeniably strong would that evidence be if all crime ceased abruptly upon the arrest of this one man!

"It would not be the penitentiary for Buck Thornton," she thought suddenly, her face whiter than it had been when she had overheard Pollard and Broderick. "The ranch would come back into Henry Pollard's hands, the men who have committed these crimes would be able to keep the thousands and thousands of dollars they have taken from stages and stolen cattle, and Buck Thornton would go to the gallows!"

It was unbelievable, it was unthinkable, it was impossible! And yet . . .

"And yet," she whispered through her white lips, "it is the truth!"

She sprang to her feet, her hands clenched at her sides, her eyes blazing. Buck Thornton had been good to her and in return she had done much to give him over into their hands, she had insulted and reviled him, she had sworn to the sheriff that he had robbed her. Now suddenly she felt that she could never sleep again if she did not atone to him.

She was already at the door, her hat and gloves in her hand, ready to run down stairs, to saddle her horse, to ride to Thornton with word of warning, when a new thought came to her.

They were waiting, they were going to wait ten days; that much she had overheard. Waiting for what? For some new crime, for the monster crime of all, for the last play for the last and biggest stake?

She, too, would wait. Not ten days but until she might slip away without this danger of being seen, of her errand being guessed. In the meantime she would learn what she could.

She had not forgotten that Henry Pollard was her uncle. The thought added its bitterness. But she remembered, too, the look she had seen upon Pollard's face when she had told him that Thornton had robbed her, she remembered the look of cruel satisfaction she had surprised there more than once, and she knew that were he more than uncle, closer than uncle, she could not act otherwise than she must act now.

Then, suddenly, she sank down upon her bed, alone and lonely in the thick darkness, weary and vaguely afraid.

"Buck Thornton," she whispered, "I am afraid I need your help as much as you need mine now!"

CHAPTER
TWENTY-TWO

The Yellow Envelope Again!

Old Man King, red eyed with wrath, had gone out after the cattle rustlers in his own direct fashion, seeking to follow the trail of running steers through the mountain passes, his eye hard, his rifle ready, his mind eager to suspect any man to whom that trail might lead. But he found only confused tracks which ran toward the state border line and which vanished before even his sharp eyes, leading nowhere.

Young Bud King, his own anger little less than his father's, went forth on another trail, not after the running steers but after a man. And he went to the town of Dead Man's Alley. Mentally he had made his list of the men to whom one might look to for the commission of the crime which had driven the Bar X outfit to action. Being no man's fool, young King planned to go first to the source of the stream, as it were, and thence to travel downward seeking to see who had muddied the waters. And his "one chief bet" was that the source was in Hill's Corners.

The result of Bud King's investigations, so far as he was concerned, was little different from that of his father's and negligible. But his journey to the town of the bad name was of vast importance to others.

Winifred Waverly, upon the morning after the dance, came down late to her breakfast, and found that Pollard had waited for her. Although he was not in the habit of offering her this little courtesy, she thought nothing of it at first, having enough of other matters in her brain, perplexing her. But before the meal was over she knew why Henry Pollard had waited for her.

It was plain to her that he realized that some real importance might be attached to the matter of her having seen Buck Thornton last night, of having danced and talked with him. On the ride home he had not referred to the cattle man nor had she. Now, in great seeming carelessness but with his eyes keen upon her, he spoke lightly of the dance, mentioned that he had seen Thornton talking to one of the men at the schoolhouse door and wondered why he had gone so early.

She managed to look at him innocently and to say carelessly as he had spoken:

"I had a dance with him. He didn't say anything about leaving so soon." She even achieved a little laugh which sounded quite natural, ending, "He seemed rather put out that I did not receive him like an old friend!"

"You did not accuse him of having robbed you?"

"Not in so many words," quietly. "But I was certainly not polite to him! For a little I thought that he was going to return your money to me."

"Why?" Pollard asked sharply, and now she was sure of his readiness to suspect her of holding back something from him.

"He said," she went on, her interest seeming chiefly for her bacon and eggs, "that he was returning something to me I had left at the cabin at Harte's place. I couldn't think of anything but your money."

"What was it?"

"A spur rowel. It had been loose for several days, and dropped out in the cabin. He brought it back to me."

From this they passed on to speak of other incidents of the dance and of other people, but the girl saw that her uncle's interest waned with the change of topic. Then, her heart fluttering in spite of her, but her voice steady enough, Winifred said lightly:

"I think I'll go for a little ride after breakfast. My horse needs the exercise, and," she added laughingly, "so do I."

"Good idea," he returned, nodding his approval. But then he asked which way she was riding, and finally volunteered to go with her, assuring her smilingly that he had nothing of importance to do, and adding gravely, that he would feel safer if she were not out alone in this rough country.

So he rode with her and after an hour of swift galloping out toward the mountains, for the most part in silence, they came back to the town. Pollard left her at his own gate and rode back through the street, "to see a man." But he returned almost immediately and for the rest of the day did not leave the house. It was a long day for the girl, filled with restlessness and a sense of being spied upon, of being watched almost every moment by her uncle. And before the day was done, there had come with the other emotions a little thrill of positive, personal fear.

It was midafternoon. The silence here at this far end of the street hung heavy and oppressive. She had gone up and down stairs half a dozen aimless times, eager for something to do. The long hours had been hers for reflection, and after weighing the hundred little incidents of these last few weeks, now there was no faintest shadow of a doubt that Henry Pollard was at least guilty of criminal complicity in a scheme to send an innocent man to the penitentiary if not to the gallows; she was more than half persuaded that Pollard was in some way seeking to shield himself by using Thornton as a scapegoat; she had got to the point where she began to wonder if Henry Pollard and Ben Broderick shared share and share alike both in the profits of these crimes and in their actual commission.

She came down stairs for a book, having at last finished the one in her room, resigned to inactivity for another day, perhaps for two or three days, until her uncle's watch upon her movements was less keen and suspicious. She reflected that if she read something she might coax her thoughts away from considerations which he could not understand in their entirety, and which terrified her when she thought that she did understand.

In her quest she passed down the hall and to Pollard's office at the front of the house. The room was by no means private; she had gone into it many times before; sometimes it was used as a sitting room. She had thought that her uncle was in it, but when she came to the open door she saw that it was empty.

She went to the long table at which Pollard wrote his few letters. Upon one end of it, at the far end from the pen and ink, were some books and old magazines, piled carelessly. Yesterday she had seen here a fairly recent novel the title of which promised her an interesting story. A glance showed her the book, lying open, where Pollard had evidently been reading it. And in the same careless glance she saw something else which sent the blood into her face and made her turn swiftly, apprehensively, toward the door.

There, beside Pollard's chair, was his waste paper basket, filled to overflowing with crumpled papers. And, thrusting upward through the papers, catching her eye because the papers were white and it was another colour, was a long, yellow envelope. An envelope exactly like the one in which Mr. Templeton had put the bank notes she was to carry to her uncle!

Obeying her swift impulse she stepped to the basket and drew the envelope out. It was not only like the one she knew, yellow and cloth lined, but it was the same one! She knew that beyond a hint of doubt. For she remembered how, while sealing the thing for her, Mr. Templeton had laid it down on his table, upon his ink-wet pen, how he had carelessly blotted it. And here was the blot!

She came swiftly around the table. Her back was toward the open door. And . . .

Henry Pollard was standing behind her, watching her! She did not see him, she could not be sure that she had heard his soft step on the hall carpet, but she *knew* that he was there. She seemed to sense his presence with the subtle sixth sense.

CHAPTER
TWENTY-THREE

Warning

She felt her heart beating wildly . . . if at that second he had spoken to her she could not have found immediate voice in answer were it to save her life. But further, she knew that if he gave her one second longer she could control herself. For the first time it came upon her in a flash that she had a personal interest in what these men did. They sought to play her for their dupe, their fool; they counted upon making her a sort of innocent accomplice, they dared to count upon her to help them. To make their own positions safe they were dragging her into the dirty mess that they had made.

Her anger steadied her. Her brain had gone hot with it; now it went cool, cold. She was holding the envelope in her hands when Pollard came to the door; now she tossed it back to the basket carelessly and still kept her back to the door. She was humming a little song softly when she picked up the book she had come for and turned with it in her hand as though to leave the room.

But in spite of her second of preparation she started when she saw Henry Pollard's face. She had known that it could look hard and cruel, that it could grow dark and threatening. But she saw now a look in the hard eyes, about the sinister mouth, which sent a spurt of terror up into her heart. Here was a man who could kill, would kill if he were driven to it. She read it in his eyes in that flash of a glance as she might have read it in big printed letters. If he came to believe that there was actual danger to him from her knowledge he would find a way to keep her silent.

"Well?" Pollard said steadily.

He came into the room and closed the door softly behind him. Now there was no tell-tale expression in his tone and all expression had gone out of his eyes.

Even then, though her heart beat quickly and the colour wavered in her cheeks, she managed to look at him steadily and to answer collectedly:

"It looks like I'd been playing Paul Pry, and that you'd caught me, doesn't it?"

She even laughed softly, and went on:

"I came down for a book. Then I noticed this." She picked up the envelope again, holding it out toward him. "You see I recognized it!"

"There are lots of yellow envelopes," he answered colourlessly, his eyes sharp points of light upon hers. "What about it?"

"I am not a lady detective," she smiled back, taking a sudden keen delight in the knowledge that she had taken the right tack, and that she was puzzling Pollard. "But it is quite obvious that you've got your money back! Why didn't you tell me?"

"There are lots of yellow envelopes," he repeated, speaking slowly, and she knew that his brain was as busy as her own. If the moment held danger for her, then it held danger no less for him. "They are common enough. What makes you think that this one . . ."

"Oh, but I know," she broke in lightly. "You see I remembered Mr. Templeton getting this smudge of ink on it. He called my attention to it, the dear, precise old banker that he is, and wanted to give me a clean one. Did Mr. Thornton get frightened and bring your money back?"

For a moment he did not answer. She knew that he was measuring her with those shrewd eyes of his, looking for a false sign, just the twitch of a muscle to tell him that she was playing a part. And she gave no sign.

"No," he said at last. "Thornton did not bring it back. And even if you were a lady detective you might make a mistake now. I haven't seen a cent of the money."

She lifted her eyebrows in well simulated surprise.

"But the envelope?"

Now he spoke swiftly and she knew that he had made up his mind that she was hiding nothing, that she knew nothing, for there was a note of relief in his words.

"I had his cabin searched last night, while we all were at the dance. It was found there. There was no sign of the money!"

Again she tossed away the envelope as though it no longer had any interest for her.

"A man," she said contemptuously, "who would not destroy a piece of evidence like that, is a fool!"

The matter was dropped there; one would have said it was forgotten by both of them. For the rest of the day Winifred Waverly appeared to be much interested in her book, Pollard seemed busy in his office or upon the street. But the girl realized that the man was taking no chances and that there was going to be little chance of her riding the twenty miles to the Poison Hole without his knowing of it. She let the day go with no thought of making the trip, satisfying herself with the knowledge which she had gleaned from the conversation she had overheard at the schoolhouse, and with the comforting thought that she had ten days yet.

Upon the second day following the dance she saw Broderick and Pollard talking earnestly out under the pear trees. Broderick, at his boots whipping impatiently with his riding whip, did not come to the house as was his custom, but going back to the gate flung himself upon his horse and rode away. That same afternoon he came again, and this time Cole Dalton, the sheriff, was with him. They were met by Pollard at the front door, and for an hour the girl in her room could hear their low voices in the room below her.

The third day came and went and she saw no one but Pollard and Mrs. Riddell. Pollard was unusually silent, and again and again she saw that his eyes were hard, his mouth cruel. She began to forget that he was kin to her; she began to see only that here was a man playing his game with high, very high, stakes, that he was watchful and determined, that he was not the sort to let anything, no matter what, stand between him and the thing he had made up his mind to do. She saw that he was growing nervous and sensed that he was in that frame of mind when men act swiftly and unscrupulously. She took no step about the house that Pollard did not know of it.

The fourth day came, and her own nerves were strained to snapping. If she could only do something! She must do something. But what? If Broderick were the guilty man, and from a score of little things, she knew that he was, then Henry Pollard was no less guilty. If Pollard were a part of the horrible scheme, how about Cole Dalton, the sheriff? She began to think that she saw why the months had gone by and Dalton had made no arrests! If he was one of them, if the man paid by the county to defend the county against outlawry were hand and glove with the outlaws, to whom then could she turn?

But at last, upon the evening of the fourth day, when her spirit was ready for some desperate measure unless fate came to help her, fate did help and young Bud King called. He had spent the day in Hill's Corners upon the quest of any information which might tell him who the man was who had run off his father's cattle. Having learned nothing, and being a wise young man after his fashion, he had determined not to go home entirely profitless, and so came to see Pollard's niece.

She saw him as he rode slowly down the street. In a flash she guessed that he came to see her, divined too that Pollard would give her little opportunity of talking to young King or any other man, alone. She was at her window where she sat so often. Before Bud King's horse had been tied at the gate she had written a hasty note, had thrust it into an envelope, and had scrawled on the outside:

"Please carry this right away to Buck Thornton. Don't let any one see. It is very important."

Then she ran down stairs, slipping the note into the bosom of her dress, hastening to be at the door when the Bar X man knocked lest Henry Pollard turn him away, saying that she was not at home.

As she opened the door, and Bud entered, hat in hand and flushed of face, Pollard came to the door of his office. Winifred, shaking hands warmly, asked King in, and remarking that her uncle was only reading, invited him into the office. Pollard, she knew, had no reason to suspect what she had in mind, and she would give him no reason. Before Bud left she would find a way to give him the note.

The three sat down, and Bud, never letting his wide hat out of his hands, sat twirling it and shifting his boots and looking and talking for the most of the time at Pollard. He was a young man, was Bud; girls had been few in his life, and this calling upon a young woman in broad daylight was a daring if not quite a devilish thing.

Winifred found room here for smiling amusement. Pollard did not want to be bothered with King and showed it so plainly that had King not been so alive to the presence of the girl at whom he looked with the tail of his eye and so nearly oblivious of the presence of the man whom he sat facing, he must have noted it before he had been in the room five minutes. Bud did not care to talk with Pollard, whom he agreed perfectly with Buck Thornton in calling a rattlesnake, and yet he talked rather wildly to him of branding and fence building and stray horses and hold-up men and the weather and last year's politics. And Winifred, for a little, watched both men with mirthful understanding.

But as the minutes slipped by and Pollard gave no sign of leaving the room, as silences fell which were too awkward to go unnoticed and which the girl had to fill, she began to be afraid that Pollard's watchfulness was going to prove too much for her and that she would fail in the plan which had seemed so simple. But she must not fail! Four days of the ten had gone. She must find some way to keep Bud King here until something carried Pollard out of the room if only for a moment, and during that moment she must give the note to King.

She was sure that Pollard did not, could not suspect that she meant to say anything to King, or that she counted on having him carry a message for her. But she knew, too, that Henry Pollard was taking no chances he did not have to take. He was a man to play close to the table.

She had time to determine that she *would* succeed in this one vital point, time to hope, to fear, to lose hope a dozen times, before her chance came. She heard a step on the walk under the pear trees, Broderick's step, she thought swiftly, despairingly. Usually Pollard kept the front door locked; she had not locked it after she had let Bud King in. Pollard would know it was Broderick and would merely call, "Come in," not even leaving the room for the one necessary moment. Broderick would come in, Bud King would go soon and she would have no chance of doing the thing she had sworn to herself that she would do.

Her one hope was that she had mistaken the step and that it was not Broderick. When the man outside came up the steps, she heard his spurs jingle on the porch and saw that Pollard too was listening intently.

"Come in," called Pollard. "The door's open, Ben."

Why, why hadn't she locked the door? Now there would be two men to watch her, now it would be impossible . . .

But fresh hope leaped up into her heart, though she could scarce believe her ears when Broderick's voice in answer was like the snarl of a beast, harsh with anger, snapping out his words fiercely:

"Come out here. I want to talk with you outside. And, for God's sake, man, hurry!"

Pollard, too, started. Bud King looked up with wondering eyes from his swinging hat. Pollard, with the briefest sign of hesitation, went out of the room and to the front door.

No sooner had he gone than the girl, her face flushed, her eyes brilliant with the excitement in them, snatched the paper from the bosom of her dress and, tiptoeing to King, forced it into his big hand. Not a word did she speak, not so much as a whisper. But she laid her finger upon her lips, glanced from him toward the door, and tiptoed back to her seat. And Bud King understood in part while he could not understand in full, and thrust the note into his pocket.

When a moment later King rose to go she went with him to the door. She caught a glimpse of Ben Broderick's face, though he hid it from her instantly, whirling about upon his heel; she felt sick and dizzy with a sudden dread of she knew not what. For his face was dead white and horribly drawn with the rage that blazed in his eyes and distorted his mouth, and she saw, standing up in his soul, that thing which one may not look upon and misread: that rage that drives a man to kill. And she saw, too, that a white bandage was tied about his head, under his hat brim, and that the bandage was red with blood.

CHAPTER
TWENTY-FOUR

The Gentleman from New Mexico

Thornton returned rather early that night to the ranch cabin. That he came in at all, instead of remaining far out upon the range border as his men were doing, was because tomorrow he planned on riding to Dry Town where he would raise the four thousand five hundred dollars for Henry Pollard, and he wanted to make an early start.

He left his horse at the barn, passed the bunk house and was crossing the little footbridge which spanned Big Little River, going straight to his cabin upon the knoll, when he saw that while the bunk house was dark there shone a light from his cabin window. Wondering who his guest might prove to be he strode up the knoll. The cabin door was open, he could see his lamp burning upon the table, and sitting upon his chair, hands clasped behind head and cigar smoking lazily, was a man he had never seen before.

He came on, still wondering, until his tall form passed through the doorway and stood over the smoker. The man turned a little, watching him as he drew near.

"Howdy, Stranger," Thornton said quietly.

"Mr. Thornton?" smiled the other. "You see I've been making myself at home."

216

He rose and put out a hand, a small, hard, brown hand which the cowboy accepted carelessly and released marvelling. Its grip was as strong as his own, the muscles like rock.

The man was of medium stature, looking small beside the towering form of his host. He was dressed quietly and well, trousers still preserving the lines left by the tailor's iron, his coat fitting closely about the compact muscular shoulders, his soft shirt white and clean. He was a sandy haired man of forty, perhaps, clean shaven, square jawed, with very bright, very clear brown eyes.

All this Thornton saw at one swift glance. He tossed his hat to the table, pulled another chair toward him, and sat down.

"Glad you made yourself at home," he said then "Find anything to eat?"

The stranger nodded.

"I've been here three hours, and I was hungry. So I raided the bunk house."

"That's right." He brought out his paper and tobacco, making his cigarette slowly, his eyes alone asking the other his business.

"I want a little talk with you, Mr. Thornton. But maybe I'd better wait until you've eaten?"

"Had my supper an hour ago," Thornton replied. "Made camp with the boys before I came in. Fire away, Stranger."

"All right. First thing, my name's Comstock."

The keen eyes which had measured the cowboy as he came through the door were very bright upon him now. Thornton nodded. The name meant nothing to him.

"Don't get me?" laughed Comstock. "Well, well, it's a shock to vanity, but after all one's fame is a poor crippled bird that doesn't fly far." He paused a moment, then added quietly, as though this other information might help his "bird" to fly. "My stamping ground's New Mexico."

Thornton's look showed nothing beyond a faint curiosity; one would have said that he was as little interested in this man's stamping ground as in his name.

"One more try," laughed Comstock easily, "and I'll give up. Two-Hand Billy Comstock . . . Aha, I get you now!"

For now Buck Thornton started and his eyes did show interest and a sudden flash of surprise. For fifteen years Two-Hand Billy Comstock, United States Deputy Marshal, had been widely known throughout the great South-west, a man who asked no odds and gave no quarter, one whose name sent as chill a shiver through the hard hearts of the lawless as a sight of the gallows would have done. And this man, small, well dressed, quiet mannered, as dapper as a tailor's dummy . . .

"If you *are* Billy Comstock," grunted Thornton, "well, I'm damn' glad to know you, sir!"

"If I *am*?" grinned Comstock. "And why should I lie to you?"

"I'm not saying that you are lying," returned the cowboy coolly. "But I'm getting in the habit these days of being suspicious, I guess. But if you *are* that Comstock and want to see me, I'd come mighty close to guessing what you want. But before I do any talking I want to know."

"Sure," Comstock nodded. And then, smiling again, "Only, Mr. Thornton, I'm not in the habit of carrying around a trunk full of identifications."

"You don't need them."

Billy Comstock's name he had made himself, and it had carried far. There were few men in half a dozen States in this corner of the country who did not know why he was called "Two-Hand Billy" and how he had earned his right to the nickname. His fame was that of a man who was absolutely fearless, and who carried the law where other men could not or would not carry it. To him had come the dangers, the sharp fights against odds that had seemed overwhelming, and always he had shot his way out with a gun in each hand, and no waste lead.

"I never saw the man who could beat me to my gun," went on Thornton quietly, no boastfulness in his tone, merely the plain statement of a fact. "If you are 'Two-Hand Billy Comstock' you ought to do it."

The two men were sitting loosely in their chairs at opposite sides of the room, the table with the lamp between them. Comstock's hands were again clasped behind his head. Thornton lifted his arms, clasping his own hands behind his head.

Comstock smiled suddenly, brightly, seeming to understand and to be as pleased as a child with a new game.

"I'll count three," said Thornton. "We'll both go for our guns. If I get the drop on you first," with a smile which reflected the other's, "I've a notion to shoot you up for an impostor!"

"If you get the drop on me first," grinned Comstock, "and *don't* shoot me up, I'll make you a present of the best gun you ever saw."

Thornton counted slowly, with regular intervals between the words. "One," and neither man moved, both sitting in seeming carelessness, their hands behind their heads. "Two," and only their eyes showed that every lax muscle in each body grew taut. "Three," and then they moved, the two men like two pieces of the same machine driven unerringly by the same motive power.

Not the hands alone but the entire bodies, every muscle leaping into action in a swiftness too great, too accurate for it to have been fully appreciated had there been a third man to see. Thornton slipped sideways from his chair, dropping to his knees upon the floor, and his two hands flashed downward. The left hand sped to the opening at the left hip of his chaps, and to the pocket beneath; the right hand into the loose band at his stomach. And the hands seemed not to have disappeared for a fraction of a second when they were flung out in front of him, and two heavy double action revolvers looked squarely into Comstock's smiling face.

Comstock had scarcely seemed to move. He still sat loosely in his chair, its front legs tilted back supported by his heels. But his hands had gone their swift, unerring way to the pockets of his coat, and into the barrels of the revolvers looked the blue steel barrels of two big automatics. And both men knew that, had this been no play, but deadly earnest, there would not have been the tenth of a second between the pistol shots.

"Pretty nearly an even break," laughed Comstock, dropping his guns back into his pockets.

Thornton rose and stood frowning down into the uplifted eyes of his visitor.

"It doesn't take a bullet long to go ten feet," he said a little sternly. "One man doesn't have to get his gun working half an hour before the other fellow." He came around the table and put out his hand. "Shake," he said. "You could have got me. And I guess you're Two-Hand Billy, all right."

Comstock's eyes were bright with frank admiration.

"I don't know so well about getting you," he answered. "I played you to slip out on the other side of your chair. And," with his frank laugh, "I wouldn't care for the job of going out for you, Mr. Thornton."

"Real name, Buck," laughed the cowboy. "And now, let's talk."

"First name, Billy," returned Comstock. "And we'll talk in a minute. First thing though, there's some mail for you!"

Thornton's eyes went the way of Comstock's, and saw a piece of folded notepaper upon the table, held in place by the lamp. He took it up, wondering, and read the few words swiftly. As he read the blood raced up into his face and Comstock smiled.

"I must see you," were the hastily written words. "I have wronged you all along. I haven't time to write, I am afraid to put it on paper. But there is great danger to you. Come tonight. I will be under the pear trees in the front yard, at twelve o'clock.

"WINIFRED WAVERLY."

Thornton whirled about, confronting Comstock.

"Where'd this come from?" he demanded sharply.

"Special delivery," smiled Comstock. "A young fellow, calling himself Bud King from the Bar X, brought it."

"When?"

"About an hour ago. He said he couldn't wait and couldn't take time to look you up, and I told him that I'd see that you got it."

Thornton read the short note again, frowning. This girl, only a few nights ago, had called him a liar, had angered him as thoroughly as she knew how, had sent him from her vowing that he was a fool to have ever thought of her, and that he'd die before he'd be fool to seek again to see the niece of Henry Pollard. And now this note, speaking of having wronged him, telling him that she was afraid to write all that she wanted to tell him, warning him of danger to him, asking him to meet her in Hill's Corners . . . at her uncle's house . . . at midnight!

He knew nothing of the danger to which she referred, but he did know that for him there was danger in going into Dead Man's Alley even in broad daylight. There came to him a swift suspicion that this note had never been written by the girl whose signature it bore, that it had been dictated by a man who sought to lure him to a spot where it would be an easy matter to put a

222

bullet in him in safe, cowardly fashion. Suppose that he went, that he entered Pollard's place, and at such an hour? Pollard, himself, could kill him, admit the deed and claim that he was but protecting his own premises. Any one of the Bedloe boys could shoot him and who would know?

Another suspicion, allied to this one, came and darkened the frown in his eyes. Was it possible that Winifred Waverly had written it, acting at Pollard's command? that she was but doing the sort of thing he should look to one of Pollard's blood to do?

Comstock, saying nothing further, now seemed entirely engrossed in his cigar. Thornton, the note in his fingers, hesitated. A third time he read the pencilled words. Then he folded the paper and slipped it into his pocket.

"If a man wants to know anything real bad," he said at last, "it's up to him to go and find out, huh, Billy Comstock?"

Comstock, turning his cigar thoughtfully, answered: "That's right, Buck."

Thornton glanced at his little alarm clock. It was not yet half past eight.

"I've got to be in the Corners by twelve o'clock," he said as he went back to his chair. "I'll ride Comet, though, and can make it handily in two hours. Now, what's the line of talk?"

Comstock's look trailed back to his cigar.

"I'm after a man," he volunteered.

"That's a safe bet. What man?"

"Not poor little Jimmie Clayton," smiled Comstock. "He's only a weak little fool at the worst, and wouldn't be a bad sort if he had somebody around all the time to steer him right."

"Who is he?" retorted Thornton steadily ... remembering.

"He's the man you owe a debt of gratitude to," laughed Comstock. "He put some bullets through you one night down Texas way, found that he'd slipped up and that you'd put your money into a check, and then played safe by nursing you through it! The man who broke jail a month or so ago, and beat it up here to you to see him through. I'm *not* after him."

"You seem to know a whole lot," answered Thornton noncommittally, neither voice nor face nor eye showing a hint of surprise or other emotion. And yet he was thinking swiftly, that if this man spoke the truth he had a score to settle with Jimmie Clayton.

"Oh, it's my business to know a whole lot," resumed Comstock, answering the look in Thornton's eyes. "I just say that I'm not after Jimmie Clayton as I don't want you to think that you'll be giving away anything on a friend. The man I want," and he tilted his chair back a little farther, drew up his carefully creased trousers with thumb and forefinger and crossed one leg over the other, "is a man who got away from me seven years ago. Down in New Mexico."

"Name?" asked Thornton bluntly.

"His name doesn't matter, I guess. He had three during the time that I knew him, and I suppose he's had half a dozen since."

"Before you go any further," interrupted Thornton, "tell me why you came to me at all?"

"Banker Templeton of Dry Town is a friend of mine. We went to school together. He's the man who led me to believe, to hope," he added softly, "that the man I want is working this country now. I told Templeton that I wanted to make a little visit to this neck of the woods. And he gave me your name."

"I see. Now, about your man?"

"I'm going to ask you a string of questions, Thornton. We haven't over much time and any way there wouldn't be any use now in my stopping to explain just what I'm driving at and why I want to know this and that. If you'll just answer what I ask . . ."

"Fire away."

For a little they smoked on in silence, Two-Hand Billy Comstock's expression suggesting that he was planning precisely the course his inquiries were to take before beginning.

"Let's start in this way!" he said at last. "What men around here do you know real well, well enough to call friends?"

"I've been here only a year," Thornton told him. "I don't know many men here real well. Friends? Outside Bud King and the boys working for me I don't know any I'd call friend."

"Then," placidly suggested, "how about enemies? A man can make a good many enemies in a year and not half try."

"If you'll change that to men I know pretty well and don't like, and who don't like me, I can name a name or two."

"Let's have 'em."

"There's Henry Pollard, to begin with."

"The man you're buying from. First, how old a man is he and what does he look like? Next, what do you know about him?"

Thornton described the man, guessed at his age, and told what he knew of "Rattlesnake" Pollard. Comstock seemed interested in a mild sort of a way, but neither now nor later, as Thornton spoke of other men, did he give any sign of more than mild interest.

"Who are Pollard's friends?" was the next question.

Thornton named Ben Broderick, two other men who do not come into the story, and Cole Dalton, the sheriff. And as he named them, Comstock asked him to give an estimate at their ages, to tell what he knew of them and to give as close a personal description as he could.

Having finished with Pollard and his friends he spoke of the Bedloe boys. And United States Deputy Marshal Comstock listened throughout with the same mild interest, merely asking questions, offering no opinions.

"One last question," he said finally. "If you had a guess who'd you say was the bad man this county wants?"

"If any stock's missing from my range," was the blunt answer, "I'd look up the Bedloe outfit."

Comstock, offering no opinion, smiled and sank into a thoughtful silence.

At half past nine o'clock Thornton got to his feet and took up his hat.

"I'd better be riding," he said, putting out his hand. "Make yourself at home."

226

But Comstock came to the door with him.

"If you don't mind I'll ride along," he offered carelessly. "I think my trail runs into Dead Man's, too. And by the way, Thornton," he added a little sharply, "my name's just plain Richard Hampton for the present. And my business right now is ... my business!"

Thornton nodded that he understood and together they left the cabin.

CHAPTER
TWENTY-FIVE

In the Dark

It was a pitch black night, the stars hidden by dense drifting clouds, and intensely still. Buck Thornton and Two-Hand Billy Comstock, riding side by side with few words, turned straight out across the fields, the marshal reining his horse close in to that other horse he could scarcely see and leaving to the cowboy the task of finding their way.

They rode slowly until they turned into the level county road and then swifter that they might come into Hill's Corners before it was midnight. When at last the twinkling lights of Dead Man's Alley winked at them Comstock struck a match and looked at his watch.

"Fifteen minutes of twelve," he said. "You're on time. And I guess you can do the rest of your riding alone? So long. I'm apt to drop in on you at the ranch any day."

Comstock had planned to ride straight to the Brown Bear saloon, to invest in a stack of chips, and to spend the evening "seeing the town." And Thornton, understanding that if the note from Winifred Waverly were truthful in all that it said and in all that it suggested, it would be as well if he were not seen tonight, turned out along the outskirts of the village to come to Pollard's house without riding through the main street.

"Easy, Comet, easy," he muttered to his horse, having no desire to come to the appointed place before the appointed hour. "We've got fifteen minutes and then won't have to keep the lady waiting. If she's there, Comet!"

For even yet his suspicions were not all at rest, already he rode with reins and quirt in the grip of his left hand, the right caught in the loose band of his chaps. It lacked but a few minutes of midnight when he entered the dark, silent street in which was Henry Pollard's house.

Here were a few straggling houses with many vacant lots between and no single light to show that any were awake, no gleam from a window to cut through the darkness which was absolute. Thornton drew his horse to the side of the road where the grass had not been worn away by the wheels of wagons and where the animal's footfalls were muffled, hardly to be heard a score of paces away. Twice he stopped, frowning into the gloom about him, seeking to force his eyes to penetrate the impenetrable wall of the dark, straining his ears to catch some little sound through the silence. But there was nothing to see save the black forms of houses and the pear trees in Pollard's yard, shapeless, sinister shadows something darker than the emptiness against which they stood; no sound save his horse's breathing, the faint creak of his own saddle leather, the low jingle of bridle and spur chain.

"Almost too still to be true," he told himself. "But," with a grim tightening of his lips, "too infernally dark for a man to pick me off with a shotgun if he wanted to!"

Fifty yards from Pollard's front gate he stopped his horse, swung down noiselessly from the saddle and tied Comet to a tree standing at the edge of the road; his jingling spurs he removed to hang them over the horn of his saddle. Then he went forward on foot, walking guardedly, his tread upon the grass making no sound to reach his own ears, and came to Pollard's gate.

It was so dark under the pear trees that the obscurity was without detail; he must guess rather than know where the tree trunks were; it was hard to judge if they were ten feet or fifty feet from him. There might be no one here to keep tryst with him, while on the other hand a dozen men might be waiting.

For perhaps two or three minutes he waited, standing motionless at the gate. No faint noise came to him, no hint of a shadow stirring among those other shadows as motionless as they were formless. The night seemed not to breathe, no sound even of rustling branches coming to his ears from the old pear trees.

"It's twelve o'clock, and after," he thought. "If she's coming she ought to be here now."

Still he waited. And then when he knew it must be ten or fifteen minutes after the time Winifred had set, and remembering that she said specifically "under the pear trees," he moved forward suddenly, jerked the gate open and stood in Pollard's yard.

The little noise of the gate whining upon its worn hinges sounded unnaturally loud. His footfall upon the warped board walk which led to the front door snapped through the silence like a pistol shot.

"If there's anybody laying for me here he knows now that I've come," he told himself. And with no hesitation now, yet with no lessening of his watchfulness, he came on swiftly until he stood under the pear trees and within ten feet of the front porch.

It was still about him, intensely still, and black-dark. He stood leaning forward a little, peering into the darkness, listening for a sound, any sound. He knew that it must be half past twelve, that for close upon half an hour he had waited here. Half an hour filled with quick, conflicting thoughts, suggesting a dozen explanations. Was the note really from Miss Waverly? Had she acted in good faith in sending it? What was the danger of which she spoke? Why had she not come, and why had she set an hour like this? Was it a mere hoax?

"If I could only have a smoke," he muttered, "it wouldn't be so bad waiting to see what the play is."

But still he waited, determined not to leave until possessed of the certainty of there being no need of staying longer. Cautiously he approached the house until he could have put out his foot to the first of the steps leading up to the little porch. There he stopped, telling himself that doubtless he was just playing Tom-fool here in his enemy's garden. Less and less did he like the idea of prowling about the place of Henry Pollard at this time of night.

But now at last there was a sound to vibrate against the empty silence in his ears, a little sound which at first he could not analyse and could not locate. He could hardly be sure whether his senses had tricked him or if he actually heard it. It seemed rather that he had *felt* it. His body grew very tense as he tried to know where it was, what it was. But again the silence was heavier and more oppressive than before.

At last, through the void of the absolute stillness, it came again. Now he knew what it was although not even yet could he be certain whence it came. It was a cautious step . . . it might have been a man's step or a woman's. No muscle of his rigid body moved save alone the muscles which turned his eyes to right and left.

At first he thought that there was some one moving toward him from behind, some one who had perhaps just come in through the gate or had been hidden in the straggling shrubbery. And the next instant he knew that the sounds were in front of him, that what he heard was some one walking in the house, tiptoeing cautiously, and yet not silently because the old boards of the floor whined and creaked under the slow tread. Had the night been less still, had his ears been less ready for any sound the faint creak-creak would not have reached him.

"Woman or man?" was his problem. "Winifred Waverly or Henry Pollard?"

There came a second sound and this he recognized; the scraping of dry wood against dry wood, the moving of the bars which the countryside knew that Henry

Pollard used as the nightlock upon his doors. Thornton drew back a little, step by step, slowly, silently, and stopped under the pear trees. Now he was ten feet from the first of the front steps, ten feet from the board walk.

When a man must trust everything to his ears for guidance his ears may tell him much. Thornton knew when the bars were down and when the door was opening very slowly. And then, suddenly, he knew that there was a third person out here in the garden close to him, and that this person . . . man or woman? . . . was moving with as great a slow caution as himself and the other some one in the house. There was the crack of a twig snapping underfoot . . . silence . . . slow cautious steps again.

The cowboy moved again, a bare two steps now, and stopped, his back against the trunk of the largest of the pear trees, his eyes running back and forth between the door he could not see and the moving some one he could not see at the corner of the house. His widened nostrils had stiffened, as though he would scent out these beings, and his eyes were the alert eyes of an animal in the forest seeking its enemy through the denseness of a black undergrowth.

The door was open, the soft step was at the threshold. The other step at the corner of the house had stopped. In the new silence the cowboy could hear his own deep, regular breathing. He could see nothing, he knew that his body pressed against the tree trunk could not be seen, and his hands were ready. He began to long for a pistol shot, for the spurt of red fire, for anything that would mean certainty and would release the coiled springs of his tense muscles.

But the still minutes dragged by and there was no certainty of anything save that the some one at the door and the some one at the corner of the house at Thornton's right were standing as still, as tense, as himself. A little sense of the grim humour of this game three people were playing in the dark, this Blind Man's Buff which he was waiting to understand, drew his lips into a quick, fleeting smile.

Now at last came the first bit of certainty. The some one at the door moved again, came to the steps and down into the garden, taking the steps slowly, with long pauses between. This some one was a man. Dimly Thornton saw the blur of the form, but more than his eyes his ears told him that this tread, though guarded, was too heavy for a girl like Winifred Waverly.

"Pollard," he told himself swiftly. "Not ten feet away. And if he comes this way . . ."

The man at the steps stopped and in the long silence Thornton knew that the two other people playing this grim game with him were listening even as he was, trying to force their eyes to see through the shadows. Then the heavy tread again, and Thornton thought that it was coming nearer. Then a pause, the step once more, and Pollard, if Pollard it were, had turned the other way and keeping close to the house was moving toward the far corner. The steps grew fainter as they drew farther away, and he knew that the man had gone around the corner of the building.

That other person at the other corner of the house, at Thornton's right, had heard and understood, too. The cowboy heard steps there again, quick steps, almost running, soft, quick breathing not a yard away, and bending forward a little, knew that Winifred Waverly had come to keep her tryst with him.

"Miss Waverly?" he whispered softly.

She was at his side, close to him, so close that he could feel the sweep of her skirts against his boots. She, too, had leaned forward, her face lifted up to his, her eyes seeking to make sure who this man was.

"Buck Thornton?" she whispered back.

"Yes. What is it?"

"Here. Quick!" She had thrust a folded paper into his fingers, closing them tightly upon it. "Now, go! Do what I tell you in it. Henry Pollard suspects something; he is looking for me. Go quickly!"

She was already passing him, hastening toward the steps and the front door.

"Wait!" he commanded, his hand hard upon her arm. "I don't understand . . ."

"For God's sake let me go!" Only a whisper, but he thought he heard a quiver of terror in it, he knew that her arm was trembling violently. "He'd kill me . . . Oh, my God, go!"

"If there is danger for you . . ."

"There is none if you go now . . . if he doesn't find me here. Please, Buck . . ."

She jerked away from him and went swiftly to the steps. He could hear her every step now so plainly his heart stood still with fear that Pollard must hear, too.

He heard her go to the door; she passed on, and so became one with the blot of darkness within the house. Then he drew back, slowly, half regretfully, back toward the gate, stopping for a last time under the trees there. And after a very long time he heard Pollard's steps again. The man had made a tour of his grounds, keeping rather close to the house, and now mounted the steps with no effort at silence, slammed the door and dropped the bars into place. It was as though he had flung them angrily into their sockets. Thornton went out of the yard and to his waiting horse.

"She says to go away, to leave her there alone with Pollard," he muttered dully. "And something's up. She said he'd kill her if he knew that she was talking to me . . ."

He hesitated, his horse's tie rope in his hand, of half a mind to go back, to force his way into Henry Pollard's house, to demand to know what was wrong, to take the girl away if there were real danger to her. But then the urgent pleading in her voice came back to him, her insistence that he go, that with him gone there would no longer be any danger for her. Slowly, regretfully, he swung into the saddle. He had made up his mind. He would obey her at least in part, he would go where he could read the paper she had given him, and then perhaps he would understand.

"Any way," he said under his breath, "she's a real girl for you."

He rode swiftly the five hundred yards through the dark street which ran as nearly parallel with the main street as two such crooked streets could approximate parallelism, until he was behind the Here's How Saloon. Here he dismounted and, leaving his horse with reins thrown over his head to the ground, strode off toward the side door of the saloon.

Under the window he glanced in swiftly. Chance had it that the cover was off of the little used billiard table and that two men, in shirt-sleeved comfort, were playing. Both men he knew. They were Charley Bedloe and his brother, the Kid.

The Bedloe boys were intent upon their game, the Kid laughing softly at a miscue Charley had made. Charley was chalking his cue angrily and cursing his luck and neither of them glanced toward the window. Thornton, drawing back a little so that he would not be seen did they happen to look his way, unfolded the paper Winifred had given him.

"Watch me play out my string, Charley!" he heard the Kid call banteringly. Then he heard nothing more from the room, nothing to tell him of another man not ten steps from him in the darkness, for his whole mind had been caught by Winifred's first words.

"I have wronged you from the beginning," she had written. "I thought that I had seen you that day on the trail behind me. You denied it. I thought that you were lying to me. While you were out after the horses a man, masked, came into the cabin and robbed me of the five thousand dollars I was taking to Henry Pollard. I *thought that it was you!* The man was dressed as you were dressed, his grey handkerchief even was like yours. Now I know it was a man named Ben Broderick who robbed me, and that he wanted me to think that it was you.

"Can't you see the whole scheme? Broderick and the men who are with him, have been committing these crimes. And pretty soon, in a few days, in five days I think, they will be ready to make the evidence show that you are the man who has done it all."

There was more; there were several sheets of paper, closely written. Thornton saw the names of Henry Pollard, of Cole Dalton. But he read no further. In one instant the mind which had been so intent upon these things a girl's writing was telling him forgot Winifred Waverly, Henry Pollard, Broderick everything except that which was happening at his side.

For, while he read, there had been the sharp crack of a revolver, he saw the spit of angry reddish flame almost at his side, and as he saw he dropped to his knee, Winifred's note in his left hand, his right flashing to his own revolver. For his first thought was that a man had crept up behind him, that it was Pollard, that he was shooting at him.

But almost with the flash and the report of the gun he knew that this man was not shooting at him. There came the crash and tinkle of broken glass, one of the small panes of the window beside which Thornton had been reading dropped out, and almost before the falling pieces had ceased to rattle against the bare floor he heard the sound of running footsteps behind him. The man who had fired had made sure with one shot.

Then Thornton heard the Kid cry out, his voice hoarse and inarticulate, and with the cry came a moan from Charley Bedloe. Charley staggered half across the room, his two big hands going automatically to his hips. He had come close to his younger brother, staring at him with wide eyes, and then slipped forward and down, quiet and limp and dead.

Thornton's one first emotion, one so natural to a man who takes his fight in the open, was a boundless rage toward the man who had murdered another man in this cold blooded fashion, taking his grim toll from the darkness and without warning. He whirled about, his own gun blazing in his hand, and as fast as his finger could work the trigger sent six shots after the flying footsteps.

The footsteps were gone. Again the cowboy looked swiftly in at the window. He saw that Charley Bedloe was dead; the Kid, his face contorted, hideously twisted to his blended rage and grief, stood staring about him helplessly. Then, the moment of paralysis gone, the Kid suddenly leaped over his brother's body and ran to the window.

"It's Buck Thornton!" roared the Kid. Both of his big guns were already in his hands. "Take that, you . . ."

Then Buck Thornton, making most of an unforeseen situation, did a thing that he had never done before in his life, which he never would do again. He turned and ran, stumbling through the darkness into which one leap carried him.

For he knew that the Kid had no shadow of a shred of doubt that he had killed Charley Bedloe, he knew that if he did not run for it, run like a scared rabbit now, why then he'd have to kill the Kid or the Kid would kill him. He had no wish to meet his death for the cowardly act of another man and he had no wish to kill Kid Bedloe because another man had murdered his brother. If there were anything left to him but to run for it, he did not know what it was.

He found his horse, leaped into the saddle and turned out toward the north.

"The Kid sure had his nerve, running right up to the window after Charley dropped," he muttered, with the abrupt beginning of the first bit of admiration he had ever felt for a man whom he had appraised as even lower in the scale than "Rattlesnake" Pollard. "The boy is game! And now he's going to come out after me, and there won't be any talking done and it's going to be Kid Bedloe or me. And," with much certainty, but with a little sigh, half regretful, "the Kid is just a shade slow on the draw. Sure as two and two I've got to kill him. Oh, hell," he concluded disgustedly. "Why did this have to happen? Haven't I got enough on my hands already?"

CHAPTER
TWENTY-SIX

The Frame-Up

Thornton returned to his cabin long before the first faint streak of daylight, and not once during the night did he think of sleep. At his little table in the light of his coal-oil lamp he read over and over the hurried words which Winifred Waverly had been driven to put on paper for him. At first his look was merely charged with perplexity; then there came into it incredulity and finally sheer amazement.

"The pack of hounds!" he cried softly when he had done, his fist striking hard upon his table. "The pack of low down, dirty hounds!"

For now, in a flash, he saw and understood beyond the limits to which the girl's vision had gone, grasping explanations denied to her. She had told him everything which she knew or suspected, saying somewhere in her account, "I know now that my first judgment of you, before I was deceived into thinking Ben Broderick you, was right. I know that you are a man and a gentleman. I know that you are 'square.' So now, if you think that you owe me anything for what I am doing for you, I want you to remember that Henry Pollard is my uncle, my dead mother's brother, and to make things no harder for him than he has made them for himself."

With no other reference to her relation to the man, with no further hint of a plea for herself, she went on to tell what she knew of Pollard and Broderick, of their meetings with Dalton whom, she thought, they had completely deceived, of the talk she had overheard that night at the schoolhouse. She said nothing of her own precarious position at Pollard's house. When he finished reading Buck Thornton's eyes were very bright.

"A real woman," he muttered. "A real man's sort of girl! I doped her up right at the first jump, and then I went and insulted her by thinking that she was like 'Rattlesnake' Pollard! Lord, Lordy! What a difference!" And then, very gently, his eyes clouding a little, he muttered over and over, under his breath: "Poor little kid!"

But ever his thoughts came back to the tangle into which day by day he himself had been moving deeper and deeper. He saw how simple the whole matter had been, how seemingly sure of success. Broderick was close enough to him in size and form to make the scheme eminently practicable. It was easy for Broderick to dress himself as Thornton dressed, boots, chaps old and worn, big black hat and grey neck handkerchief. It was simple enough for Broderick, here in this land of cattle and horses, to find a horse that would be a fair match for any horse which Thornton rode. He would allow himself to be seen only at a distance, as upon the day Winifred Waverly had seen him, or indistinctly at night, and when the time came and the arrest was made there would rise up many men to swear to Buck Thornton . . . Broderick himself had already said that he had been robbed of a can of gold dust. He would be ready to swear that Thornton had robbed him. Pollard would add his word . . .

One by one he remembered episodes which until now had meant nothing. Cattle had been stolen from the ranges all about him; no single cow was missing from the Poison Hole. He had thought that this had been because of his own great vigilance, his night-riding over his herds. But what would a jury say? He remembered that the last time he had seen Old Man King, just a few days ago, when King had remarked drily upon the fact that no cattle were missing from Thornton's range, there had been a swift look of suspicion in the old cattle man's shrewd eyes. Already he was suspected. How many men besides King were ready to believe the worst of Buck Thornton, a man who had been in their midst only a year?

There were many days in the life of Buck Thornton as in the lives of other cattle men hereabouts when he was absolutely alone with his horse, when he rode far out day and night upon some range errand, when, perhaps he went two or three days together and saw no other man. Thornton remembered suddenly that when he had first heard of the murder of Bill Varney, the stage driver, he had just returned from such a lonely ride, a three days' trip into the mountains to look for new pasture lands. If these men planned to commit these crimes and then to throw the burden upon him, he saw how simple a matter it would be for them to select some such occasion as this when he could not prove an alibi.

"They've come mighty close to getting me," he muttered sternly. "Mighty damned uncomfortably close!"

He saw further. Winifred Waverly had said frankly that she had sworn to the sheriff that she knew it was Buck Thornton who had robbed her. They were managing to hold Cole Dalton off, and they had a reason. What? Perhaps to work their game as long as they dared, to make a last big haul, or to have their chain of evidence welded so strongly link by link that Thornton could not free himself from it and that no faintest breath of suspicion might reach them. Pollard would be in a position to prove that Thornton had paid him this five thousand only to take it back; it would give him a chance to break the contract, to regain possession of the Poison Hole and to keep the other ten thousand dollars already paid in as forfeited . . .

Why had they chosen him to bear the brunt of their manifold crimes? That, too, was clear to him. With him in the penitentiary or gone to the gallows the whole episode would be closed, the men who had put through the monumental scheme would be in a position to enjoy their boldly acquired profits with no fear of the law so much as searching for them. It was necessary to them that some man suffer for their wrong doing. Now: why Buck Thornton in particular? The reasons were forthcoming, logical and in order: he was a man whom Pollard hated; already Pollard regretted having sold the

Poison Hole ranch for twenty thousand dollars; he wanted it back; Thornton happened to be a new man in the country and new men are always open to suspicion; he happened to be close enough to Ben Broderick in size and form and carriage to make the deception easy. And, thought Thornton, there was one other reason:

The undertaking of these men had already grown too big, the work too extensive, for it to be handled by two men alone. They had confederates; that was inevitable. Blackie, the saloon keeper in Dry Town, was one of them, he felt sure. The Bedloe boys, always ready for deeds of wildness and lawlessness, were others. The Bedloe boys hated him as keenly as did Pollard, and they were not the kind to miss an opportunity like this to "break even" with him. It was noteworthy that he had had no trouble with them since he had shot the Kid's revolvers out of his hands at John Smith's place last winter; they had left him entirely unmolested; the three of them who he knew were fearless and hard and vengeful, had not sought in any way to punish him. Here was the reason.

He went back to Winifred Waverly's letter. She had ended by saying,

"I know that Henry Pollard suspects me of knowing more than I have admitted to him; I suppose I did not entirely deceive him about that yellow envelope. He is watching me all the time. That is why I have written this to be ready to give it to you if I get the chance, if I dare not talk with you. Don't try to see me. I am in no danger now, but if you came, if he knew that we were seeing each other . . . I don't know."

At last when Thornton got up and went to his door day was breaking. He returned to his table where his lamplight was growing a sickly, pale yellow in the dawn, and holding Winifred's letter over the chimney burned it. He took her other little note from his pocket and let the yellow flame lick it up. Then, grinding the ashes under his heel, he put out the light and went again to the door.

The recent shooting at the Here's How Saloon by some man who had stood almost at the cowboy's elbow, he had for a little forgotten as he pondered on his own personal danger and admitted that the case was going to look bad against him in spite of what he might do. But now, for a moment, he forgot his own predicament to become lost in frowning speculation upon the night's crime.

He knew that men like the Bedloes, hard men living hard lives, have many enemies. There were the men whom they had cheated at cards, and who had cheated them, with whom they had drunk and quarrelled. It was clear to him that any one of a dozen men, bearing a grudge against Charley Bedloe, but afraid to attack in the open any one of these three brothers who fought like tigers and who took up one another's quarrels with no thought of the right and the wrong of it, might have chosen this method.

Yes, this was clear. But one thing was not. The night had passed and neither the Kid nor Ed Bedloe had called to square with him. He did not understand this.

For he did not believe that even their affiliation with Broderick and Pollard would have held the Kid and Ed back from their vengeance now. It was patent that the Kid had leaped to the natural conclusion that he had killed Charley Bedloe; he understood the emotion which he had seen depicted in the Kid's twisted face as Charley staggered and fell at his brother's feet. It was a great, blind grief, unutterable, wrathful, terrible, like the unreasoning, tempestuous grief of a wild thing, of a mother bear whose cubs had been shot before her eyes. For the one thing which it seemed God had put into the natures of these men was love, the love which led them to seek no wife, no friend, no confidante outside their own close fraternity. And yet the night had passed and neither the Kid nor Ed had come.

"Something happened to stop them," mused Thornton. "For a few hours only. They'll come. And I'd give a hundred dollars to know who the jasper was that put that bullet into Charley."

He went back into his cabin, put his two guns on the table, threw out the cartridges, and for fifteen minutes oiled and cleaned. Then, with a careful eye to every shell, he loaded them again. When he once more threw his door open and went outside his eyes were a little regretful but very, very hard.

He was inclined to believe that Winifred was mistaken in judging Ben Broderick's to be the brains of this thing. He thought that he saw Pollard's hand directing. Until now he had fully expected to go to Dry Town, to raise the four thousand five hundred dollars with which to make his last payment upon the Poison

247

Hole ranch. Now he more than suspected that this was but a play of Pollard's to get him out of the way while the last crime be perpetrated, to have him out upon one of his lonely rides so that he could prove no alibi, perhaps even to rob him of the four thousand five hundred dollars before he could come with it to Hill's Corners. Now he made up his mind that he was not going to give Pollard this one last chance he wanted. For, he felt convinced, if he did succeed in getting through with the money without a bullet in the back, and if he actually brought it to Pollard the latter would tell him that he had changed his mind, and so the rash act would have been done uselessly. Having no way of holding Pollard to his bargain he had little wish to make the long ride to Dry Town and back.

Thornton for several days had planned to ride out to the borders of his range and see his cowboys, giving them full instructions for work to be done during the week which followed in case he should not be able to give more time to them. Now, with a great deal to think about, he was not averse to a solitary day in the saddle.

Of late he had noted how the cinch of his working saddle was weakening; some of the strands had parted even. He should mend it now, but he had no time to lose, and he did have another saddle, which he did not use twice during the year and which for months now he had not even seen. He had put it out of the way, high up in the loft. He went down to the barn meaning to get it and make the exchange. If he was going to have some hard riding during the coming days it was as well if he used this saddle, the best he had ever seen. Rather too ornate with its profuse silver chasings and carved leather for every day's use, a heavy Mexican affair which he had won in a bronco "busting" competition down in Texas four years ago.

He came up into the loft, half filled with hay, and went to the far end where the saddle had hung upon its peg. It was gone. He stood staring at the peg in surprise. Surely he had left it here, surely he had not removed it. He tried to think when he had seen it last. And he remembered. It had been two or three months ago, and he knew that he had left it here, he even remembered the trouble he had had in drawing it up after him through the small trap door. Now where was it?

His first suspicion was that one of his men had been using it. But he knew that that was impossible. He would have seen it, and moreover one man does not take another man's saddle without saying by your leave.

"The thing is worth three hundred dollars, easy," he muttered. "It would be funny . . ."

He went to the loose hay heaped at the wall and began to kick it about, half expecting to have his boot strike against the silver tipped horn or the heavy tapaderos. And then at last did the swift, certain suspicion of the truth flash upon him. He came upon a small soap box hidden far under the loose hay. He drew it out, whisking away the straw which half filled it. After the first start of amazement and a swift examination of the contents, he understood.

"A plant!" he cried angrily. "A damned cowardly plant! Lord, Lordy, but they're making a clean job of this!"

Upon the top of the pile, the first thing he took into his hands, was a heavy silver watch. It bore a name, scratched within the case, and the name was that of Jed MacIntosh, the man who, Blackie had told him, had been "cleaned out" in Dry Town. There were two bank notes, one for ten dollars, one for twenty, and both were soiled with dark smears that told of dry blood. There was a little, much worn memorandum book, with many pencil-scribbled entries in it, and upon the fly leaf it bore the name of Seth Powers, the man who had been robbed in Gold Run and who had been found beaten into unconsciousness. There was a small tin can; in the bottom of it some pine pitch, and adhering to the pitch a fine sifting of gold dust. A can, he knew, Ben Broderick would identify as the one of which he had been robbed! There were other articles, two more watches, a revolver, an empty purse, which he could not identify but which he realized keenly would be identified when the time came.

Suppose that the time came now! Suppose that he should hear the sheriff's voice calling upon him, that a posse should come upon him and find him with this box in his possession! What chance would he have?

His face went white with the anger which surged up within him and the desire leaped up, strong and bitter, to get in his two hands the man who had framed him and to choke the treacherous life out of him. Then, suddenly, he was cool again, seeing the present danger and the urgent need of prompt action.

First he made certain that there was no other damning bit of false evidence concealed in the hay or any where in the loft. Then, taking the box under his arm, he went down into the stable. Here again he made careful search, spending an hour in a stubborn search. Then leaving the box in a manger, straw-covered, he went back to the cabin on the top of the knoll. His eyes, running to the four points of the compass, told him that there was no other man within sight.

Taking off his boots and socks he waded out into the middle of Big Little River, carrying a shovel and the box. In the soft, sandy soil he made a hole deep enough to hold the box which he put into it. Swiftly he filled it with stones, placed a big, flat rock over it, saw that there was no sign of his work as the sand and mud drifted in to fill the little hollow, and then went back for his boots. The shovel he put again against the bunk house wall.

When, at last, he had mended his cinch and rode Comet out towards the east and the mountains upon the flank of the Poison Hole, he had made up his mind what he was going to do.

"It's a gamble," he told himself coolly. "But I guess I've got to gamble now. And I'm going to play it heavy."

CHAPTER
TWENTY-SEVEN

Jimmie Squares Himself

A horseman was riding toward him upon the far bank of the Big Little River where it straightened out beyond the cabin. He recognized the horse and a moment later the rider now waving his hat to him, and knew that it was Two-Hand Billy Comstock returning. He turned and rode slowly to meet the officer.

"Back already, Comstock?" he called carelessly. "What luck?"

"Bully luck," grinned Comstock, replacing his hat and looking as fresh and well groomed as though he were but this minute up from bed and a long sleep. "First let me tell you the news." He slipped his hand into his breast pocket and took out an envelope. "More mail for you, Thornton! You're doing a big correspondence, it seems to me!"

In spite of him a quick flush ran up to Thornton's brow. For his first thought was that Winifred Waverly . . .

"Wrong guess, Buck," chuckled Comstock, his good humour seemingly flowing from an inexhaustible source. "It's from a man."

"Who?" demanded Thornton sharply, putting out his hand.

252

Comstock's amusement welled up into open laughter.

"It's a prime joke of the Fates," he cried cheerfully. "Here is William Comstock, United States Deputy Marshal, carrying a message from no less a person than Jimmie Clayton, jail bird, crook and murderer! A man wanted in two states!"

"Clayton!" said Thornton in amazement. "You don't mean to tell me . . ."

"Oh, he'd never seen me, you know. Nor I him. But then I've seen his picture more than once and I know all about him. He's keeping low but he took a chance on me. I was just a whiskey drummer last night, you know, and happened to let it out that I was riding this way this morning on my way to Dry Town. So Jimmie slipped me the letter! Read it."

Thornton took it, wondering. The envelope was sealed and much soiled where Jimmie Clayton's hand had closed the mucilaged flap. He tore it open and read almost at a glance:

Deere buck come the same place tonight I want to put you wise. Theare is sum danger to you buck. Keap your eyes open on the way. I will be there late tonight.

j. C.

Thornton looked up to see the twinkling eyes of Two-Hand Billy Comstock watching him.

"You had better tell me what he says," said Comstock coolly. "I don't know but that I should have been well within my rights to open it, eh? But I hate to open another man's private mail."

Thornton hesitated.

He must not forget that Comstock was an officer — that even now he was upon a state errand — that it was his duty to bring such men as Jimmie Clayton to justice. He must not forget that Clayton had been a friend to him — or, at least, that he had credited the crook with a feeling of friendship and the care of a friend.

True, Comstock, who seemed to know everything, had said in a matter-of-fact way that it had been Jimmie Clayton who had shot him that night between Juarez and El Paso. But nothing was proven. He had long thought of Clayton as a man to whom he owed a debt of gratitude, and now with the man, hunted as he was, his sympathy naturally went out to him, evil-doer as he knew him to be.

Evidently Comstock read what was passing in the cowboy's mind.

"I'm not asking you to squeal on him, Buck," he said quietly. "Look here, I could have taken him in last night if I had wanted to. I could have got him a week ago if I had wanted him. But I didn't want him — I don't want him now. I'm hunting bigger game."

Still Thornton hesitated, but now his hesitation was brief. He swung his horse around toward the cabin.

"Let's ride back, Comstock," he said shortly. "I want a good long talk with you."

Not another word about the matter did either man say as they unsaddled or as they went up the knoll to

254

the cabin. Not a word until the fragrance of boiling coffee and frying bacon went out to mingle with the freshness of the new day. Then as they sat at table and Comstock began to soak the biscuits Thornton had made in the bacon gravy, they looked at each other, and their eyes were alike grave and equally stern.

"First thing," began Comstock, "let me finish my news. Charley Bedloe was murdered last night."

"I know."

"The devil you do? All right. Then here's something else. His brother, the Kid, they call him, swears that you killed him."

"I know," nodded Thornton as quietly as before.

Comstock made no pretence of hiding his surprise.

"I thought you had left before the shooting happened. I was all over town; no one saw you . . ."

"Except the Kid. He did. He saw me outside the window through which somebody shot Charley."

Comstock returned his attention to his biscuit and gravy.

"I'm a failure as a news monger," he grunted. "Go on. *You* tell *me*."

And Thornton told him. Before he had finished Comstock had pushed back his chair and was letting his coffee go cold. For Thornton had told him not alone of what had happened at the Here's How Saloon last night, but of the work that Broderick and Pollard were doing, of all of his certainties and his suspicions, of the "planted" evidence he had found in the hay loft, of the missing saddle. Only he did not mention the name of a girl, and he remembered that Pollard was her uncle and spared him where he could.

"What a game! By high heaven, what a game!" Comstock pursed his lips into a long whistle. Then he banged his first down upon the table, his eyes grown wonderfully bright and keen, crying softly, "I've got him, I've got him at last, and he's going to pay to the uttermost for all he has done in the last seven years . . . and before! Got him — by thunder!"

"Pollard?" asked the cowboy quickly.

"No. Not Pollard."

"Then Broderick?"

"Not Broderick."

"Bedloe? . . . The Kid?"

"What does his name matter? I'll give him a dozen names when the time comes, and by heaven he's got a crime to pay for for every name he ever wore!"

He grew suddenly silent and sat staring out through the open door at the distant mountains. At last he turned back toward Thornton, his eyes very clear, his expression placid.

"Guess why they are waiting five days more before springing their mine?" he asked abruptly.

"Yes. I figured it out a little while ago, after I found the truck in my loft. In five days it'll be the first of the month. On the first of the month the stage from the Rock Creek Mines will be worth holding up. It carried in ten thousand dollars last month. At times, there has been a lot more. Just as sure as a hen lays eggs, it is due to be robbed on the first; they'll find something here to prove I was the hold up man, and I . . ."

256

"And you go over the road for life or take a drop at the end of a rope? And they quit being badmen and buy ranches? That it?"

"That's it. It's a gamble, but . . ."

"But it's a damned good gamble," laughed Comstock softly. "You ought to be sheriff, Buck."

But Buck, thinking of how blind to all this he had been so long, how not even now would he have his eyes open were it not for a girl, longed with an intense longing for the end of this thing when she might be free to go from the house of a man like Henry Pollard, when he might be free to go to her and . . .

"How does it happen," he asked suddenly, "that you are not after Jimmie Clayton?"

"When I'm out for a big grizzily," returned Comstock, "I can't waste my time on little brown bears! That's one thing. Another is that Jimmie Clayton never had a chance of getting away. If he lives ten days he'll be nabbed, and he won't live ten days. He's shot to pieces and he's sick on top of it. I told you last night the poor devil is a fool and a tool rather than a real badman. If he's got a chance to die quietly, why let him die outside of jail. It's all one in the end."

Thornton had always felt a sort of pity for Jimmie Clayton; it had always seemed to him that the poor devil was merely one of the weaker vessels that go down the stream of life, borne this way and that by the current that sweeps them on, with little enough chance from the beginning, having come warped and misshapen from the hands of the potter. And now Jimmie was about to die. Well, whether it had been

Jimmie Clayton or another who had shot him that night down in Texas, he would heed the entreaty of the letter and go to him for the last time.

So that night, when darkness came, Thornton left Comstock at the cabin and rode out towards the mountains, towards the Poison Hole and the dugout at its side.

It was dark, but not so dark as last night, there being no clouds to blot out the stars. And the moon was slipping upward through the trees upon the mountain top when Thornton came at last to the lake. As before, he was watchful and alert. Clayton was Kid Bedloe's friend, and Clayton had always struck him as a man in whom one could put little faith. It was quite in keeping with what he knew that Jimmie's note had been written at the instigation of Kid Bedloe himself and that he was to be led out here where Kid Bedloe and Ed might be in waiting for him. It was quite possible, even probable. But he thought it more than likely that for once Jimmie Clayton was acting in good faith.

The Jimmie Clayton whom he found alone a little after moonrise was very much as he had found him that other night. The fugitive lay upon the bunk in the darkness of the dugout, and only when he was assured that it was Buck Thornton come to him did he light his stub of candle. As before Thornton entered and closed the door after him to look down on the man with a sharp twinge of pity.

"How're they coming, Jimmie?" he asked gently.

"Can't you see?" replied Clayton with a nervous laugh. "I'm all in, Buck. All in."

258

If ever a man looked to be "all in" it was poor little Jimmie Clayton. He threw back his coat for Thornton to see. There upon the side was the stain of blood hardly dry upon the shirt. His eyes were hollow, sunken, fever-filled, his cheeks unthinkably drawn, yellow-white and sickly, the hand which fell back weakly from the exertion of opening his coat showed the bones thrust up as though they would pierce the skin.

"You've been shot again?" demanded the cowboy.

Jimmie shook his head.

"The same ol' hole, Buck; Colt forty-five. It won't heal up, it breaks out all the time. I can't sleep with it, I can't eat, I can't set still." He had begun manfully, but now the little whimper came back into his voice, his shaking hand gripped Thornton's arm feebly, and he cried tremulously, "I wisht I was dead, Buck. Hones' to Gawd, I wisht I was dead!"

"Poor little old Jimmie," Thornton muttered just as he had muttered the words once before, gently, pityingly. "Is there anything I can do, Jimmie."

Jimmie drew back his hand and lay still for a little, his eyes seeming unnaturally large as he turned them upwards, filled at once with a sort of defiance and an abject, cringing terror.

"Nothin'," he said a little sullenly. His eyes dropped and ran to the fingers of his hand which were plucking nervously at his coat. He parted his lips as though he would say something else and then closed them tightly; even his eyes shut tight for a moment. Thornton watched him, waiting. It was easy to see that Jimmie

259

Clayton had upon the tip of his tongue something he wished to say, and that he hesitated . . . through fear?

"What is it, Jimmie?" Thornton asked after a while.

Jimmie lifted his head quickly, his eyes flew open with a look in them almost of defiance as he blurted out:

"Do you know who shot you . . . that time down in Juarez?"

"Was it you, Jimmie?" asked Thornton.

Jimmie's eyes grew larger; all defiance fled from them and the terror came back.

"You . . . you think . . ." he faltered. "You thought all along . . ."

"Was it you, Jimmie?"

The voice was soft, the eyes gentle and now a little smile accompanied the words. It was so easy to forget what had happened so long ago, to disregard it when one looked into this man's eyes and saw there the end of the earthly story of a man who had not been a good man because he had never had a chance, who had never really earned his spurs as a Western badman, because he was of too small calibre, who was after all a vessel that had come imperfect from the hands of the potter. Now Jimmie answered, his voice hushed, his eyes wide, his soul filled with wonderment:

"It was . . . me, Buck!"

"Well, Jimmie, I'm sorry. But it can't be helped now, can it? And I'll forget it if you will." He looked at the worn, frail form, and knew that Comstock was right and that little Jimmie Clayton was lying in the valley of the shadow of death. So he added, his voice very low and very gentle, "I'll even shake hands if you will, Jimmie."

Jimmie closed his eyes but not quick enough to hide the mistiness which had rushed into them. His breathing was irregular and heavy, its sound being the only sound in the dugout. He did not put out his hand. Finally, his voice steadier than it had been before, he spoke again.

"You've been square with me, Buck. I want to be square with you . . . There's a frame-up to get you. Now don't stop me an' I'll talk as fast as I can. It hurts me to talk much." He pressed a thin hand upon his side, paused a moment, and then went on.

"I think Broderick's the man as has been putting over most of the stick-ups around here for quite some time. Him and Pollard in together. I ain't squalin' on a pal when I tell you this, neither," with a little flash of his old defiance. "Broderick's no pal of mine. The dirty cur. He could of got me clear . . . He wanted to make 'em give me up, to git the reward . . . Their game is to make folks think you been doing these things, and to send you up for 'em."

He stopped to rest, but even now did not look to see what effect his words had upon his hearer.

"I don't know much about it," he went on after a moment. "You can find out. But I do know they stole a saddle of yours, and a horse. They're going to stick up the stage out of Rock Creek Mines next week; there's going to be some shooting, and a horse is going to get killed. That'll be your horse, Buck. An' it'll have your saddle on."

He had told his story. He told nothing of how he knew, and Thornton did not press him, for he guessed swiftly that somehow the telling would implicate Kid Bedloe, who was a pal ... and little Jimmie Clayton was not going to squeal on a pal.

Half an hour after he had come to the dugout Thornton left it. For Clayton would not talk further and would not let him stay.

"I got a horse out there," he had said irritably. "I can get along. I'm going to move on in the morning. So long, Buck."

So Thornton went back to his horse, wondering if, when tomorrow came, Jimmie Clayton would not indeed be moving on, moving on like little Jo to the land where men will be given an even break, where they will be "given their chance." His foot was in the stirrup when he heard Clayton's voice calling. He went back into the dugout. The light was out and it was very dark.

"What is it, Jimmie?" he asked.

"I was thinking, Buck," came the halting answer, "that ... if you don't care ... I *will* shake hands."

Thornton put out his hand a little eagerly and his strong fingers closed tightly upon the thin nervous fingers of Jimmie Clayton. Then he went out without speaking.

CHAPTER
TWENTY-EIGHT

The Show Down

Upon the first day of the month the stage leaving the Rock Creek Mines in the early morning carried a certain long, narrow lock-box carefully bestowed under the seat whereon sat Hap Smith and the guard. Also a single passenger: a swarthy little man with ink-black hair plastered down close upon a low, atavistic forehead and with small ink-black eyes. In Dry Town beyond the mountains, to which he was evidently now returning from the mines, he was known as Blackie, bartender of the Last Chance saloon. This morning he had been abroad as early as the earliest; he seemed to take a bright interest in everything, from the harnessing of the four horses to the taking on of mail bags and boxes. In a moment when Hap Smith, before the mine superintendent's cabin, was rolling a cigarette preparatory to the long drive, Blackie even stepped forward briskly and gave the guard a hand with the long, narrow lock-box.

Keen eyed and watchful as Blackie was he failed to see a man who never lost sight of him or of the stage until it rolled out of the mining camp through the early morning. The man, unusually tall, wearing black shaggy chaps, grey soft shirt and neck-handkerchief and a large black hat, kept the stage in view from around the corner of the wood shed standing back of the superintendent's cabin. Then, swinging up to the back of a rangy granite-coloured roan, he turned into the road.

"We're playing to win this time, Comet," he said softly. "And, as we said all along, Blackie's the capper for their game. Shake a foot, Comet, old boy. Maybe at the end of a hard day's work we'll look in on . . . her."

When, an hour later, the stage made its brief stop in Miller's Flat to take on mail bags Blackie was leaning out smoking a cigar and looking about him alertly. A lounger near the post office door turned to watch in great seeming idleness. His eyes met the bartender's for a second and he nodded casually.

"How's everything?" he asked in the customary inconsequential manner of casual acquaintanceship.

"Fine," said Blackie in a tone of equal casualness. "Couldn't be better."

The stranger slouched on his way, climbed into the saddle of the horse he had left by the door, and rode off . . . And Buck Thornton, from the bend in the road where he had halted Comet under a big live oak tree, noted how the horseman rode on his spurs when once he had passed from the sight of the stage driver.

"Taking the Red Cañon trail," he marked with satisfaction. "Carrying the word to Broderick and Pollard that there's been no slip-up and that the box is really aboard. And now . . . Shake a foot, Comet; here's where we put one over on Blackie."

The man who had passed the time of day with the saloon man had disappeared over a ridge and out of sight; Thornton consequently rode swiftly to overtake the stage. Before the four running horses had drawn the creaking wagon after them a half mile Hap Smith stopped his horses in answer to the shout from behind him and stared over his shoulder wonderingly.

"What the hell . . ." he began. And then with a shade of relief in his tone and yet half hesitatingly, the frown still on his face as Thornton rode close up, "It's you, is it? I thought for a minute . . ."

"That it was Broderick?" laughed Thornton. "You didn't think so, did you, Blackie?"

Blackie drew back and slipped his hand covertly into his coat pocket. Thornton, giving no sign that he had seen, said briefly to Hap Smith:

"You've talked things over with Banker Templeton? And with Comstock?"

"Yes," said Hap Smith, his thick, squat figure growing tense where he sat as though with a sudden nervous bracing within. "Yes."

"And you expected me here? You will give me a free hand?"

"Yes," cried Smith ringingly. "Damn 'em, yes. Go to it, Buck!"

Thornton turned stern eyes upon Blackie.

"I can shoot twelve holes through you before you get your hand out of your pocket," he said crisply. "You damned stool-pigeon! Now, suppose you pull your hand out . . . *empty!* . . . and stick it up high above your head. Think it over, Blackie, before you take any fool chances."

His left hand held Comet's reins gathered up close as he spoke; his right rested lightly on the horn of his saddle. Blackie plainly hesitated; a tinge of red warmed his swarthy cheek; his eyes glittered evilly . . . Then suddenly he whipped out his hand, a revolver in it . . .

But Thornton, for all of the handicap, fired first. His own right hand went its swift, sure way to the gun swinging loose in its holster under his left arm pit; he jabbed it forward even as he swung himself to one side in the saddle, and fired. The revolver slipped from Blackie's hand and clattered down to the bed of the wagon while Blackie, crying out chokingly, his face going white with fear, clutched at his shoulder and gave up the fight.

With scant time allowed in their plans to waste on such as Blackie he was made to lie down in the bottom of the wagon, his wrists bound, his wound very rudely bandaged, his body screened from any chance view by the boxes and mail bags and a handkerchief jammed into his mouth. Within ten minutes Hap Smith was clattering on, his and the guard's mouths and eyes grim and hard, and Thornton had again dropped behind, just out of sight around the first bend in the road.

"And now, my boy," muttered Hap Smith to his friend the guard, "keep both eyes peeled and your trigger-finger free. Hell's goin' to pop in considerable less'n no time."

266

Nor was the stage driver unduly pessimistic. Half an hour after Blackie had gone down among boxes and bags the lumbering vehicle thundered into one of the many deep gorges through which the narrow road wound. Here was a sharp turn and a bit of steep grade to take on the run if the stage were to keep to schedule time. But suddenly and with a curse from Smith and a sharp exclamation from the guard, Hap slammed on his brake. A newly fallen pine tree, three feet thick, lay across the road.

The guard's rifle was ready in his hands; in a flash Hap Smith had dropped his reins so that they were held only by the ring caught over the little hook at the back of the seat and had whipped out his own big ugly revolver. His eyes ran this way and that; in his soul he knew well enough that no mere bit of chance had thrown the obstruction across his way. But never a head nor an arm nor a rifle barrel rewarded his look. Until, suddenly, heralded by a curt shouted command, a man rode out into the open road from the mouth of a cañon.

"Don't be a fool, Smith! Take a little look-around first!"

It was a voice eminently cool and steady and insolent. Though his gun rose slowly Hap Smith heeded the note of arrogance and, with a hard finger crooking to the trigger, looked about him again. And this time not in vain. Yonder, from across the top of a boulder, a rifle barrel bore unwaveringly upon the breadth of his chest; ten feet higher up on the mountainside where there was a pile of granite rocks and a handful of scrub brush, a second rifle gave its sinister silent warning; two other guns looked forth from the other side of the road . . . in all, at least five armed men . . .

Hap Smith's eyes went back to the man sitting his horse in the middle of the road, just across the fallen pine tree. A tall, powerfully built man dressed quite as Hap Smith and the guard had been told to expect: black, shaggy chaps, grey shirt and neck-handkerchief; broad black hat; red bandana across his face with wide slits for the eyes. And yet both of the men in the stage stared and were on the verge of uncertainty; had they not been prepared both would have sworn that it was Buck Thornton on Buck Thornton's horse; and later they would, no doubt, have sworn to Buck Thornton's saddle.

Five to two, seemed the odds, with all of the highwaymen saving the one bold figure screened from view and so holding the advantage of position. And yet, for once, the odds were not what they seemed.

For now there came abruptly, and utterly with no sign of warning, the answer to the last big play of Ben Broderick and Henry Pollard and the rest. Into the road out of the same cañon from which the masked man on the horse had come now rode two more men, side by side and with a thunderous racket of pounding hoofs beating at rocky soil, their heads up, their faces unhidden, their eyes hard and bright and their right hands lifted a little. Two-Hand Billy Comstock and Buck Thornton, come at the top speed of a swinging gallop to alter the odds and take a hand. And as Thornton's horse's hoofs struck in the dust of the road and the masked rider swung about, startled in the moment of his supreme arrogant confidence, it looked to those who saw as if there came Buck Thornton on one big grey horse racing down upon another Buck Thornton on that big grey's mate. With but a hundred yards between them . . .

"Pull the rag off your face, Broderick!" shouted Thornton savagely.

And oddly enough Ben Broderick, with a swift realization that a bandana hiding his face now could no longer befriend him and might flap across his eyes at a time when he should see straight and quick, yanked it away. And with the same gesture, he jerked his lifted gun down and started firing, straight at Thornton.

Of the five rifles trained upon those in the stage not a one was silent now. Hap Smith jumped to his feet and fired as fast as he could work the trigger; the man at his side leaped down into the road, crouched at the wagon wheel and poured shot after shot into the brush whence he had seen the muzzles of two guns. Before Ben Broderick's pistol had broken the silence Buck Thornton had fired from the hip; and Two-Hand Billy Comstock, his reins on his saddle horn, was freshening his right to his title, firing with one gun after the other in regular, mechanical fashion.

Hap Smith was the first man down; he toppled, steadied himself, fired again and collapsed, sliding down against the dash board and thence to the ground. His horses had plunged, leaped and in a tangle of straining harness tugged this way and that a moment and then with the stage jerking and toppling after them went down over a six-foot bank and into the thicket of willows along the creek bed. With them went Blackie, his face showing a moment, grey with fear . . .

Hap Smith, alive simply because the trampling horses had whirled the other way, lifted himself a half dozen inches from the road bed, struggled with his gun and fainted . . . The guard saw a head exposed from behind a tree and sent a 30–30 rifle ball crashing through it; on the instant another bullet from another quarter compacted with his own body and he went down, shot through the shoulder . . .

Thornton's eyes were for Ben Broderick alone. And, it would seem, Broderick's for Thornton. But in their expressions there was nothing of similarity; in Thornton's was a stern readiness to mete out punishment while from Broderick's there looked forth a sudden furtiveness, a feverish desire for escape.

Broderick had never drawn to himself the epithet of coward. But now he knew what he was doing, where wisdom pointed and what was his one chance. There was still a good fifty yards between him and the man who rode down upon him, a long shot for a revolver when the horses which both men bestrode were rearing and plunging wildly. Broderick bent forward suddenly, whirled his horse, drove his spurs deep into the grey's sides and in a flash had cleared the fallen log, shot around the bend in the road and, taking his desperate chance with all of the cool defiance of danger which was a part of the man, sent his mount leaping down the steepening bank, into the willow thicket and on across. Shouting mightily and wrathfully, after him came Buck

Thornton. But Broderick had the few yards' headstart and, for the moment his destiny was with him. Thornton saw only a thicket of willows wildly disturbed as Broderick went threshing through them and knew that for the present at least Broderick was beyond pursuit.

Swinging about angrily he rode back to join Comstock. Already the battle there in the cañon was over, the smell of powder was gone from the still air, the last reverberating echo of a shot had died away. And in the road lay three men, two of them severely wounded while the other was already dead. Stooping over this man, a queer look in his eyes, stood Comstock.

"I hankered to bring him in alive," he muttered. "But, after all it's just as well. And it had to be him or me."

"Pollard?" asked Thornton quickly. But Comstock shook his head. Then Thornton, riding close, looking down from the saddle, saw the white upturned face. This time as his eyes came back to Comstock, Comstock nodded.

"Cole Dalton, sheriff," he said gravely. "Yes. And he's the man I came all this way to gather in, Buck. I've been after him for seven years, never guessing until lately that he was out here working the old Henry Plummer game of sheriff and badman at the same time. He's kept under cover, that being always his way; you'd never have thought that Pollard, Broderick, Bedloe were all tools . . . But, I got him, Buck. At last."

A moment only Thornton stared incredulously. Then his shoulders twitched as though this was a matter which could not concern him at present and he had other things to think of.

"Pollard?" he asked shortly.

"Over yonder." Comstock nodded toward the patch of brush on the mountainside. "Shot through the head."

"And the others? One was the Kid, wasn't it? . . ."

But now the Kid answered for himself. He rose to his knees among the stunted manzanita bushes not twenty steps from them and for a moment knelt there, his big bulky body wavering as he tried to bring his rifle to rest at his shoulder, his eyes peering out wildly from a blood smeared face. But his gesture was awkward and slow and uncertain; he was too badly hurt to shoot straight or quick, and Thornton, swift and sure and yet merciful withal, was before him. The Kid's rifle clattered to the ground; the Kid's left arm, the bone broken, dropped uselessly to his side. He tried to steady the gun with his one good arm alone, but it shook hopelessly. He dropped it and turned bloodshot eyes on Thornton.

"Damn you," he said tonelessly. "Better do a clean job, you white-livered coward, or I'll see you hang yet for killin' Charley . . ."

"I was outside when he was shot," said Thornton coolly. "I saw just as much as you did. Somebody shot him from behind me."

"Liar!" jeered Bedloe. "An' . . ."

"Don't be a fool, Bedloe," snapped Comstock. "The man you want is the same man we want; only the other day he had a quarrel with Charley and got a bullet alongside the head . . ."

"Not Ben Broderick!" gasped the Kid stupidly. "Not him!"

"I think your little friend Jimmie Clayton knew," said Comstock. "And you ought to know that Thornton isn't that kind."

With widening eyes the Kid stared at him. At last he got again to his knees; finally and shakily to his feet.

"Jimmie tol' me to watch him," he muttered thickly. "An' him an' Charley *did* have words . . ."

He stared at them stupidly, hesitated, pondered the matter. Then he turned and went lumbering down the road. Comstock, stepping forward swiftly, called out:

"I say, Bedloe! None of that . . ."

But Bedloe neither turned again nor paused. Thornton's hand shut down hard on Comstock's arm.

"He's going after Broderick," he said sharply. "Don't you see? He'll know where Broderick is. And we don't. Besides . . . I don't know just why we should stop him . . . If Broderick did kill Charley . . ."

Comstock went back to administer to Hap Smith and the guard. Thornton watched the Kid go to a horse hidden in a clump of trees; then as Bedloe rode down into the road and passed on whither it led, sitting slumped-forward and seeming at each step about to fall, Thornton rode after him. The Kid did not so much as look around; perhaps it mattered to him not in the least just then who followed or how many . . . so that they left him to ride on ahead . . .

* ★ *

It was straight into the town of Dead Man's Alley that the Kid's way led. The high sun glared down into a deserted street when he and Buck Thornton, a hundred yards behind him, passed by the Here's How saloon and the Brown Bear and at last drew rein at Henry Pollard's gate. A couple of men at the lunch counter stared curiously after the Kid; they even got down hastily from their high stools and stared more curiously still when they saw who it was who followed.

"They've rode hard, them two," said one of the men thoughtfully. "Their horses is all in."

"The Kid ahead an' Buck Thornton followin'!" grunted the other musingly. "An' the Kid never lookin' around!"

He shook his head and, long after both of the riders had passed out of sight down the crooked street these two men looked after them wonderingly.

At Pollard's gate the Kid dismounted stiffly. Now for the first time Thornton came up to him.

"If you think Broderick's in there," he said sharply, "you'd better let me go ahead. You're in no shape, Bedloe . . ."

"You go to hell," said Bedloe heavily. "He's mine."

He stepped forward and pulled open the gate. Here he paused just long enough to drag his revolver from the holster at his hip. With the weapon in his hand, swaying in his long-strided walk, he went to Pollard's front door. Just behind him, almost at his heels, came Thornton.

As he tried the door cautiously the Kid looked over his shoulder with a show of teeth.

"He's mine," he snarled again. "You keep your hands off."

Thornton offered no answer. The Kid, having ascertained that the door was locked, drew back, steadied himself with his hand against the wall, lifted his foot and with all of the power in him drove his heavy boot against the lock. Something broke; the panel splintered; the door gave a little. But only a little; the heavy bar which Henry Pollard used was in its place.

"Again," said Thornton. "Together! . . . Quick!"

So together Buck Thornton and Kid Bedloe, two men who had long hated each other, struck savagely at Pollard's barricade. And such was the weight of the two men, such the power resident in the two big bodies, that a hinge gave and after it an iron socket screwed to the wall was torn away from the woodwork, and the door went down.

Gathering all there was of strength left in him Kid Bedloe pushed to the fore and went down the hall; and Thornton followed at his heels. In this fashion they came to the door of Pollard's study and saw through it, since it had been flung wide open and so left.

In a far corner of the room was Winifred Waverly, her face dead white, her body pressed tight into the angle of the walls, her hands twisting before her, her eyes going swiftly to the two entering figures from that other figure which had held her fascinated. Upon the floor, just rising, knelt Ben Broderick. He had tossed a rug aside and had lifted out the short sections of half a dozen strips of flooring, disclosing a rude wooden vault below. Here was the accumulation of loot, here where the Kid had known Broderick was to be found.

For a very brief yet electrically vital and vivid moment there was no sound in the room, wherein never a single muscle twitched. And then there were no words and only three sharp pistol shots. Broderick had seen what lay in the Kid's eye, a look to be read by any man; he had snatched his gun up from the floor beside him and had fired, point blank. There is no name for the brief fragment of time between his shot and the Kid's. But Ben Broderick had shot true to the mark, and the Kid was sinking; Bedloe's bullet had gone wide . . . And then the third shot, Thornton's . . . and as the two men fell, Kid Bedloe and Ben Broderick, they pitched forward toward the centre of the room and the big body of the Kid lay across the body of Ben Broderick. As the Kid died his eyes were upon Thornton, and in them was a look of content and of gratitude!

"Again he tried to kiss me . . . He is all brute. He . . . he told me you were dead . . . Oh, dear God, dear God!" cried the girl, shrinking back, covering her face with her hands.

Thornton, his face set and white and grave, came to her. She was trembling so that he put his arm about her. She sobbed and caught at him as a child might have done. His arm tightened, holding her closer.

"Let me take you away," he said gently.

With never a look back to see what long hoarded booty there in the hole in the floor had drawn Ben

Broderick back to Pollard's house, he turned and with his arm still about her, led the girl from the room, from the house and out to his horse at the fence. She moaned again and drooped against him. He gathered her up into his arms tenderly. And with a tenderness which was to become part of the man, he held her close while he swung slowly into the saddle.

"Winifred Waverly . . ." he began.

There he stopped, looking with puzzled eyes down into her white face. God knew how much she had gone through, what fear Ben Broderick had put into her heart. But at the least now she had fainted.

"She's all alone," muttered the cowboy. "All alone. And somebody's got to look out for her . . ."

He turned slowly and rode down the crooked street, carrying her lightly in his arms. And now, more than ever, did the two men at the lunch counter stare.